SLIPPERY

'Spanking time!' Mr Spottiswood declared, rubbing his hands together as he got up without even waiting for Poppy to have a drink.

Poppy glanced at Sabina, who merely nodded towards the chair in the centre. Mr Spottiswood sat down on it, beaming with satisfaction as he patted his lap.

'Over we go, my dear,' he said, 'bum up for the boys, eh, that's how we like 'em. Which way around would you like her, Mistress Sabina, bum first or face first?'

'Face first,' Sabina answered. 'I'd like to see her expression while you spank her.'

I bit down a little involuntary thrill at the thought of watching Poppy's face as she was punished. Already she looked deeply sulky, but that didn't stop her draping herself across Mr Spottiswood's legs. He immediately raised one knee, making her bottom lift and part, now the highest part of her body except for her curly piggy tail, which was wobbling faintly.

'Very sweet, and it does suit you,' Mr Spottiswood remarked as he gave the tail a tug and let it spring back into position. 'Now, we're going to play a little game. It's called Spare my Blushes.'

'You didn't say anything about perverted games?' Poppy protested, lifting her head to look at Sabina.

Sabina smiled and took a sip of her drink, watching Poppy's expression change between hope and worry before she answered.

'You're being punished, Poppy. I expect Mr Spottiswood's game will add to that, don't you?'

Why not visit Penny's website at
www.pennybirch.com

By the same author:

A TASTE OF AMBER
BAD PENNY
BARE BEHIND
BRAT
DIRTY LAUNDRY
FIT TO BE TIED
IN DISGRACE
IN FOR A PENNY
JODHPURS AND JEANS
NAUGHTY NAUGHTY
NURSE'S ORDERS
KNICKERS AND BOOTS
PEACH
PENNY IN HARNESS
PENNY PIECES
PETTING GIRLS
PLAYTHING
REGIME
TEMPER TANTRUMS
TICKLE TORTURE
TIGHT WHITE COTTON
UNIFORM DOLL
WHEN SHE WAS BAD
TIE AND TEASE
WHAT HAPPENS TO BAD GIRLS
BRUSH STROKES

THE INDIGNITIES OF ISABELLE
THE INDISCRETIONS OF ISABELLE
THE INDECENCIES OF ISABELLE
(Writing as Cruella)

SLIPPERY WHEN WET

Penny Birch

This book is a work of fiction.
In real life, make sure you practise safe, sane and
consensual sex.

First published in 2007 by
Nexus
Thames Wharf Studios
Rainville Road
London W6 9HA

www.nexus-books.co.uk

Typeset by TW Typesetting, Plymouth, Devon

Printed and bound by CPI Bookmarque, Croydon

ISBN 978 0 352 34091 7

One

My knickers were coming down.

I knew it from the expressions on their faces, Poppy's full of mischief, Sabina's cruel. It must have shown on my face too, because Poppy giggled as she put a square golden package down on the table.

'Happy birthday, Gabrielle,' she said, pulling out a chair and turning it sideways on.

'You are going to spank me, aren't you?' I asked.

'It's your birthday,' she answered me.

'Birthday spankings are traditional,' Sabina added, 'at least for girls like you, so let's not have any nonsense.'

'I have a client due in twenty minutes,' I pointed out, 'perhaps if . . .'

'No nonsense,' Sabina repeated. 'Kneel on the chair. Bum up, panties down.'

'Yes, but . . .'

'Do it!' she snapped, and I found myself reacting by instinct, but still talking as my knees settled on the hard surface of the kitchen chair.

'Just quickly, perhaps . . .'

'Do you ever shut up?' Sabina demanded. 'Poppy, stick her panties in her mouth, that should keep her quiet.'

'Sabina, please, I . . .'

1

'You're only making it worse for yourself,' Poppy interrupted me. 'Come on, bend over and let's have that pretty bottom bare.'

I obeyed, but it was impossible not to make a face as I bent forward to rest my arms on the table, raising my bottom into spanking position.

'That's better,' Poppy said as she began to ruck my skirt up.

I didn't answer, giving in to the pleasure of having her expose my behind as my skirt was turned up around my waist and my knickers eased slowly down. As my bottom came bare Poppy kissed each cheek, and for a moment I thought she was going to bury her face between them, only for Sabina to give a meaningful cough. Poppy giggled and pulled away, levering my knickers down and off. I'd given in, and lifted my knees obligingly as she stripped me, to leave me with my naked bottom stuck out towards them.

'Back in, Gabby,' Sabina ordered, 'let's have those cheeks open.'

Again I reacted to her voice by instinct, pulling my back in to make my cheeks spread and show off the lips of my sex and the wrinkled pink knot of my anus. They liked to make me show everything, arguing that when a woman is to be punished she should be completely stripped of her dignity. I understood, and was happy to play their game for what they gave me, although my own pleasure was not in the supposed humiliation of my exposure, but simply in my nudity.

'Open wide,' Poppy giggled, showing me my knickers.

She had them balled in her fist, and as my mouth came wide she'd quickly pushed them in, forcing me to make spit and suck on the dry cotton to get them comfortable. That was humiliating, to be gagged with my own underwear to shut me up while my bottom was smacked, but I knew it was for the best. I always make a fuss. I can't help it.

Sabina had pulled out another chair and sat down, watching as Poppy prepared me. I thought they'd start, and was surprised Sabina wasn't going to do the spanking. She usually did, for both me and Poppy. Punishing us was her favourite thing. Now she just watched as Poppy pushed the small golden box under my face and tugged a piece of ribbon loose to let it fall open. Inside was a small but perfectly made cake, just a few centimetres across, iced with plain chocolate and topped with swirls of dark brown chocolate cream.

'Happy birthday,' she said again, took me by the hair and jammed my face into the chocolate cake.

I never even had a chance to react, let alone resist. The chocolate cream squashed against my skin, the icing beneath broke, and sticky cake smeared out across my features. I'd heard the squelch as my face went in, I heard their laughter as Poppy began to rub my head in the mess, and I heard the first smack of her hand on my bottom as she started to spank me. She'd taken me completely by surprise, robbing me of any chance I might have had of retaining my dignity as I was punished. Instead I lost control immediately, wriggling in her grip and waving my hands in futile remonstrance, kicking my feet and treading up and down with my knees.

The bigger the fuss I made the more they laughed, and the more they laughed the harder Poppy spanked, still rubbing my face in the ruined cake as my bottom bounced to the stinging slaps. Nor did she stop the smacks, but carried on, which added an ever rising sense of resentment to my emotions as my bottom was slapped up to a burning, smarting ball.

'What a sight!' Sabina crowed, struggling to get her words out through her laughter. 'OK, that's enough, Poppy. Let her have some cake now.'

The spanking stopped and my head was pulled up, Poppy keeping a firm grip in my hair as I spat out my soggy knickers and gasping in the chocolate-scented air. I couldn't see a thing, my glasses smeared with cake, and I quickly took them off. My bottom was on fire, hot and throbbing, but my sex had begun to react, leaving me badly in need of a touch and theirs to do with as they pleased. The moment I'd got my breath back I began to nibble up bits of chocolate cake with my lips, hoping that if I was playful and submissive they'd take pity on me.

'Good girl,' Sabina said as she stood up. 'Hmm, you're juicing nicely.'

I gasped as she slid a finger into my vagina, wiggling it about to see how moist and ready I'd become. Poppy giggled to discover how excited she'd made me, and put a hand back to my bottom, first to plant one more admonishing spank across my cheeks and then to stroke my heated skin. They both knew full well what I wanted, but I realised they might prefer to have me seated on my hot bottom and aroused sex while I talked to Stephen Stanbrook about his life after divorce.

'Please,' I managed, 'be kind to me.'

'Shall we?' Poppy queried, even as she let a finger stray to my anus, tickling the little hole to make my muscle contract.

'Maybe,' Sabina answered, easing a second finger in up my vagina, 'if she asks very nicely.'

'Please,' I repeated. 'Please do it.'

'Please do what?' Poppy demanded, still holding me firmly by my hair as she tickled my anus.

'Masturbate me,' I asked, my frustration bubbling

4

up as I realised they were going to tease me into begging for it and maybe still leave me in need.

'You can do better than that, Gabrielle,' Sabina chided and she had slid a third finger into me, holding me open behind as she slipped her spare hand in under my belly.

'I ... I beg you,' I managed. 'Make me come, please?'

'Not good enough,' she said, but her hand was cupping my mound, her fingers pressing firmly to my smooth, shaved skin and half of her hand in up my vagina.

Poppy had penetrated me too, the top joint of her finger wiggling in my anus, helping to make my breathing ragged as I tried again.

'Please! Please make me come, Sabina ... Poppy. Please? It's not fair to leave me like this, and I did let you spank me ...'

'Don't whine, Gabrielle,' Sabina chided. 'Just ask, but use some dirty words.'

Poppy giggled and a sob escaped my lips. They knew my weak spots only too well.

'Come on,' Poppy urged, 'nice and rude.'

'Rub me off,' I tried. 'Fist me and rub me off ... you can tickle my bottom too, Poppy, and put your finger in.'

'Try harder,' Sabina ordered, but she had begun to massage my pubic mound and ease her hand in and out of my now gaping sex. 'Come on, we all know you're not as prissy as you make out.'

My answer was a gasp, because Poppy had pushed her finger in up my bottom, giggling in delight as she felt around inside my rectum. I was nearly there, needing only a few touches to my clitoris, but Sabina had her fingers spread, deliberately tormenting me as she spoke again.

5

'Go on, Gabrielle, you're not getting away with this. Tell me what you want.'

'You can do it,' Poppy insisted. 'Come on, the way a man would, some dirty bastard.'

'Rub me,' I answered. 'Rub . . . rub my pussy until I come. Please, Sabina, rub my pussy off while Poppy fingers my bottom . . . my bum . . . my bumhole . . .'

I broke off with a sigh as both of them increased the vigour of their motions. Poppy let go of my hair and began to smack my bottom again, and Sabina, a cheek each. It no longer hurt, just serving to increase my arousal, but still they wouldn't touch that vital spot between my lips.

'Please?' I sobbed. 'Do it . . . just do it. Rub my pussy while you finger my bum and spank me. Make me come, please . . . rub my pussy . . . frig me . . . frig my cunt, my dirty cunt . . . yes, thank you, thank you so much.'

Sabina had given in, easing her fingers between my sex lips to rub on my clitoris. Poppy laughed to see me so eager, probing deep up my bottom as my cheeks and the muscles of my thighs began to contract.

'Don't stop, or I will,' Sabina warned and I was babbling filth as the full bulk of her fist pushed in up my vagina.

'No, don't stop, frig me off . . . frig my dirty cunt, Sabina . . . and my bum, Poppy, right in up my box . . . my dirt box . . . my hamster run . . .'

I was coming, my whole body tight as I rode the waves of ecstasy generated by Sabina's finger, my head full of what they were doing to me and what they'd done: taken off my knickers and stuck them in my mouth, pushed my face in my own birthday cake, spanked me and made me talk dirty while they masturbated me to orgasm with both my holes penetrated. They let me do it, holding my body as I shivered and gasped my way through orgasm, neither of them speaking until I was done.

'Hamster run?' Poppy asked, amused yet not without a touch of disgust. 'Where did you get that from?'

I immediately began to blush.

'I'm sorry, but you did say to talk dirty. It's something Jeff Bellbird said, and you know what he's like.'

'That's for sure,' Sabina agreed, 'filthy fat bastard, and speaking of Jeff, you've got a card from him, a big one.'

'I thought he was in Japan?' Poppy queried.

'It's from Japan.'

'That was thoughtful of him,' I said, surprised that Jeff even knew my birthday, let alone remembered it. 'I'll have a look when I've cleaned up. Could you do the floor and the table, please? Stephen Stanbrook will be here any minute.'

The bell went, precipitating an immediate flurry of activity as I struggled to make myself decent and Poppy cleaned up the mess. Sabina mainly gave instructions, which was typical of her behaviour recently. Aside from the detail with my birthday cake, what we'd done had been typical of the sort of sex the three of us had been having of late. Sabina was always firmly in charge, with myself as her plaything and Poppy at some point in between.

Even when we had the occasional male playmate to visit she remained strictly dominant, although she didn't mind handling the occasional cock. She wouldn't even pose or take a playful spanking, but she did at least know how it felt. Jeff Bellbird had done it, and she'd never forgiven him. He hadn't asked either, but simply assumed that because she was a friend of mine and Poppy's, it would be acceptable to punish her for making a remark about his weight. It hadn't just been a few swats over her clothes either, but bare, and in front of several people. That still rankled, and he was the one male among my friends she would never play with at all.

Since we'd met Sabina nearly two years before, she had slowly but surely stamped her authority on our relationship, gaining in confidence and skill until it was much more about us fulfilling her needs than the other way around, at least on the surface. Deeper down, so much of what she now liked to make us do, or the ways she liked to punish us, were exactly the things we had hoped for when we first met.

I had changed too, growing more confident and accepting of her right to spank me, also taking on much of the culture associated with submission and punishment. Her rich East End accent and vocabulary had also affected me, moving the formal English I'd learnt as a child in France and working as a therapist in London towards the colloquial.

Stephen was a little early, and I just managed to let him in within time for his appointment. I was still checking for crumbs in my hair as I pressed the communicator, and I was glad it was him. Unlike the great majority of my clients he knew that my relationship with Poppy was unconventional, having been referred to me by Jeff, who knew exactly what we liked. Considering the smell of chocolate and sex that both open windows and air freshener had failed to conceal, it was just as well, and I still found it hard to put on my professional manner when he came in, with Poppy and Sabina now in a bedroom.

'Good morning, Gabrielle,' he said, and kissed me.

It was not what I'd been expecting at all, as our last session had largely consisted of me listening to him enlarging on the woes of his divorce settlement.

'You seem greatly improved,' I ventured, motioning him to my couch.

He didn't take it, but settled himself into one of the black leather armchairs instead, always a sure sign with clients that they're feeling good in themselves. The way he immediately relaxed with his hands folded easily across his stomach also suggested confidence, even complacency, very different from the nervous fidgeting of the time before. I gave him an encouraging smile as I took the other chair.

'I'm more than just improved,' he stated. 'I'm the happiest man alive, and the luckiest. In fact, I won't be needing your services any more . . . not that I don't appreciate your efforts of course, and I think it's fair to say you've done more to keep me sane over the last three years . . .'

He paused, noticing the huge, canary-yellow envelope Sabina had carelessly put down on my work table. Jeff, with characteristic childishness, had written the W and the Os in my address so that they appeared to be bottoms and breasts. I put it quickly aside, trying not to blush as I tried to explain.

'A birthday card, from Jeff Bellbird.'

Stephen nodded with what I hoped was understanding.

'Is it your birthday?'

'Yes, today.'

'Many happy returns.'

'Thank you,' I answered him, and went on, determined to get back on track. 'You were saying?'

'That I'm the happiest man alive,' he repeated. 'I've met the most wonderful woman, my Tasanee, a true jewel. Do you know, she is the first person to accept my sexuality without qualification? I feel so liberated! To be able to express my dominance in this awful, repressed . . . crushed society, it is wonderful, marvellous . . .'

He went on, and I listened. I have never calculated what proportion of my work consists of simply listening to my clients, but it must be something in the region of half. It is also essential, both in allowing them to speak with absolute freedom and to enable me to gain a deeper understanding of the situation.

Essentially, Stephen had used an internet service to secure himself a Thai bride. She was apparently a natural submissive, a masochist, and eager to support him in his role as dominant male and sexual master. I didn't criticise. A basic tenet of Rogersian therapy is that so long as nobody else is being endangered the client's well-being is paramount. The morality of Stephen's actions was not my concern, let alone with respect to the subjective expectations of British society. Nevertheless, I promised myself I would find an opportunity to speak to Tasanee herself as soon as I could, just to be sure.

Sabina was rather more forthright in her assessment, emerging from the bedroom before the sound of Stephen's footsteps had faded on the stairs and speaking immediately.

'He's bought himself a fucking sex slave, hasn't he? What a bastard!'

Poppy came out as well, her face flushed with a mixture of outrage and excitement. I drew a sigh.

'I do wish you two wouldn't listen while I am with clients. It is confidential.'

'The dirty pig!' Sabina went on, ignoring me completely. 'I bet she's really young too.'

There was more than a little jealousy mingled with the disapproval in her voice, but I didn't say anything, not wanting to risk another spanking, which she was all too likely to dish out if I challenged her in any way.

'You're going to make sure she's OK, aren't you?' Poppy asked.

'Yes, of course,' I assured her, and reached for my cards in an attempt to change the topic of conversation.

There were several, from my parents and a few old friends in France, more from the UK, and Jeff's. I opened it last, expecting something rude and probably in execrable taste. What I got was a large card showing two girls in the *hentai* style, one with green hair, one with blue, but both naked except for white knee-length socks, shiny black shoes, and nappies. Both were also in the same pose, knock-kneed and with their bottoms stuck out towards the viewer while they were looking back over their shoulders with expressions of acute shame. The seat of each girl's nappy showed a tell-tale bulge of grotesquely exaggerated size, leaving no doubt whatsoever about what they'd done.

'Cute!' Poppy giggled, craning over my shoulder to see. 'Trust Jeff.'

'I always said he was a pervert,' Sabina put in. 'What's this?'

Some pieces of paper had dropped out of the card as I opened it, a small, glossy brochure and four of what appeared to be tickets. Sabina picked up the brochure.

'Wyddon Manor,' she read, 'luxury accommodation for the discerning holidaymaker or the perfect spot for a conference. Wyddon Manor is set deep in the beautiful and secluded Plynlimon Mountains, at the very heart of romantic Wales, and yet within easy access of Aberystwyth . . . I think he's bought you a week in a holiday cottage, Gabby.'

'Sort of, yes,' Poppy agreed, looking at one of the tickets. 'The Institute, where all your fantasies come true. The Institute is a secure environment in which to explore your sexuality in the company of like-minded individuals, an environment where the normal rules of society are replaced by SM convention and ... blah ... blah ... blah ... blah ... in rural Wales, catering and accommodation included ... blah ... blah ... Admit One – £400. Four hundred pounds!'

'That's not bad for an SM boot camp,' Sabina pointed out, 'and that's what it is, obviously.'

'It's a pretty generous birthday present, all the same,' Poppy insisted. 'Four tickets at four hundred each!'

'It seems suspiciously generous,' I suggested as my instinctive gratitude gave way to concern. 'Jeff can be generous, yes, but he usually has an ulterior motive.'

'So?' Poppy responded. 'It sounds fun, and anyway, what's Jeff going to do? He's in Japan.'

'That's true,' I admitted, 'but still ...'

Poppy had taken the brochure, and came to sit beside me. It showed a large house built of grey stone, with high gables and more chimneys than seemed really useful. There was a small, flat lawn surrounded by a garden sculpted into the hillside, with dense pine woods rising steeply behind. It was certainly pretty, although at once wild and somewhat austere, and reminded me rather of southern Germany.

'It certainly looks lonely,' Poppy said.

'There's probably a village or a Youth Hostel or something right behind where the photographer's standing,' I pointed out.

'Don't be such a pessimist,' she answered. 'It's obviously not overlooked, or they wouldn't have set it up there, would they?'

'Do you suppose the owners know what it's being used for?' I queried. 'I'm not sure if ...'

'Don't tell me you're not going to go?' she interrupted. 'Come on, Gabby, don't be a spoilsport. I'll come, and Sabina, and maybe Sophie, or June or somebody. It'll be great.'

'Yeah, we should go,' Sabina agreed. 'Why not?'

'When is it for?' I asked cautiously.

'The week after next,' Poppy told me.

'In that case it's impossible,' I pointed out. 'I have appointments, and we're going to see Hurst's interpretation of the Ring Cycle, and . . .'

'Oh come on, Gabby,' she insisted. 'Jeff's been really generous.'

'That is all very well, but as I said . . .'

'You can change your appointments around, and we can see the opera another time. Come on, please?'

'I want to go,' Sabina put in.

'Why don't the two of you go then?' I suggested. 'Perhaps I can come down at the weekend?'

'Gabby!' Poppy protested.

'You're coming,' Sabina stated.

'I am sorry, but I can't.'

'You're coming,' she repeated.

She'd stood up, her strong, dark face once more setting in the cruel smile I'd grown so used to. Poppy giggled as she realised Sabina's intention. I spread my hands in a resigned shrug.

'It's not that I don't want to, Sabina, only that I cannot afford the time.'

'You're coming,' she insisted, 'or do I have to deal with you first?'

'It won't make any difference,' I protested, trying to fight down the bubble of chagrin that was forming in my throat. 'Please, Sabina . . .'

'Do her, Sabina!' Poppy urged. 'She'll soon change her mind.'

'I've just been spanked!' I protested.

'That wasn't what I had in mind,' Sabina answered, and her grin had changed from cruel to downright fiendish.

I wasn't sure what she was going to do to me, only that it would certainly be painful and probably humiliating too, so I got up quickly.

'No, Sabina, not now!' I protested. 'This evening, maybe, but I've got another client in an hour ... less than an hour ...'

'That's plenty of time,' she answered, and darted forward.

I'd been expecting it, and dodged behind the chair, which would have been fine if Poppy hadn't stuck a foot out to trip me up. Sabina's fingers clutched the sleeve of my jacket as I fought for balance, but I got away, dashing into the bathroom, but too slowly to shut the door on them. I couldn't help laughing as I backed slowly away, but I was still trying to talk my way out of what I had coming to me.

'Not now, you two, please? I'll do whatever you like this evening, I promise, but not now!'

'We want you to come to Wales,' Poppy replied.

'But I can't ...'

'Oh yes you can, you're just being difficult.'

'You're going to,' Sabina added.

I'd backed up against the toilet, which was as far as I could go.

'Please?' I tried, but they'd already grabbed me.

I was still protesting as I was dragged down on to the bathroom floor, but I couldn't stop laughing, and I knew that unless I managed to sound genuinely upset I was going to get it. Sure enough, I'd quickly been pinned down on the floor, with Poppy sitting on my legs as Sabina straddled my waist. She was too strong for me, and all I could do was wriggle feebly as she turned around and settled herself into

14

position with the full denim-clad ball of her bottom directly over my face. Reaching down, she pulled my glasses off, leaving me feeling even more vulnerable.

'Are you going to come?' she asked.

'Sabina, I . . .'

My voice was cut off as she lowered her bottom into my face, rubbing the seat of her jeans against my cheeks as I struggled to turn away. After a moment she rose again, but her hands had gone to the buckle of her belt.

'Are you going to come?' she repeated.

'I would, Sabina, but . . .'

'Oh dear,' she interrupted. 'You're a slow learner, aren't you, Gabrielle?'

Poppy giggled and adjusted her position a little, freeing my skirt from beneath her. Sabina began to undo her belt as Poppy rucked my skirt up. I struggled a little, but they had me well and truly pinned down and I soon gave up, instead trying to fight down my feelings of consternation and helplessness as my skirt was pushed up over my hips and Sabina eased her jeans down to expose lacy red knickers barely covering the full, golden brown cheeks of her bottom.

'Tell me you're going to come,' she demanded, 'or I sit it in your face.'

'Look, Sabina, I . . .'

She sat down, smothering me between her cheeks so well that I could feel the line of panty material where it covered her anal region and her sex, which she'd begun to grind against my chin. I heard Poppy give a little purr of delight to see me get my face sat on, then Sabina spoke.

'Pull her knickers down.'

I tried to fight, wriggling my hips and trying to kick

15

my legs, but it was no good at all. Poppy took hold of my knickers. Again Sabina wiggled, rubbing her bum in my face, before once more lifting it, but not far, so that my face was just inches from her big, fleshy cheeks.

'Well?' she demanded. 'Do you give in, or do I have to make you kiss my arsehole first?'

'It's not that, Sabina . . .'

'You really are a glutton for punishment, aren't you? Stick something up her, Poppy.'

'Which hole?'

'Both, why do things by halves? Well, Gabby, last chance?'

I didn't even answer, fairly sure they'd do it anyway and pretty well surrendered to my fate. Sabina settled her bottom back in my face as Poppy went to work, climbing off my legs so that she could roll me up and get at my sex. My knickers were quickly pulled down, exposing my sex, and I was left, with Sabina holding my legs up, both my sex and bottom fully exposed. I heard the faint pop of the fridge door being opened, then Poppy's voice.

'I'll lube her up with some butter, and . . . ooh, she's got courgettes!'

'They're too big, Poppy!' I protested, my words coming out muffled by my faceful of bottom, 'and anyway, I was going to make ratatouille for dinner.'

She didn't even bother to reply, and Sabina ground her bottom a little more firmly into my face to shut me up. I knew I was helpless, but I couldn't help but wriggle as I heard Poppy close the fridge door once more, my apprehension now bordering on fear at the thought of being made to accommodate a courgette up my bottom. She'd be careful, I knew, but I'd picked the courgettes myself, and they were particularly fat ones.

'Do stay still, Gabrielle,' Sabina chided. 'If you don't want it, all you have to do is say you'll come to Wales.'

I tried to answer, but her bottom was pressed firmly into my face, and a moment later I felt Poppy's fingers between my legs, then the cold, uneven shape of a piece of butter, which she eased in up my vagina. A second followed, applied to my anus and stuck just a little way in, so that my hole was open around it, with the heat of my body already melting both pats to make them slippery and my twin holes accessible. I began to wriggle again, and Poppy laughed out loud for the view I was giving her.

'Up she goes,' she said happily, and obviously indifferent to whether I'd given in or not.

Something round and firm pressed between my sex lips, a little high, and then directly on my buttery hole, which began to spread. I hadn't even needed lubricating, my vagina giving easily to the thick courgette and both Sabina and Poppy giggling as they watched it go in, with me still wriggling beneath them. Melted butter squashed out as I was penetrated, to trickle down from my vagina to my anus and between the cheeks of my well-spread bottom.

'Now fuck her,' Sabina said eagerly, and Poppy had begun to move the courgette inside me.

She was pushing it a little deeper every time, and faster, until I was arching my back in pleasure and gasping against Sabina's musky bottom flesh despite myself. Only when she stopped fucking me, leaving the courgette as deep up my hole as it would go, did my apprehension return. Again I tried to speak, but Poppy's finger had already found my anus, worming its way in up the buttery little hole. Sabina spread my legs a little wider and rolled me higher still so that she

17

could watch my anus opened and I was held like that, completely vulnerable.

'Don't worry, Gabby,' Poppy said gently, 'you're quite a bit looser than you used to be.'

My answer was a muffled sob, then another gasp as she slid two more fingers into my now open anal ring. I was doing my best to relax, but the thought of the fat, hard courgette being put up me was making it difficult, with my ring twitching and tightening on Poppy's fingers as she gently eased my hole.

'She looks pretty sloppy,' Sabina said, 'won't that do?'

I wanted to point out that to the best of my knowledge she'd never had anything up her bottom hole bigger than the tip of my tongue, but I knew I'd only get a lecture on her dominance and the courgette would go up anyway, so held my peace, trying to fight down my feelings as my anus was slowly but surely prepared for buggering. At last she spoke.

'That's open enough. Push it out, Gabs.'

There was no choice but to obey, deliberately pushing to make my bottom hole pout and so accept the tip of the courgette, which she'd now touched to the puffy, moist central hole. I felt myself spread, easily at first, then suddenly tense as my ring reached its full size. My muscles went stiff by instinct and Poppy immediately took the pressure off, only to push again, a little more firmly, withdraw, and push one more time.

It went in, my bottom hole spreading wide on the thick, green stem of the courgette. I felt my rectum fill as she pushed it up, doubling the feeling of being plugged and leaving me completely and utterly helpless beneath them, not just physically, but mentally. Poppy began to fuck me again, moving both courgettes slowly in and out of my now gaping holes as Sabina spoke.

18

'Now you're going to lick my arse, Gabrielle.'

She lifted up a little, once more presenting me with the full, dark spread of her bottom, her cheeks now wide, with only the minuscule red knickers to cover her most intimate parts.

'I'll be nice and give you one last chance,' she said. 'Are you coming?'

I didn't even bother to answer, too far gone to want to resist. She had already put her thumbs into the waistband of her knickers, and barely waited a moment before giving a disappointed tut as she began to push them down. I watched her bare herself, my vision already dizzy with pleasure from the two fat courgettes working in my holes as the full, nude spread of her bottom came bare in my face. She took them down only as far as they would go with her legs spread across my body, but it was far enough, the wrinkled, jet black star of her anus plainly visible between her open cheeks, and also the twin curve of her puffy, excited sex lips.

'Lick it, lick my arsehole,' she demanded, and she sat on my face.

Now she was nude, with nothing to keep my tongue from her flesh, while I was far beyond resistance. I began to lick immediately, lapping at the little fleshy bumps of her anal star and probing her hole with my tongue. She sighed in pleasure and reached back to pull her cheeks wide, allowing me to push my tongue deeper still up into her bottom hole, licking for all I was worth and swallowing down the thick, feminine taste as I made spit in my mouth.

She seemed to have forgotten about Wales, now moaning and gasping for the pleasure of having her bottom licked and rubbing herself against my face to get more friction. Poppy was still moving the courgettes inside me as I licked, but stopped suddenly, leaving both deep inside, just as Sabina rose a little to release my trapped arms. Both of them knew there was no fight left in me and they were right. I took hold of Sabina's bottom, holding her heavy, rounded cheeks wide across my face so that she could play with her breasts and sex while I licked her anus.

'That's right, you lovely little tart, Gabrielle,' she sighed, 'lick it well. You love my bum in your face, don't you, you slut?'

I was far too busy to answer, but nodded my head as I continued to lick and probe. Poppy pushed close, rubbing herself against me, her sex now bare and warm and wet against the flesh of my thigh, and as Sabina went quiet I knew they were kissing as they used me. Poppy put a thumb to my clitoris, masturbating me, and I almost immediately felt myself go tight on the thick, heavy loads in my vagina and anus. I couldn't have stopped it if I'd wanted to, my body going into hard, involuntary contractions as I began to come, completely helpless beneath them, wave after wave of ecstasy sweeping through me until I thought I'd pass out.

Yet I'd never stopped licking, and Sabina was going to come too, moaning and wriggling herself into my face, one finger busy between her sex lips. Her cheeks tightened in my face, her anus began to pulse on my well-intruded tongue and she was there, the wet from her sex running down my chin and neck as my own orgasm rose once more in response to hers. I couldn't see what Poppy was doing, but I could feel her pressed close to me, and I heard her moan as she too came.

Sabina finally lifted her bottom off my face, allowing me to gasp in air as she spoke.

'That was good. Thanks, Gabby, you really know how to lick arse.'

'She gets enough practice,' Poppy answered, her voice still raw from her climax, 'but we were supposed to be making her give in about Wales, not getting off.'

'That's true,' Sabina admitted. 'How about it, Gabby?'

'Sabina, you know . . .'

'Oh, for goodness' sake! Say you're coming to Wales, or . . . or I'm going to pee on you, right in your face.'

'What, you're coming?'

'No, but you can pee in my face if you like.'

Two

We drove down to Wyddon Manor on the Saturday, leaving in the early hours of the morning so that we could get well clear of London before the traffic began to build up and make the best of our time there. Sabina was driving the new Mini her father had bought her on her twenty-first birthday and we were soon off the motorway and driving through the Herefordshire countryside.

I was given the map and led us deep into Wales before turning south on a narrow, twisting A road between steep grey-green hillsides and gloomy looking pine forests. I hadn't seen a building in miles, and no human beings either, save those in the occasional car and one distant group of hikers. I had at least found Wyddon Manor on the map, at the end of a track marked as unpaved and with woods on three sides, but the map only went so far to prepare me for the reality when we arrived. The brochure hadn't done it justice, either.

The house stood well back from the road, with the drive coming off a hairpin bend and rising steeply, so that only the roofs were visible and those only for a moment. The gardens were a maze of hedges, tiny steep lawns and flights of steps cut in the same grey stone as the house, with only one big area of flat grass directly in front of the house, while the trees hemmed it in to within fifty metres on every side save the front. A service yard at the back served for a car park, where Sabina stopped.

There didn't seem to be anybody about at first, and the three of us stood in the yard for a moment, feeling slightly lost, before a woman stepped out from the back door. She was tiny, certainly no more than one metre fifty tall, and petite as well, also strikingly pretty in a classically oriental fashion, with fine features, large dark eyes and glossy black hair hanging down to the backs of her knees in a pony-tail. Her dress was no less striking; thigh boots with thin steel heels, a pair of minuscule shorts so tight the outline of her sex showed clearly beneath, while most of her tiny buttocks seemed to have spilt out at the back, an equally tight halter top half-unzipped at the front to show off what cleavage she had, and matching collar and cuffs set with pointed steel studs. A long, double-strand tawse was clipped to her shorts. All of it was either black leather or steel, creating a striking effect slightly spoiled by the bright yellow clipboard she was holding.

She glanced at her clipboard, then spoke.

'I am Mistress Kimiko. On your knees to me, dirt sluts!'

She spoke in a sharp, high voice, somehow peremptory, so that I felt a desire to obey at the same instant as my immediate resentment. I wasn't sure quite how best to answer her in any case, but Sabina had no such doubts.

'Who do you think you're talking to?' she demanded, her voice full of very real aggression.

For one brief instant the girl looked puzzled, but with another glance at her clipboard she replied, no less authoritative than before.

'You are Sophie Cherwell, yes, dirt slut?'

'No, I'm Sabina Ranglin, and if you call me that one more time . . .'

'Many apologies,' Kimiko broke in, although she didn't sound as if she meant it. 'You are the Domina, yes?'

'Yes,' Sabina replied, only slightly mollified.

Kimiko once again consulted her clipboard, lifting the top sheet of paper to glance at the one beneath.

'There should be four girls,' she said after a moment, 'Mistress Sabina and three dirt sluts, Poppy, Gabrielle and Sophie. Sophie is missing?'

'Sophie's coming by train,' I told her. 'She should be here this evening.'

'Quiet, dirt slut!' Kimiko snapped.

'Excuse me, Kimiko,' Poppy answered her, giggling, 'but I think the expression you want is "dirty slut", not "dirt slut".'

'I know what I am saying!' Kimiko snapped back, rounding on us. 'Miss pig-girl Poppy and Gabrielle who likes to make pee-pee in diapers. I was addressing your Mistress, also. You do not speak unless spoken to, and when you speak, you call me Mistress, always!'

I was going to say something, and so was Sabina, but Poppy had hung her head and folded her hands into her lap.

'Yes, Mistress,' she replied, her voice meek and submissive, but with just the faintest hint of mockery.

Kimiko didn't seem to notice.

'That is better,' she said. 'Show me respect, always, and maybe I will beat you less . . .'

'Poppy is my playmate, not yours,' Sabina cut in, 'Gabrielle too, and if they need to be punished I'm going to be the one who does it.'

Kimiko turned to Sabina, her perfect little face full of very real anger. Her hand moved towards her

25

tawse, but she stopped, perhaps thinking of the likely consequences of trying to use it when her head didn't quite come up to Sabina's chin. Instead, she spoke again, as if reciting a litany.

'The first rule of the Institute is that the house Mistress must be obeyed at all times. She may also punish as she pleases. If you do not agree with this, you are not welcome here.'

'I'm not being pushed around by you, you little . . .,' Sabina began, but Poppy cut her off.

'Come on, Sabina, it's only play, and I'm sure we have a stop word and everything, don't we Kimiko, er . . . Mistress Kimiko?'

'The stop word is red,' Kimiko answered, 'but only to be used if there is too much pain or something goes wrong.'

'Maybe so,' Sabina said, 'but I'm a Domina and I'm not being told what to do by anyone, and I'm definitely not being punished!'

Kimiko shrugged.

'You must accept the rules or leave.'

Sabina hesitated, her mouth set in annoyance, but Kimiko spoke again before she could find an answer.

'I will make a deal. Take one stroke from my tawse now and I will not ask to punish you again, but I must be allowed to beat your sluts, whenever I please.'

'That sounds fair,' Poppy responded.

Sabina looked at Poppy in outrage.

'Well it does,' Poppy insisted. 'Come on, Sabina, don't spoil the fun. Tell her, Gabby.'

I'd been somewhat taken aback by Kimiko, but was coming to realise that what she was saying made sense.

'I think we should accept the rules,' I said, 'so long as we have a stop word. Otherwise we will not fully appreciate the experience.'

'Thanks a lot, you two!' Sabina responded.

'Stick out your bottom,' Kimiko ordered as she unclipped the tawse from her shorts.

'I didn't say you could . . .' Sabina began angrily, and then stopped. 'Oh all right, I suppose so.'

Her expression had grown sulky as she turned sideways on to Kimiko and pushed her bottom out, her full cheeks straining the denim of her jeans to make what even I had to admit was a tempting target for a smack. Unfortunately Kimiko wasn't satisfied.

'Take down your jeans,' she ordered.

'My jeans?' Sabina answered. 'You didn't say anything about taking down my jeans.'

'Girls are beaten bare, always,' Kimiko pointed out.

'Not this girl!' Sabina answered.

Kimiko lifted several sheets on her clipboard, consulting a page of small, dense type before she replied.

'You must be bare. That is the Master's word.'

'Master?' Sabina demanded. 'Fuck that! You, maybe, but no man, not ever.'

'The Master's word must be obeyed,' Kimiko insisted, 'but he is not the one to beat you, I am. Now take down your jeans, or go.'

Kimiko's voice was full of glee, also stern. Clearly she wasn't going to back down, but Sabina's mouth was working in bitter consternation as she faced the prospect of taking her jeans down for the strap. Finally she spoke.

'Oh for fuck's sake!'

She was already wrestling with her belt buckle, and a moment later had it loose and her trousers pushed down, exposing the full golden brown ball of her bottom, with just a tiny, bright green thong to cover what remained of her modesty.

'Go on then, if you have to!' she snapped.

'Panties down,' Kimiko ordered.

'What?' Sabina demanded. 'No way!'

'Panties down,' Kimiko repeated. 'Remember, girls are beaten bare. You are not bare.'

'Yes I am!'

'You are not. Bare means your panties are down.'

'What difference does it make? I've only got a thong on, it's not as if I'm covering anything!'

'It makes all the difference, in your head,' Kimiko answered, 'as I suspect you know very well. Do you make Poppy and Gabrielle take their panties down?'

'You bet she does!' Poppy chimed in before Sabina could answer. 'We get ours pulled down every time, don't we, Gabby?'

'Just you wait, Poppy,' Sabina hissed as her thumbs went into the waistband of her thong. 'OK, I'll take them down, but you're a real bitch, do you know that, Kimiko?'

'That is why the Master chose me,' Kimiko answered calmly as Poppy giggled in anticipation of the punishment she would get in turn. 'Now stick out your bottom.'

Sabina looked ready to cry as she pushed her knickers down and stuck her bottom out, allowing her big cheeks to part. From behind I could see both the jet black star of her anus and the lips of her sex, a display Kimiko made sure to enjoy before lifting her tawse. Poppy and I both stepped back to let Kimiko get a proper swing and the tawse came down, landing across Sabina's bare bottom with a meaty smack. The tawse drew a squeal of shock and pain from its victim, at the sound of which Kimiko clicked her tongue in contempt.

'So,' she said, 'you like to dish it out but you cannot take it yourself. That is often the way. Would you like another few strokes?'

'No I would not!' Sabina snapped, pulling up her thong and jeans all at once in her haste to get covered.

'You are a liar,' Kimiko responded calmly. 'Your cunt is juicing.'

'Bitch!' Sabina answered, but she didn't deny it, maybe because both Poppy and I had seen that it was true. 'Right, you two, get our stuff. Where are our rooms, Kimiko?'

'You are in the Green Room,' Kimiko answered. 'You two sluts are in the girls' dormitory. All on the first floor.'

She had attached her tawse to her shorts again and I felt a touch of relief, only for it to fade. I'd been expecting her to find an excuse to apply it to my bottom just as she had to Sabina's, if only to exert her dominance. She hadn't, but that didn't mean I wasn't going to be punished, just not yet. As I helped Poppy unload the car I was thinking of the pain of a strapping, which was really more than I enjoyed and usually brought me to tears. I did want to make myself subject to discipline from both Kimiko and Sabina, but that didn't stop me feeling seriously apprehensive. There is no pleasure for me quite like giving myself over to another woman's control, completely, but for some reason I have never been able fully to understand, they always seem to want to punish me physically, and I have very little tolerance for pain.

Kimiko led us into the house, through the kitchen area and out into a fine hall panelled with old, dark wood. A flight of stairs led up to a landing from which corridors led to both left and right while a narrower stair continued up to the next floor. After indicating which corridor we should take, Kimiko went off on her own business and we were left to find

29

our rooms. Each room was labelled in fading gold letters, and we quickly found the Green Room, which looked out over the gardens with the valley and hills beyond. It was light and airy, with a big, comfortable bed and a thick carpet, also good furniture and a private shower and loo. Sabina had been sulking after being forced to take the strap, but cheered up immediately, bouncing on her bed with a happy smile.

'This is more like it!' she said. 'Five-star accommodation all the way. I'm going to enjoy this.'

'Let's find our room,' I suggested to Poppy as I put Sabina's case down.

From what Kimiko had said I was expecting an austere dormitory room, perhaps with bare boards and a row of metal-framed beds. It was very different. The plaque on the door read 'Nursery', which was evidently what the room had been when Wyddon Manor was a private house years if not decades before. Within, the room stretched right across the end of the house, with windows on three sides and magnificent views over the hillsides and the forest. There was a perfectly good carpet too, and five smart new pine beds, a little small but perfectly comfortable. Clothes had been laid out on two of them, on one a school uniform of tiny red tartan skirt, white blouse, white knee socks, a red-and-white-striped tie and polished black shoes, and on the other a flounced pink baby-doll dress and a nappy.

Poppy hadn't noticed, because she'd gone to look at a set of printed sheets pinned to a notice board and entitled 'Rules and Duties'. I stood looking down at the big puffy disposable, feeling excited and doubtful all at once. It had been a while since I'd been put in nappies, what with one thing and another, but I do like it. Nothing else can provide that wonderful sense of having completely divested myself of responsibility which means so much to me. I wondered if I'd be made to spend the whole week in nappies, a thought that sent a strong shiver through me. Wyddon Manor still felt unfamiliar, making it hard to feel completely comfortable with the idea, especially if it was going to be in front of other guests, yet once again I knew that the only way fully to enjoy the situation was to give myself over completely.

'They seem to know a lot about us?' Poppy queried from behind me.

'Jeff would have told them,' I pointed out, 'after all, it is supposed to be geared to our fantasies.'

'Jeff's idea of our fantasies anyway,' she responded, 'which I suspect has a lot more to do with his imagination than either of ours. So I get to be a naughty schoolgirl, do I?'

'I think the school uniform is for Sophie,' I told her, having just spotted what was on a third bed at the far end of the room.

She walked over, her mouth coming open in surprise and indignation as she picked up a small rubber pig's snout and a curly pink tail. There was also a pair of shoes, a bit like clogs, but carved at the ends and painted pink so that they resembled trotters, and a little bottle of some sort of resin on her bedside table, but no clothes as such. I couldn't help but smile.

'I think you're supposed to be a pig,' I pointed out.

'Why me, why not Sophie?' she demanded.

'Kimiko did call you Miss pig-girl.'

'I've hardly ever been a piggy-girl! No more than Sophie has, anyway. You wait until I catch Jeff. I'll kill him.'

That didn't stop her putting her bags down by the bed and starting to undress. I followed suit, a little reluctantly as I would have preferred to know more about what I was letting myself in for. Beneath the baby-doll was a pair of short pink socks, loosely knitted from a thick wool, two hair bands and two ribbons, also pink, and a dummy. I was feeling a little sticky after the long journey and went to shower first, in a communal bathroom opposite Sabina's. There were fresh towels, soap, and even shower gel, presumably all of which came as standard with the house.

By the time I'd finished Poppy was stark naked and was admiring her rear view in the mirror as she held the flat piece of rubber where the pig's tail attached to the base of her spine. She'd already put her snout on, giving her naturally round face a wonderfully piggy look, while her full, soft bottom was perfect to go with the little curly tail.

'It does suit you,' I told her, sitting down on the bed. 'What are the rules about then?'

'The usual stuff,' she said casually. 'You know, how we have to do as our Mistresses say and the punishments we get if we're disobedient or naughty. We're supposed to do the cooking and cleaning too, apparently.'

'I'd expected that.'

'There's other stuff too. I didn't read all of it, but I don't suppose there's anything unexpected. I think the poison dwarf is a professional dom, actually, just from the way she acts.'

'Kimiko? Perhaps you're right, although she seems genuine enough.'

'Oh she's a sadist all right, nothing fake there. She loved making Sabina take it on the bare. I just think she's more used to paying clients than playmates.'

'Maybe. I wonder who this Master is?'

'Some male dom with a big ego and a small prick, I suppose.'

I had finished drying myself and opened my bedside table, hoping Jeff had remembered to give Kimiko proper instructions. He had. There was a bag of fresh nappies, baby powder and cream, even a shaving kit, although I had one in my luggage. Again I felt a sharp thrill at the thought of being able to play safely for a whole week, which was again followed by a touch of uncertainty. For now at least, I could afford to indulge myself, in a house dedicated to unusual sexual practices, 'where the normal rules don't apply', as the brochure had said, and with just Poppy, Sabina and Kimiko.

'Would you powder me?' I asked.

'Sure,' Poppy answered, 'just as soon as my tail's stuck on. This gum takes ages to dry.'

I took my glasses off and lay face down on the bed, with my excitement for the familiar little routine she was about to put me through rising within me. It's always good and somehow always fresh, never fading with familiarity, and more like hunger or thirst than a typical thrill. After a moment she came over, taking the powder and cream from the cupboard with the brisk efficiency of long practice.

'Bum up,' she ordered.

As I lifted my hips to present my bottom I had closed my eyes in sheer bliss. They stayed that way as Poppy shook powder over my cheeks and between, applied a few gentle pats to spread it around, then held them apart to apply a blob of cream to my anus. Her finger slipped a little way inside as she lubricated me, just enough to leave me with that lovely creamy sensation but not so much as to make me loose or uncomfortable.

'Stick it up a bit more and I'll do your pussy from behind,' she offered.

I couldn't help but sigh as I obeyed, lifting my hips further still and setting my knees apart to allow her to powder between my legs. She shook the powder on and put a cupped hand to my sex with a few of the gentlest possible pats, and for one instant her finger brushed between my lips.

'Would you?' I asked, but got a smack on my bottom for my trouble.

'Patience,' she told me. 'Now roll over.'

She was still holding the powder, and quickly shook some out on to my tummy as I turned over on the bed, before grabbing my ankles and lifting my legs into nappy-changing position. I took hold of myself under my knees, helping her as she applied a little more powder and a trio of slightly firmer smacks to my bottom cheeks. Working with that same practised speed, she took the nappy Kimiko had set out for me, slid it underneath my back, slapped my legs gently apart and folded it up over my sex. Even as she fastened the tabs around my hips I was sighing in pleasure for the feeling of the thick, puffy material encasing my bottom and sex – for me, at once the most relaxing and most erotic sensation of all.

'There we are,' she said, 'all clean and tidy, only I suppose you need me to diddle you now?'

My answer was to stick my thumb in my mouth and let my thighs come up and apart, showing her the plump bulge of nappy material between them and offering what lay beneath. She gave a little sigh, the perfect nurse, clinical, yet ever so slightly impatient with my intimate needs. I'd begun to suck my thumb as she slipped a hand in around the side of my nappy, quickly finding my sex and setting to work on my clitoris with a firm, no-nonsense motion, masturbating me because I needed to be masturbated, nothing more.

It took just moments, bringing me to a sweet, sharp orgasm of pure physical pleasure, from the motion of her fingers, from being almost nude, but most importantly from being in my nappy. Inevitably she wanted the same treatment, and I returned the favour with her kneeling on my bed, her bottom stuck high with her piggy tail wobbling above her cheeks as I used my tongue on her anus and sex until she too had come.

I had wondered why Sabina hadn't come in to play with us, and it turned out that she was asleep on her bed, worn out by the early start and the long drive. We left her there, and after a moment's hesitation began to explore. I would have felt considerably less self-conscious nude than in my nappy and baby-doll dress, while for Poppy it was the other way around, no doubt a deliberate choice on Jeff's part. Nevertheless, there didn't seem to be anyone else about, aside from Kimiko, and our confidence gradually increased.

The house was pretty much symmetrical, with a master bedroom in the centre and another set of rooms like our own in the opposite wing, while the ground floor had all the usual rooms and an extension to the kitchen at the back. The upper storey had evidently been the original servants' quarters, with a long bare corridor and a row of identical and sparsely furnished rooms, now intended for youth groups or perhaps hiking parties.

We found Kimiko in the sitting room with her boots off and her feet up, reading a book in Japanese. She hastily reasserted her dominance by shouting at us and making us stand with our hands on our heads while she admired the way we looked, but was happy to tell us that we were safe to go outside. The woods belonged to the manor, while only the very lowest part of the garden could be seen from the road.

Despite her assurances, going outside made us both feel nervous and excited. We were holding hands as we explored the gardens, which had a dozen private little places among the hedges and tall, grey stone walls. There was also what had once been a stable block to one side, but to our disappointment was now locked and apparently not in use. Beyond were the woods, with a broad, flat path leading in among fully grown pines that created a gloomy, resin scented space beneath them. We walked in among them, moving gradually up the slope, and were soon hidden from view completely.

It was a magical place, somehow unearthly, and just being there dressed as I was made me feel both liberated and secure. I promised myself I'd walk nude in the woods later in the week, but for the time being it was enough to know that my baby-doll failed to cover my nappy, which gave me an exquisite sense of vulnerability in perfect balance with the safety of being where I was and with Poppy.

The woods were huge, leading right up on to the hillside, where they opened out to a rocky slope which in turn rose to a skyline of grey crags. Nobody was visible, and when we found an ancient gate in the wall we went through just for the pleasure of going naked under the open sky before scurrying quickly back as a line of hikers appeared over the ridge. We were laughing together as we walked back, but a little nervous too, and walking considerably faster than we had before.

We were quite close to the house when we heard Kimiko's high-pitched screech demanding to know where we were. I increased my pace, genuinely keen not to provide her with an excuse to apply her tawse to my bottom, and we met her as we came out of the woods.

'You must learn your duties,' she said immediately. 'You are always to be on hand when you are needed.'

'I'm sorry, I didn't know we were needed,' I told her.

'You have to tell us these things,' Poppy added.

'Speak to me properly, dirt sluts!' she snapped. 'All rules and duties are written down in your dormitory. You must learn quickly.'

She was fumbling her tawse loose but didn't tell me to stop, so I hurried past. I still caught the smack, laid across the seat of my nappy so that I didn't feel a thing. Poppy was less lucky, with no protection as the tawse caught her low on one fleshy cheek, but she merely giggled and broke into a run down the path, much too fast for Kimiko to follow in her heels.

'Sorry, Mistress,' I said, keen to acknowledge her authority and thus hopefully avoid a beating.

'Get indoors,' she ordered, 'and go to the sitting room. You too, pig-girl!'

I hurried after Poppy, in at the back door, wondering if I was going to be punished. Dominant women often seem to know that I'm genuinely scared of the pain, which brings out the worst in so many of them. I was imagining how it would feel to take my nappy down and present my bottom for the tawse, probably in front of Poppy and Sabina, and was completely unprepared for the sight that greeted me in the sitting room. There were other people there, five of them, all complete strangers, and all men.

Poppy was standing in the doorway, her back to me, one hand over her breasts and the other over her sex, taken completely by surprise. I came to a halt behind her, my face flushing with embarrassment despite myself, only for Kimiko to come up behind me and push Poppy and myself forward.

Every face had turned to us as we stumbled into the room, men old and young, tall and short, fat and thin, all staring at Poppy's naked body and mine. I managed a weak smile, desperately trying to tell myself that they would all be there for the same reason as I was, and that therefore I had no reason to feel embarrassed. It didn't work.

'You will meet the other guests,' Kimiko stated, clearly enjoying our discomfort. 'Hands on your heads, both of you, now!'

I obeyed, as it didn't make any difference. Poppy hesitated, seemed about to speak and then changed her mind, raising both arms slowly and linking her fingers in among her dark curls. I could almost feel the men's eyes as they looked us up and down, although most of their concentration was reserved for Poppy's breasts. She'd gone pink, the flush spreading not just over her face but down her chest too, while even as I watched her nipples began to poke out, growing quickly to erection. One of the men swallowed, another suddenly looked down, as if ashamed of his enjoyment of our exposure. Kimiko came up beside me.

'This is Gabrielle,' she announced, picking up her yellow clipboard from a table and consulting it before she continued. 'She is a slut and should be treated as one.'

The men nodded, some eager, some sheepish, their eyes flicking between me and Poppy as Kimiko went on, reading from her clipboard.

'She likes to wear a nappy, and to use it. She likes to be naked. She likes to be spanked, but not hard. She likes to piddle in public. If you wish to watch, you must ask.'

My face had been growing slowly hotter as she spoke, while the men's expressions had become increasingly lewd, all except for one, who didn't seem able to look at me at all. Mistress Kimiko continued.

'If you wish her services you must ask myself or her Mistress, Sabina, who is resting at present.'

'Services?' I queried.

'Read your duties,' she answered and would have continued but I interrupted her, now genuinely alarmed.

'Sorry, Kimiko . . . Mistress Kimiko, but what sort of services?'

'Everything is written down, stupid girl!' she snapped. 'Read it.'

'Yes, but . . .'

'Shut up! You have a stop word, don't you? What else do you want?'

I went quiet, but I was feeling far from reassured as she went on and I scanned the men's lecherous faces. Two were conventionally good looking, but that made little or no difference. Men do almost nothing for me, as such.

'The one with the fat breasts is Poppy,' Kimiko went on. 'She is also a slut and to be treated the same. Her Mistress is Sabina. She likes all sorts of corporal punishment. She likes role play, particularly to be a pig, a pony, or a dog. Again, you must ask if you wish her services.'

Poppy and I exchanged a glance, at once worried and puzzled. One of the men had raised his hand.

'Er . . . Mistress Kimiko,' he asked. 'If we have to ask all the time and we may be turned down, how can we be sure we get what we've been promised?'

'And paid for,' another put in, triggering nods of agreement from two more.

'You will get it. I will make sure,' Mistress Kimiko assured him.

'Get what, exactly?' Poppy queried.

A new voice sounded, a familiar one, Sophie Cherwell.

'Relax, you two, we only have to toss them off once a day. Have fun with it.'

She kissed Poppy, then me, and came to stand between us, her hands going to the top of her head without having to be asked. The men simultaneously swivelled their gazes to her, even the one who didn't seem to want to look glancing up briefly. It wasn't surprising, as she was in her school uniform, only with her tiny skirt worn so high the front of her knickers showed, while her blouse was undone to her waist and she very obviously had no bra.

'That is right,' Mistress Kimiko confirmed, trying to sound dominant but more relieved. 'Each guest is entitled to one orgasm every day, with assistance.'

It was completely outrageous, but with Sophie being so casual about it and given my right not to be involved still intact I decided against speaking out. Sophie giggled as the men were told that she was more or less public property and enjoyed spanking and humiliation, and I let myself relax a little. Kimiko moved on, seeming to forget her role as Mistress as she compared the five men with the notes on her clipboard and read out their names.

'We have here, from nearest me, Mr Petherick. Then is Mr Spottiswood and Mr Greene. In the armchair, Mr Masham, and standing behind him, Mr Noyles.'

I managed a smile as I looked them over, hoping my nervousness wasn't too obvious and wondering how I would react if Sabina demanded that I do anything rude with them. It was hard to gauge their sexualities, and Kimiko didn't seem about to enlighten us, despite the embarrassing detail with which she'd revealed ours. Mr Greene, at least, seemed to be submissive, either that or extraordinarily shy, unable to lift his eyes to us despite being fully clothed while we were either naked or clearly on sexual display. Otherwise he was about as nondescript as it is possible to be, middle-sized, middle-aged and from his dress, middle-class. I could easily imagine him as a bank manager.

Next to him on the sofa was Mr Spottiswood, who was somewhat older, also smaller but quite solidly built. He was also balding, but far from nondescript due to a pair of bright, piercing eyes that seemed not merely to penetrate my flimsy baby-doll dress, but touch my flesh beneath. His fingers were constantly in motion, fidgeting together as if he couldn't wait to get his hands on what he could see.

Mr Masham was at least physically appealing, perhaps thirty and with a hard, muscular body to judge by what I could see between the sides of his open leather jacket. His trousers were also leather, encasing lean, powerful legs, while his hands seemed strong and capable. There was a heavy gunmetal chain around his neck, he wore rings and had an elaborate cross tattooed high on one cheek, while his unusually dark eyes and neat, triangular beard gave him a rakish, even devilish aspect and more than a suggestion of cruelty.

Despite being much the same age and smartly dressed, there was something about Mr Noyles that gave me the creeps, for all my efforts to tell myself it was an irrational reaction. He was tall with dark hair and a clean-cut face, but somewhat lanky, with a slight stoop. Worse, he had one of the most enormous pairs of hands I'd ever seen, with long, unpleasantly meaty fingers that reminded me of J. R. R. Tolkien's description of the creature Gollum. Unlike Mr Greene, he had no difficulty in admiring our bodies, but his gaze was shifty and indirect as if he wanted to look without us realising.

Then there was Mr Petherick, a man who bulged in every direction but was either in denial of his obesity or had been putting on weight rapidly and grown out of his clothes. Both his trousers and shirt were plainly too tight, while a double ream of fat had squeezed out from the top of his collar. Aside from a nasty little moustache he was completely bald, so that with his bulges of fat his head gave the impression of a squat candle that had softened and spread in the heat. He had small, round glasses.

They all seemed to be expecting us to do something, or at least for Mistress Kimiko to do something with us, but she merely clapped her hands.

'Time to prepare dinner, sluts, chop chop!'

'What about them?' Poppy queried, jerking a thumb at the men.

'Do not question me!' Mistress Kimiko snapped back.

'Yes, but . . .'

'Touch your toes, pig-girl!'

Poppy hesitated, and might not have done if Sophie hadn't spoken up, laughing.

'You put yourself right in that one, Pops. Come on, bum up!'

Poppy made a face but bent down, touching her toes with some difficulty to leave her bottom pushed well out with the rubber piggy tail wobbling above her cheeks. Mistress Kimiko stood away, making very sure the men could see, which meant using the tawse backhand. I watched the first smack, delivered accurately but not too hard, so that Poppy barely gasped, then turned my attention to the men, hoping to see which were the real sadists and which simply lecherous.

Mr Greene had hidden his face, apparently unable to watch a woman beaten, but the other four were looking. Mr Noyles seemed as if he didn't want to be seen peeping, while Mr Spottiswood was the exact opposite, gloating openly over Poppy's fate. Mr Masham was smiling, his face alight with sadistic glee. Mr Petherick's eyes looked as if they were about to pop out of his head.

Poppy took her strokes as well as ever, four of them, each laid plum across the full, cheeky target of her bottom and leaving her decorated with a set of broad pink lines, but barely drawing a squeak from her lips. When she was allowed up she stuck out her tongue at Mistress Kimiko's back the moment the tiny domina had turned at the sound of the doorbell.

'Does it hurt, darling?' Mr Spottiswood asked, his tone making it obvious he didn't want the answer to be a 'no'.

'It's nice and warm, as it goes,' Poppy told him as she gave her cheeks a rub. 'What, more guests?'

She stepped out into the passage and I followed, hoping to make it to the kitchen door before yet another complete stranger was given an eyeful of my nappy. I failed, but the person who had just come through the door was no stranger. It was Stephen Stanbrook, which was more of a relief than an embarrassment, and I was also pleased to see that he had a woman with him, presumably Tasanee. She was only fractionally taller than Kimiko, with the same dark hair and large, liquid eyes, but where Kimiko was bold she was timid and clearly submissive. Beneath her open coat she was plainly stark naked but for a pair of high-heeled black ankle boots joined together by a short chain and a dog collar from which a lead ran to Stephen's hand.

'Hello Gabrielle,' Stephen greeted me. 'Poppy, Sophie.'

He came forward, kissing each of us and taking a squeeze of Poppy's bottom, also introducing us to Tasanee before Mistress Kimiko cut in.

'You can talk later. Now you must do dinner.'

She gave Sophie a little flick with the tawse as she spoke. None of us raised any further objection, but trooped into the kitchen. It was large, and clearly intended to allow catering for quite big groups, with not only two tall refrigerators but a box freezer and the original larder, while a number of huge saucepans hung from hooks on one wall and the cupboards proved to be well stocked with utensils. There was also plenty of food, if anything more than twelve people would need for a week.

'I could do a *tarte à l'oignon* as a starter?' I suggested.

'For that lot?' Sophie scoffed. 'They can have bangers and mash and lump it. If you want to do anything fancy, we'll eat it in here while we're serving.'

'I agree,' Poppy added. 'If we have to do all the work we should get the best grub.'

'Don't you think we'll be sitting at the same table?' I queried. 'And what about Sabina?'

Poppy merely shrugged and disappeared into the larder. I could see it was going to end in tears, but that was all part of the game, while if I behaved I might be spared. At least, I would be spared for the moment. I knew only too well that at some point either Sabina or Mistress Kimiko would find an excuse to punish me, but that didn't prevent me from wanting to delay the moment for as long as possible.

There were aprons hanging on the pantry door, and we each put one on before we began to prepare the food. We talked as we worked, Poppy and Sophie peeling potatoes at the big table in the middle of the kitchen while I got the pans and the grill ready. It didn't take long with the three of us together, and when Sophie went to one of the refrigerators for the

44

sausages she discovered that the vegetable drawers were full of bottles of white wine. She soon had one open, and we began to drink as we cooked, so that by the time I was stirring milk and butter into the potatoes the alcohol had begun to take effect.

'I'll serve the spuds,' Poppy offered, extracting a large ladle from one of the drawers. 'I've always wanted to do this.'

'I bags the beans then,' Sophie said quickly. 'You can do the sausages, Gabby.'

There was a big wooden service trolley and we piled everything on to it before wheeling it out and down the corridor to the dining room, which was already full of people. Mistress Kimiko was at the head of the table, with Stephen to her right and Sabina at the far end. The others were ranged to either side, except for Tasanee, who was kneeling beside Stephen with her head hung down. Her lead was attached to the back of his chair, while instead of a place setting she had a dog bowl on the carpet in front of her. Spare places had been laid out too, showing that we were at least permitted to eat with the others.

'Grub's up,' Poppy declared, lifting the great tub of mashed potato. 'Bangers and mash.'

'What is that?' Mistress Kimiko demanded.

'Mashed potato, sausages and beans,' Poppy explained.

'What about the blue cheese salad? That is the menu.'

'Salad's off, love,' Poppy told her. 'It's bangers and mash.'

'No!' Mistress Kimiko squeaked. 'This is not right. You must follow the rules and duties.'

Poppy ignored her completely, going to Mr Greene, who was seated at the corner of the table nearest the door.

'Mash?' she asked him at the same moment as she slapped down a pile of it with her ladle, so hard it not only splashed across the plate but also spattered a considerable part of the table and his front.

'At least serve properly, pig-girl!' Kimiko snapped.

She already had her tawse out, and brought it down across Poppy's bottom with a resounding smack. Poppy barely seemed to notice, but moved on to Mr Spottiswood and out of Kimiko's reach. This time she slapped the ladle full of mashed potato down even harder, but it missed, mostly landing in his water glass.

'Stop this!' Kimiko screeched, rising. 'What are you doing, stupid girl? You must obey me and follow the rules and duties!'

'Don't get your knickers in a twist,' Poppy answered.

'Stop it, Poppy,' Sabina ordered, 'or you'll get it from me. Do sit down, Kimiko.'

Mistress Kimiko's face had gone red with anger, but she managed to control herself and Poppy began to serve more carefully. Several of the men were laughing, although Mr Greene looked as if he was about to burst into tears and Mr Spottiswood was frowning as he fished bits of potato out of his water.

'I think I should get to spank her,' he said after a moment, his voice reedy and wheedling. 'Don't you think so, Mistress Sabina?'

'I'll spank you in a minute,' Sabina answered, then seemed to reconsider. 'Maybe later, we'll see.'

Mr Spottiswood made an odd nasal noise as he turned his face to Poppy, who merely stuck out her tongue.

'You can do me in front of them, if you like,' she said. 'But I'm not having that dirty old bastard touching me.'

46

'Enough!' Kimiko screeched. 'You will learn to show respect, and for your punishment, Mr Spottiswood will spank you after dinner, in the sitting room, in front of everybody. Is that not right, Mistress Sabina?'

Poppy turned a knowing look to Sabina, who merely shrugged.

'Fair enough,' she said. 'It's your show. You're to let him spank you, Poppy.'

Poppy stopped, her mouth open in horror. She began to speak, thought better of it, began to speak again and again thought better of it, instead continuing to serve, but now quietly with her head hung low. Mr Masham gave a murmur of approval and Stephen Stanbrook said something to Tasanee, who inclined her head in agreement. I wasn't sure what Poppy had been angling for, but I very definitely did not want the same treatment myself, and served out my sausages carefully and in silence, leaving my own plate until last.

Poppy's behaviour had broken the ice, her coming spanking providing an immediate topic of conversation to which all of us could relate in one way or another. Even Mr Greene spoke up, asking if he might take the punishment in her place. He clearly regarded the idea of a woman being spanked as utterly inappropriate, confirming my view of him as not only sexually submissive but a believer in female supremacy. Sabina turned him down, but she was thoroughly enjoying her dominance, which all the men except Stephen seemed to be soaking up, even Mr Masham, who I'd assumed to be purely dominant himself. More than that, she made a point of demonstrating her control over Poppy and me, also Sophie, in what had quickly become a contest with Stephen. Unfortunately, both Poppy and Sophie were

47

inclined to be cheeky and rebellious, while Tasanee behaved with a meek and loyal obedience that drew murmurs of approval from all the men and Mistress Kimiko too. I did as I was told, both to support Sabina and avoid punishment, addressing people correctly, bending from the waist as I served drinks, keeping my eyes lowered and all the other little details Sabina had learnt and imposed on Poppy and me over the past couple of years. By the time we'd finished the bangers and mash all three dominants had relaxed into their natural roles, treating us with easy disdain as we cleared the plates.

'What's for afters, slut?' Stephen asked, sliding his hand up Sophie's school skirt as she bent to pick up a now empty dish.

'Um . . . we didn't make one . . . sir,' Sophie replied.

'Well that's no good, is it?' Stephen responded, still fondling her bottom. 'Bad girl.'

He tweaked up her skirt and tucked it into her waistband, to leave her with her knickers on show as she walked from the room. There were murmurs of disappointment from some of the other men, although the grossly overweight Mr Petherick muttered something about his diet. Mr Spottiswood suggested spankings and I felt my stomach go tight as Kimiko replied.

'Perhaps that would be appropriate, we shall see.'

'It does say three-course dinners with maid service in the brochure,' Mr Masham pointed out.

'The matter will be dealt with,' she answered.

'They need training, that's what they need,' Mr Petherick suggested.

They continued to speak, but I lost the conversation as I left the room with a stack of plates. Sophie and Poppy were already in the kitchen, bending over the open freezer.

'How about Toothsome Toffee?' Poppy suggested. 'Or Strawberry Supreme?'

'Are we giving them ice cream for dessert?' I asked.

'No,' she answered, 'we're just having some ice cream.'

'Aren't we supposed to be washing up?'

'Come on, Gabby, stop being so wet, or I'll spank you myself. That's what it is, Sophie, she's scared of getting her botty smacked.'

'Ah, diddums!' Sophie laughed. 'Come on, Gabrielle, have some ice cream.'

'But if we get caught . . .'

'We get spanked. Big deal.'

'Maybe for you . . .'

'They've got some really posh sorbets, those ones you like, Gabby,' Poppy cut in. 'There's lemon, and jasmine, and green tea.'

'Have they got Riesling?'

'Sure.'

I took the pot of sorbet, trying to tell myself that a spanking was inevitable anyway, and that I could always back out if I really had to. They decided on a tub of ice cream and shared it, feeding each other and me by spoon, until I'd begun to enjoy myself too much to worry unduly about the consequences. After all, it was Poppy who was going to be the entertainment for the evening, across the horrible Mr Spottiswood's knee.

Only when we'd finished eating did we do the washing up, not even bothering to hurry. Sophie was completely happy, looking forward to her week without the slightest reservation, but while Poppy was trying her best to be equally nonchalant I could tell she was getting nervous underneath. She had never been completely at ease with men, unlike Sophie, and while she didn't mind long-term playmates such as Jeff Bellbird I could tell that she was less than happy about punishment from Mr Spottiswood. He was not only a dirty old man, but a stranger, and effectively paying for it, which, like me, she found to add considerably to the humiliation. She had wanted to be spanked in front of him, by Sabina, but that was a different matter. To have to allow him to touch her was stronger by far.

'Oh well,' she said as we left the kitchen, 'at least he won't have the satisfaction of pulling my knickers down.'

'Only because you haven't got any on,' Sophie pointed out, and slapped her as we entered the sitting room, where the rest of the guests had gathered.

They were sitting comfortably, drinking brandy or liqueurs, which Tasanee was serving, still stark naked but for her boots and collar. Sabina and Stephen were in the two big armchairs, Kimiko by the fireplace, Mr Masham and Mr Petherick at either end of the sofa, with the other three men seated behind on wooden chairs. The sofa had been pushed back a little, and a fourth wooden chair stood at the exact centre of the rug around which everyone was gathered. With no chairs left, I went to sit on the arm of Sabina's.

'Spanking time!' Mr Spottiswood declared, rubbing his hands together as he got up without even waiting for Poppy to have a drink.

Poppy glanced at Sabina, who merely nodded towards the chair in the centre. Mr Spottiswood sat down on it, beaming with satisfaction as he patted his lap.

'Over we go, my dear,' he said, 'bum up for the boys, eh, that's how we like 'em. Which way around would you like her, Mistress Sabina, bum first or face first?'

'Face first,' Sabina answered. 'I'd like to see her expression while you spank her.'

I bit down a little involuntary thrill at the thought of watching Poppy's face as she was punished. Already she looked deeply sulky, but that didn't stop her draping herself across Mr Spottiswood's legs. He immediately raised one knee, making her bottom lift and part, now the highest part of her body except for her curly piggy tail, which was wobbling faintly.

'Very sweet, and it does suit you,' Mr Spottiswood remarked as he gave the tail a tug and let it spring back into position. 'Now, we're going to play a little game. It's called Spare my Blushes.'

'You didn't say anything about perverted games?' Poppy protested, lifting her head to look at Sabina.

Sabina smiled and took a sip of her drink, watching Poppy's expression change between hope and worry before she answered.

'You're being punished, Poppy. I expect Mr Spottiswood's game will add to that, don't you?'

'Yes, but Sabina . . .'

'Shut up. Do you as like with her, Mr Spottiswood.'

'Sabina! Look, I . . .'

I really thought she was going to use her stop word, but she trailed off, her face setting in consternation, which grew stronger as Mr Spottiswood's hand settled on her bottom. Sabina was being unusually cruel, perhaps in an effort to impress Stephen and Kimiko, perhaps as a reaction to her own humiliation at being made to take a stroke of the tawse on the bare, perhaps just to show off, or a bit of all three. Again I told myself I would be extra good, cuddling into her as we watched Mr Spottiswood fondle Poppy's bottom.

'I do like them nice and big,' he was saying, the words seeming to drool from his little, fleshy mouth. 'That's how a girl's bottom should be, big and fleshy, and you, my dear, are truly exceptional.'

He'd put his hand under her bottom, pushing up to make both her cheeks and her piggy tail wobble. Every eye in the room was on her, even Mr Greene watching from the shadows in horrified fascination. Poppy responded to his words with a little sob and once more lifted her face, pleading with her eyes to Sabina, who merely shook her head. Mr Spottiswood continued to fondle.

'I shall explain how Spare my Blushes works,' he said. 'Essentially, it is a question of which set of cheeks get reddest, those belonging to your pretty face, or these somewhat larger and ruder ones behind. I shall ask you a question, and if I am satisfied by your answer I shall ask another question, if not, it's smack-botty time!'

He gave her bottom a couple of firm pats to illustrate his words. Just the description of the awful game was enough to set my stomach fluttering. I could guess what sort of questions he would ask, and was extremely glad that it was Poppy and not me who was being punished.

'Question one,' he said. 'Do you have a big bottom?'

Mr Masham gave a lewd snigger. Mr Petherick pointed out that she could hardly deny it, which was a bit much coming from a man maybe twice her weight, but Poppy kept a stony silence, her mouth pursed and her eyes full of defiance.

'So you're a tough one, eh?' Mr Spottiswood chuckled. 'I wonder how long that will last? Maybe I'll have to spank you to tears, eh? Do you cry easily?'

Poppy still kept her mouth firmly shut, but Mr Spottiswood merely laughed. He'd never once stopped groping her bottom, his stubby fingers squeezing and stroking at her flesh. Now he began to spank, not hard, which Poppy could have taken easily, but with an awful, loitering intimacy, smacking her under her cheeks and keeping his hand in place to make her flesh wobble, all the while with his bright, piggy eyes staring at his target. Poppy took it with her face set in sullen determination, showing only the occasional flicker of shame and involuntary arousal when his fingers touched some particularly sensitive spot. He took so long I thought he'd forgotten all about his dirty little game, but finally he stopped, gave a satisfied sigh and spoke again.

'Question two. Does your cunt smell more like mackerel or cod?'

'You bastard!' Poppy gasped, her face flaming pink, and I heard Sabina give a little intake of breath.

Mr Spottiswood waited a moment, but Poppy gave an angry shake of her head. Once again he began to spank her, now using both hands, one on each cheek, and alternately, as if he was playing pat-a-cake on her bottom. She took it in silence, even as he got faster and harder, until he was drumming a rhythm out on her cheeks, the fleshy slaps echoing around the room. He'd given her a good hundred before he stopped, which left her bottom a richer pink than her face, although not by much.

'Quite the little fighter, aren't you?' he asked as he went back to feeling her now hot cheeks. 'OK, if you're so tough: question three, have you ever been buggered?'

More than one of the other men shifted position in sudden interest, but still Poppy refused to speak, her mouth pursed tight and her fingers locked into the rug beneath her. Again Mr Spottiswood gave her a chance to answer, shaking his head in mock disapproval when it became evident she wasn't going to, then once more starting to spank her.

'I bet you have,' he said, setting up the same double-handed rhythm on her bum. 'A pretty girl like you, with such a magnificent rear end? Some fellow must have been tempted to put his cock up that juicy little back hole, surely? Not telling? Well, let's have a look then?'

He stopped spanking, suddenly, to haul Poppy's cheeks wide, displaying her to the room and particularly to Kimiko and Stephen, who were directly behind. Her mouth came open in a gasp, and as he peered close to inspect her anus her face was working between misery and shock, yet she made no attempt to stop him or get off, and when he finally let go of her cheeks her breathing was left ragged and urgent.

'I suspect Mr Willy's been up the chocolate mine,' he said, looking thoroughly smug, 'but fair's fair, you wouldn't answer and you took your spanking, so it's your bottom that's red and not your face.'

In practice Poppy's face was now every bit as red as her bottom, but that didn't seem to bother Mr Spottiswood, who gave her cheeks another wobble, cocked his knee a little higher so that Poppy's anus would now be showing even without her cheeks held open, and continued with the game.

'Question four, which would you rather do, suck my cock or lick your Mistress's bum out?'

This time Poppy answered.

'Lick Sabina, of course.'

'Say it properly,' he demanded, and I caught the disappointment in his voice.

'I'd rather lick Sabina's bottom!' Poppy said firmly. 'Frankly, I'd rather lick anyone's bottom, any woman's.'

'Not a cock sucker then?' Mr Spottiswood asked. 'I'm surprised. You look like one.'

'Fuck off!'

'Oh dearie me, what dreadful language! I can see you're not disciplined nearly enough, but you will be now, believe me.'

He began to spank her again, hard now, perhaps angry at the refusal of what had obviously been an offer to fellate him. She took it as well as ever, letting out only the occasional gasp or soft mewl as her bottom bounced to slaps that would have had me kicking wildly and in tears. Unfortunately it only made him all the more determined, belabouring her bottom with the full force of his stocky arm until at last Sabina called a halt.

'That's enough, Mr Spottiswood. She'll have learnt her lesson.'

'I was only just getting started,' he protested, but stopped, contenting himself with a last stroke of her now blazing bottom before he let her up.

She scrambled hastily off his lap, to stand rubbing her bottom and trying to look back over her shoulder to assess the damage. Both her cheeks were red all over, with one or two slight bruises coming up where the harder smacks had caught her, and she was trembling ever so slightly.

'I think I'd like her to suck me now,' Mr Spottiswood announced. 'If that's OK, Sabina?'

'No it is not!' Poppy answered him.

'I was asking your Mistress,' he told her.

'You've spanked her, that will do,' Sabina put in.

'I am entitled to get it,' Mr Spottiswood pointed out, turning towards Kimiko.

Kimiko looked hesitant, and had begun to reach for her clipboard, but Stephen spoke up.

'I think I can solve that problem for you, Mr Spottiswood. Tasanee, you are to take Mr Spottiswood in your mouth, all the way.'

'Yes, Master,' she answered, a barely audible whisper.

'That's very generous of you,' Mr Spottiswood addressed Stephen, reaching out to take Tasanee's lead.

'My pleasure,' Stephen responded, 'but it must be done here, in front of everybody.'

Mr Spottiswood hesitated, clearly less than happy at having to perform in front of others despite just having shown off every intimate detail of Poppy's body, but after a glance down at Tasanee where she now knelt at his feet he nodded.

'Fair enough. Can I have the comfortable chair then?'

'Be my guest,' Stephen offered, rising.

Mr Spottiswood sat down, directly opposite me and in clear view as Mistress Kimiko pulled the spanking chair back. Tasanee went to kneel between Mr Spottiswood's thighs, her half-lowered gaze showing only a faint trace of apprehension as she turned to him. Poppy had sat down on the other arm of Sabina's chair, and the three of us cuddled close in mutual excitement, but perhaps also a need for protection. Sophie had come close to us too, but turned as Mr Masham spoke to her.

'How about you? I do like a suck from a schoolgirl, and I'm more than willing to return the favour.'

Sophie hesitated for an instant, then smiled and nodded. I could feel the speed of my heart picking up as I watched the two girls prepare to fellate the men. Mr Spottiswood had already taken his cock out, as thick and stubby as his body, with a greasy sheen to the skin and a disproportionately large helmet already poking out from a thick foreskin. Sophie did Mr Masham's for him, unzipping his fly and pulling down the front of a pair of black underpants to extract a long, pale cock, already erect. She took a moment to open her blouse, baring her breasts for him, and went down, taking him deep in her mouth and sucking with her eyes closed in concentration. Tasanee was doing the same for Mr Spottiswood, and for a moment the only sounds in the room were the soft, wet noises of the girls working on their mouthfuls. When Mr Noyles spoke it was so sudden it made me jump.

'How about you girls? Come on, your friends are doing it, so it's only right.'

He sounded resentful, accusing even, and for a moment I felt bad for not taking my share. It seemed unreasonable, when both Tasanee and Sophie were down on their knee with men's cocks in their mouth and I was only watching; only he wasn't looking at me, but Sabina.

'How about you?' he asked.

'I don't,' she said firmly.

'Oh God, OK!' Poppy said suddenly. 'I'll do it, if I have to.'

She got up, leaving me feeling guilty as she crossed to Mr Noyles, for all that I knew the spanking had got to her and that her reluctance was a pretence. He'd quickly flopped his cock out and she went down on him, sucking vigorously as if trying to get an unpleasant but necessary job out of the way as quickly as possible. I knew she was putting it on, but my feelings were growing stronger, knowing that I really ought to do my share. I wondered if Stephen would make Tasanee suck him and the other two and decided he probably would, which made me feel worse still, as if I was betraying my friends. Still I might have held back if Mr Petherick hadn't at last found the courage to speak out.

'How about me then, don't I get any? I paid too, you know.'

His voice was wheedling and full of self-pity, the worst possible thing for me. A command or a nasty remark I would have resisted, and as it was I turned to Sabina, hoping she'd rescue me from my own feelings.

'Should I, do you think?'

I wanted her to say no, but I should have known she was in a sadistic mood.

'Yes I do, and I know you want to. Get sucking, slut.'

That was it, the last of my resistance gone, and as I got down on the floor I was trying to make the best of my sense of fairness. The other girls were doing it, and so should I, while if that meant I had to suck off the least attractive man in the room then it was my own fault for holding back. Now I was kneeling at his feet, looking up into his fat red face as it broke into a knowing smile.

'Can you get your breasts out, please?' he asked. 'I like a girl to have her breasts showing.'

I managed a weak smile, no longer able to speak, and hauled my baby-doll up to show off my breasts. He gave a grunt of appreciation and moved his hands to his fly, peeling it down to pull out a thick, moist cock from beneath the overhang of his belly. I swallowed, not happy about taking it in my mouth but extremely glad it wasn't going up my pussy, let alone my bottom. He was immensely thick, considerably more so than the courgettes Poppy had put in me when they were trying to persuade me to come. He was also ugly, with thin, taut cock skin so that his veins stood out raised and dark beneath, while the base of his shaft emerged from a thick growth of reddish hair and was covered in little bumps like goose-pimples.

'Haven't I got a big one?' he chuckled. 'Come on, not scared of a bit of cock sucking, are you?'

He'd spread his legs and moved forward, holding his belly up with one hand as he presented me his cock with the other. Sabina's voice sounded from behind me.

'In your mouth, Gabrielle.'

I swallowed once, and then I'd done it, leaning forward to gulp him in, my mouth full of cock, my jaw stretched so wide it already ached as I began to mouth on the thick shaft. He gave a moan of satisfaction and settled back, releasing his belly to let it squash against my face as I struggled to suck him properly. I moved a little closer, to pull a pair of oversized balls free of his underpants, telling myself I was only doing it to make him come quickly as I began to stroke them. Above me, he had picked up his brandy glass, sipping from it as I worked on his cock.

Already he'd begun to swell, hardening and lengthening in my mouth until I was having difficulty taking his length as well as his width. At that one podgy hand settled on the back of my head, forcing me down until I felt his bulbous head squashing into my throat. I began to gag and he let me pull back, only to push down again the moment I'd caught my breath. His hand tightened in my hair and he'd begun to fuck my head, still sipping at his brandy as he moved me slowly up and down on his now fully erect cock.

I knew Sabina was watching me, enjoying my humiliation as I sucked on a man's penis, and relishing her view, with me kneeling at his feet, near naked with my breasts pulled out from my lifted baby-doll and my bottom covered in the puffy white material of my nappy, more indecent by far than if I'd been fully nude and showing everything. Nor was I the only one, four girls on their knees sucking cock, naked or in our revealing little outfits, playing the slut for the eager, dirty minded men and their mistresses. I was no better than the others, no more detached, now enjoying the big penis in my mouth as the obese Mr Petherick fucked my head, so much so that already I wanted to stick my hand down my nappy and bring myself to orgasm while I was doing it, maybe even wet myself into my hand before I started to rub, just to show how naughty I could be.

Mr Spottiswood gave a soft grunt and I knew he'd come in Tasanee's mouth, giving her a dirty, slippery reward for her obedience. Somehow I knew she'd swallow it, meekly taking a stranger's come down her throat because her Master had ordered it. I would soon be doing the same, maybe as I came. I had to do it. My hand went down my nappy and I was touching myself, rubbing the faint stubble of my skin and between my lips where it was wet and urgent, and lower, to my open, eager sex and the tiny dimple of my anus, still slippery with the lubricant Poppy had applied when she put my nappy on.

Mr Petherick gave a grunt of surprise as I forced my head back from under his hand, but not to escape, rather to take his heavy, bulbous scrotum into my mouth, sucking on his balls as I masturbated him and myself to the same rhythm. My orgasm was already beginning to rise in my head, but I slowed, knowing it would be better still for holding back. He was moaning as I mouthed on his balls, and then all of a sudden he was pulling on my hair and babbling orders at me.

'I'm going to come, get it in your mouth . . . in your mouth . . .'

I made it, just in time, coming off his balls to open my mouth wide for his load. He grabbed his cock, stuffing it into my mouth, so deep it made my cheeks bulge and holding me down by my hair, only to whip it free, jerking furiously on his shaft as more dirty words spilt from his lips.

'Keep it open . . . yes, like that, let me come in your mouth . . . let me . . . oh God, I've done it, right in your mouth, on your tongue and everything . . . oh you lovely little tart . . .'

He broke off with a sigh and slumped back into the chair. I stayed as I was, my mouth wide to show off the thick pool of spunk he'd laid on my tongue, rubbing hard as I thought of the state I was in, kneeling with my breasts out, wearing my nappy in front of the men and women who'd just watched me suck a man off. That same man had come in my mouth, and now I was coming too, my fingers busy with my sex . . . my cunt . . . my dirty, slippery cunt as I rubbed myself to a long, exquisite climax, and all the while with my mouth held wide to show off the slimy white puddle he'd done on my tongue.

Three

As I lay in bed the next morning I was thinking of
how I'd changed over the years, and in particular
since meeting Poppy. Beforehand I had always prided
myself on my openness and clear thinking. First had
come my desire for absolute liberty of body and spirit,
then my realisation that the sexual aspect of
that was best achieved by being put in nappies and
giving myself over completely into another's control.
My search for a nurse had led me to my friend
Natasha, then to Monty Hartle and to Jeff Bellbird,
who had made me understand the pleasure that can
come from accepting punishment, thus turning my
thoughts to darker and yet more secretive pleasures.
Poppy had taken me further still, until I could fully
understand what had always seemed a very English
and distinctly perverse pleasure in deliberately allowing myself to be spanked, humiliated and worse. Now
I could join her, and women like Sophie, almost as an
equal, thrilling in being put to my knees to suck a
strange man's cock, not simply as an act of physical
pleasure but to indulge in deliberate self-degradation
in a way I wouldn't even have understood before.

The only real difference was my inability to cope
with pain, but that never seemed to change, and was
now a problem. Poppy, Sophie, even Sabina, all knew

how to spank me properly, but they didn't, and Mistress Kimiko seemed to prefer to use her tawse, which I was sure would hurt. Yet it was important to play my role, and I resolved to be as good as possible in the hope that they would play fair and spare me anything extreme.

I'd woken early, worried that Mistress Kimiko might expect us to be up and about, but my watch showed nearly half-past seven and there didn't seem to be any activity at all in the big house. After serving the men, Sabina had taken all three of us to bed, enjoying us together, but we'd been too tired to do very much and had returned to our dormitory. Both the others were still asleep, Poppy with her bedclothes kicked back but her sheet twisted around her and tightly held in one hand, so that her bare bottom stuck out, the curly piggy tail still attached in the small of her back. Sophie was naked, her school uniform scattered across the floor, all except for her knickers, which she'd used to masturbate Mr Greene as Mistress Kimiko beat him with her tawse. Now only her face showed above her covers, framed in blonde hair to create a picture of innocent repose.

It would have been easy just to lie there thinking until the others woke up, but I was beginning to need the loo and wasn't in the mood to go in my nappy, which was off anyway. I got up instead, pulling on my robe and padding along the corridor to the bathroom. We'd gone up before the men and I wasn't sure who was sleeping where or using which facility, so I locked the door before going into the shower, despite feeling slightly foolish after being so open in front of them the night before. There was another copy of Mistress Kimiko's rules and duties taped to the back of the door, and I paused to read it as I dried myself, not wanting to provide any excuse for her to punish me.

There was an awful lot of it, including a wealth of obsessive detail about deportment and how we should speak to each other, much of which I was sure she didn't know, or anyone else. Certainly it hadn't been written by her, the English was far too practised. I found myself wondering who the Master was, if it might be one of the men, and if so, why he hadn't revealed himself. The rules allowed him to do what he pleased with whomever he pleased, so he didn't seem to have anything to gain from being mysterious.

One of the major rules was that I had to dress as I was told to, so I stayed in my robe, unsure if the nappy and baby-doll combination was my personal uniform for the week or if there would be others. It was just as well, because as I went downstairs to see what could be done about coffee I met Kimiko coming up. She too was in a robe and slippers, making her seem tinier than ever, but her expression was no different as she held out the pile of clothes she'd been carrying, nor her commanding tone.

'You are up, good. Take these for you and your friends. Today is maid training.'

'Could I get a coffee first, please . . . er, Mistress?'

'You get dressed first, then make the coffee, for everyone.'

'OK, if you like.'

I took the clothes, which I'd already realised were maids' uniforms, and retreated back up the stairs. It seemed a little early to be getting into role, and whatever people say about their sexuality I have yet to be convinced that anybody is so much a slave in her or his own mind that they'll gladly run errands first thing in the morning, for anybody. Unfortunately I didn't want to get punished either, and so took

65

the uniforms back to the dormitory, where I laid them out on one of the spare beds.

All three were the same size, about average for a woman, and while I realised it would have been a bit much to ask for them to be tailor made, that was distinctly awkward. Sophie would be all right, with her petite frame and more or less average figure, but Poppy was going to be bursting out at the seams.

For me it was worse. The huge, frilly knickers were a good enough fit, but the dress wasn't. After a little experimentation I found I had three choices. I could tug it up, in which case my breasts were covered but the full expanse of my frillies were showing both back and front; or I could wear it low, in which case my bottom would be moderately decent but I would be topless; or I could wear it at the natural level of my waist, in which case I was showing nipples and knickers. The third choice was the rudest, but also the least silly, and I decided it was better to be the object of arousal than of ridicule.

There were also suspender belts, stockings, garters, smart high heels and little velvet collars, all of which I put on. As I admired myself in the mirror the sense of sexual humiliation which had been rising gradually as I dressed hit a peak. I had become a French maid in the classic, or corny, style, only somewhat ruder. It was both silly and submissive, made worse because, being French, I found the whole thing faintly insulting.

Only as I went downstairs did I discover that the frills around the bodice tickled my nipples as I walked, so that by the time I got to the kitchen both were straining to erection. I had no idea how the men liked their coffee, so made it in the largest pot I could find and put it on a tray with milk, two kinds of sugar and a stack of cups. If anybody wanted tea I could point out that Mistress Kimiko had ordered me to make coffee and so I had made coffee. The only drawback was that it was rather heavy, so that I had to walk slowly and carefully.

At least, I thought that was the only drawback until I met Stephen Stanbrook in the corridor. He was in a purple silk dressing gown embroidered with golden dragons, presumably something else he'd brought back from Thailand along with his sex slave, and had just come out of the bathroom. He heard the click of my heels on the floor and turned, a smile spreading across his handsome face as his eyes moved up and down my body.

'Coffee, sir?' I offered, doing my best to sound servile rather than sarcastic.

'Maids today, is it?' he answered, and reached out to tweak my erect nipples.

I could do nothing about it, unwilling to drop the tray or to tell him to stop, and just stood there with little involuntary thrills running through my body as he teased me, rubbing my nipples with his fingers, pinching them and pulling them out, even flicking them gently with a nail. Only when I'd begun to whimper did he stop, leaving me fully turned on.

'Very pretty,' he observed. 'Yes, I'll have a coffee. Put it in my room.'

'And for Tasanee?'

'Fill a cup with milk and put it on the floor.'

He chuckled at his own wit, and stayed where he was as I continued down the passage, allowing him to watch my stocking-clad legs and the way my bottom moved in my frillies. I'd given in to my feelings, enjoying the embarrassment and excitement of my situation, and did my best to behave as I imagined he would want me to, bumping his door open with my bottom and bending at the waist to give him a good show of my knickers as I prepared his coffee.

As always, save when I'm close to orgasm, I kept part of my mind clear, and observed Tasanee as I served. My misgivings had already declined in the face of her obvious willingness the night before, and now declined further. She was curled up on a rug at the foot of Stephen's four-poster, stark naked but for her collar and lead, which were attached to one of the bed legs, and she looked blissfully happy, smiling at me as I came in and giggling when I put the cup of milk down on the floor for her. I watched as she began to lap it up, with her eyes closed and her pretty face set in something close to ecstasy. Stephen had watched me serve, but didn't speak until I had once more picked up my tray.

'Very good, Gabrielle. I must say, you're becoming quite the little trollop, in the nicest possible way, of course.'

'Thank you, sir,' I answered, and I almost meant it.

I continued my round, serving Mistress Kimiko in the master bedroom, Sabina, who was still asleep, then Poppy and Sophie, who had woken up and were laughing and joking together over their maids' outfits. Poppy was already in her dress, just about, with her breasts pushing out the bodice far beyond the limit it had been designed for and likely to pop free at any moment, while her frillies were so tight over her bottom they left a large bulge of soft pink flesh sticking out from either leg hole, which her skirt failed to cover completely. I watched Sophie put hers on, an almost perfect fit, and she was looking smug at our expense as I poured coffee.

After drinking a cup together I went upstairs. The coffee had begun to get cold, earning me a rebuke from Mr Masham, who was in what might once have been the butler's or housekeeper's room. I apologised, half dreading and half in anticipation of a spanking, but he lacked the confidence to give me discipline without asking and I escaped. It seemed likely one of them would take me to task, and as they probably wouldn't have implements to use on me my fear of the pain was bearable beside the undeniable thrill of being taken across the knee and smacked on my bare bottom. Unfortunately, of the others, only Mr Greene was awake, and he promptly apologised to me for not doing the job himself, so I was left to go back downstairs unspanked and feeling at once relieved and slightly frustrated.

Mistress Kimiko was in the kitchen, looking somewhat impatient as she consulted her clipboard, and immediately telling me off to start breakfast, with a very English choice of half grapefruit or cereal followed by sausages, bacon and fried tomatoes. It wasn't something I was particularly good at, and I was glad to hand over the cooking to Poppy when she came down. I helped Sophie serve instead, with the others gathering slowly in the dining room as we scuttled back and forth with their orders. Whatever their supposed sexualities, only Mr Greene showed the slightest concern at having us waiting on them hand and foot, and that didn't stop him tucking into a substantial breakfast. We had to wash up too, and by the time we were finished I was feeling that we were being unfairly exploited despite my gentle state of arousal. There was no time to rest either, Mistress Kimiko appearing while we were still putting the crockery away.

'It is maid training!' she snapped. 'Everybody is waiting, and only Tasanee is ready, you useless sluts.'

Both Poppy and Sophie stuck their tongues out at her back as she turned for the door, but we all followed into the sitting room once more. The tables and chairs had been pushed back, leaving a large open space where Tasanee was standing in her maid's uniform, exactly like ours but without any knickers and with her dress pinned up at the front, so that her hairless sex lips were peeping out from beneath. Next to her were Mr Greene, Mr Petherick and Mr Noyles, also in maids' uniforms, obviously their own, a sight at once so ridiculous and so grotesque I immediately found myself stifling my laughter. Poppy and Sophie were less restrained, both giggling openly as we got into line beside the others.

'Quiet!' Mistress Kimiko barked, and reached up to the mantelpiece. 'Stand to attention, backs straight, chins up, look ahead. Do not speak and do not move unless I tell you to.'

She had picked up a long, crook-handled cane and the laughter died in my throat. I stood rigid, exactly as she had ordered, with my stomach crawling as she came around in front of us, flexing the cane in her hands as she walked down the line. Beyond her Sabina, Stephen and the other two men were seated, watching us with amusement.

'This morning,' Mistress Kimiko began, 'you will learn how to be good maids. The first things you must know, a maid is there to serve, and to please. A maid is polite and attentive. A maid is obedient to every command. A maid does not question and a maid does not speak unless she is spoken to. A maid should be at all times pleasing to her Master's eye.'

She gave the three men a doubtful glance, but turned to me as she lifted her cane, using the tip to tilt my chin up until all I could see was the top of her head beneath the rims of my glasses.

'Are you going to be a good maid, Gabrielle?' she demanded.

'Yes, Mistress,' I answered quickly.

'Are you going to be obedient?'

70

'Yes, Mistress.'

'Good. What if a Master or Mistress touches you?'

'I . . . I'll let them, Mistress.'

'Wrong, stupid girl! You will not let them. For a maid, to be touched is a privilege. You will be thankful, always. What will you be?'

'Thankful, Mistress.'

I was trembling badly, sure she was after an excuse to cane me and terrified of the stinging pain. The cane tip left my chin and I was waiting for the order to take my knickers down and touch my toes, not sure if I had the courage to take it nor if I had the courage to refuse. She put the cane to my breasts, using the tip to rub my hard nipples and prod at my flesh. Her spare hand found my sex, kneading me through my frillies and then slipping down the front to feel me bare, one finger pressing between my lips and then up into my vagina.

'What will you be?' she repeated as she began to probe my hole.

'Thankful, Mistress,' I managed, a weak sob. 'Thank you, Mistress, thank you for touching me.'

'Good,' she said, 'you are a fast learner, and keen to avoid the cane, no?'

'No . . . yes . . . yes, Mistress,' I babbled, her finger now working on my clitoris.

She laughed and took her hand out of my knickers, lifting it to my face. My mouth came open automatically as I caught the scent of my own arousal. She stuck her fingers in and I sucked up my juices, still trembling, but hoping my show of submission had spared me the cane.

'Then you had better behave,' she told me, and to my immense relief moved on to Poppy, still speaking. 'Your breasts are too fat for your dress. Lose some weight.'

'Sorry, Mistress,' Poppy answered, respectful for once, and Kimiko moved on to Sophie.

'This is how a maid should look,' she stated. 'Available but smart, without bits sticking out, but what of your behaviour, girl?'

'I'm a very good maid, Mistress,' Sophie replied. 'I'm experienced too.'

'Also boastful,' Kimiko answered. 'If you are so experienced, you will show us. See if there is anything Mr Stanbrook wants. One mistake and you get the cane.'

'Yes, Mistress,' Sophie answered, and curtsied.

She stepped out of line, walked forward to where Stephen was sitting and then curtsied again.

'Is there anything I can get you, Mr Stanbrook, sir?' she asked. 'Or any way I might be of use?'

'Hmm, it's a little early for a drink,' he answered, 'and I've just had my morning blow-job, but yes, you could fetch me a glass of water, with plenty of ice.'

'Yes, sir, immediately, sir,' Sophie answered, curtsied and walked from the room with a slight wiggle and as briskly as was possible in her heels.

She was soon back, now with a small tray on which she had placed a glass of water in the exact centre of a paper doily. Approaching Stephen, she bent down, keeping her legs and upper body perfectly straight, so that her skirt lifted to show off the full expanse of her frillies as she offered him the water. He took it and she straightened up, waiting attentively for any more orders as he sipped the water.

'Good,' he stated. 'Now put the tray down and kneel beside my chair.'

'Yes, sir,' Sophie answered, put the tray on a side table and got into a kneeling position, her body upright, her hands folded meekly behind her back.

Stephen nodded, then reached out to take one rounded breast in his hand, exploring the shape beneath her bodice for a moment, then popping it free to hold it bare in his hand. Sophie stayed perfectly still, even as he ran his thumb over her nipple to bring it erect. After a moment he popped her other breast free as well, fondling them with casual intimacy until both her nipples were straining to erection and despite herself she had begun to tremble ever so slightly.

'You have nice breasts, Sophie,' he remarked after a while. 'Not too big, not too small. I think you should keep them out, don't you?'

'What you think is right, sir,' she answered immediately, not falling for the trap of giving an opinion.

Stephen chuckled, then made a little circular motion with one finger.

'Turn around, stick out your bottom.'

Sophie obeyed immediately, shuffling quickly around on her knees and pushing her bottom out to show off the frilly seat of her knickers as she lifted her skirt.

'Did I tell you to lift your skirt, Sophie?' he asked.

'No, sir,' she answered promptly. 'I thought you might like to see my knickers, sir.'

'How thoughtful,' he replied, 'but perhaps I'd like to see your bare bottom?'

'Of course, sir,' Sophie giggled, and was about to pull them down when he stopped her, taking hold of one wrist.

'Just pull them out, for now.'

She obeyed, holding the waistband of her frillies out so that he could see down the back, to where her trim cheeks bulged out in twin curves of pink girl-flesh.

'Very pretty,' he remarked, held out his glass of water and slowly, deliberately poured the full contents down Sophie's open panty pouch, ice and all.

She barely flinched, her eyes opening just a trifle wider and her breasts quivering ever so slightly to what must have been a completely involuntary tightening of her muscles. Stephen was clearly impressed, reacting with a low murmur of approval before sitting back, smiling. Sophie held her pose, the back of her knickers still held wide, with the water trickling slowly down between her thighs and spreading up the seat of her frillies, while the ice cubes created a noticeable bulge below her bottom cheeks. Stephen finally spoke up.

'Yes, not bad at all. I'll give her nine out of ten.'

'Nine?' Mistress Kimiko queried. 'Then she is to be beaten, but what was her mistake?'

A touch of alarm had shown on Sophie's face as Stephen spoke, and it changed to consternation as he explained.

'She anticipated me by lifting her skirt when I hadn't told her to do so. So yes, she should be beaten. I recommend six of the best.'

There was an immediate murmur of approval from the men, including at least two of those dressed as maids. It was grossly unfair, which showed in Sophie's face. She knew as well as I did that had she not lifted her skirt he would probably have accused her of not being willing enough, while if she had pulled down her knickers as well she'd have been caned for being insufficiently demure, or whatever had happened to come to Stephen's mind. Now she was to be beaten, but my main emotion was relief that they had picked on her and not me.

'Maybe not so experienced after all,' Mistress Kimiko taunted, indicating that Sophie should rise. 'Bend over.'

'Across my chair,' Stephen added. 'I'll hold her.'

Sophie obeyed, her mouth pursed in a resentful moue as she bent into Stephen's chair, leaving her breasts dangling bare beneath her chest and her bottom lifted with the soggy panties presented towards Mistress Kimiko. Stephen took a firm hold of her body, nestling her head against his shoulder so that she would be completely unable to move as she was beaten, save to kick her legs.

'Six strokes it will be,' Mistress Kimiko confirmed. 'Six of the best, yes?'

Again the men gave an approving murmur, and I noticed that even Mr Greene couldn't resist watching as Mistress Kimiko took down Sophie's knickers, peeling them low to leave her bottom bare to the room and the richly furred lips of her sex peeping out from between her thighs. She was wet, her pale skin glistening in the light, which I knew would make her punishment even more painful, and my stomach had gone tight as Mistress Kimiko lifted the cane.

Sophie could see, and let out the faintest of whimpers, then a shocked gasp as the first stroke was applied to her bottom, the cane landing not just across her cheeks but wrapping around one thigh to leave a long, livid welt that had quickly turned red as the cane was lifted for the second time. It must have hurt, because Sophie is tough but she couldn't help looking back, and her expression was a great deal more nervous than before. Mistress Kimiko struck down, again the cane lashed full across Sophie's bottom and her thigh too, making her yelp and sending her into a frantic little dance of pain before she managed to find her voice.

'Red! Red, red, red, red, red . . . ow! That's not my bum, Mistress, that's my leg!'

'Does it matter?' Mistress Kimiko demanded, her voice showing just a trace of doubt.

'Yes it does!' Sophie wailed. 'Just do my bum, please!?'

'Let me show you,' Sabina said, rising.

'I know how to use a cane very well, thank you,' Kimiko answered coldly.

'No you don't,' Sabina pointed out, 'or you wouldn't have hit poor Sophie's thigh.'

'I was caning men in Tokyo when you were still at school,' Mistress Kimiko answered. 'None have complained.'

'That's subbie men for you,' Sabina answered with a shrug. 'You have to do better than that for girls. Stand further back, and take aim more carefully. Tap the cane tip on her far cheek first, to make sure you know where it's going to land.'

'Thank you, Sabina,' Sophie added.

Mistress Kimiko didn't reply to either of them, radiating fury from every pore as she got into position again, but she followed Sabina's instructions, taking careful aim. She also brought the cane down even harder than before, but as it bit into Sophie's flesh the vicious stroke provoked only a gasp and a couple of little kicking motions.

'Better, much better,' Sabina remarked, drawing an angry glance from Mistress Kimiko.

Stephen had begun to fondle Sophie's breasts as Mistress Kimiko lined up the fourth stroke, making them wobble and pinching her nipples, while the bulge in the front of his trousers showed that he was reacting to holding her as she was beaten. He stopped toying with her just before the stroke landed, and let her go through a little jiggling dance before starting again, this time kissing her neck as well.

Sophie didn't respond, merely squeezing her cheeks together as she prepared herself for the next stroke, making them part as she relaxed, to hint at the fleshy pink star of her anus. She'd pushed her bottom up rather more as well, showing off the pouted lips of her sex, which for all her complaints was notably puffy and wet. With the fifth stroke she barely responded, save to kick up one leg, and as Stephen went back to fondling her breasts she had given in to his kisses.

Their mouths were open together as the sixth stroke bit in, and the rest of us were silent, allowing her to enjoy the fruits of her punishment. Only Mistress Kimiko seemed doubtful, but she made no move as Stephen eased Sophie gently down to her knees and fed his penis into her mouth. She sucked eagerly, her eyes closed in submissive bliss, one hand tugging his shaft into her mouth and the other behind her, touching her welts and stroking the bruised skin of her bottom.

As he began to stiffen in her mouth she reached back to masturbate, only for Stephen to snap his fingers at Tasanee, then point to Sophie's bottom. The Thai girl responded with a meek nod and immediately got down, sliding herself on to the floor so that Sophie was seated on her face. Every single person in the room was watching intently as Tasanee began to lick, with Sophie once more masturbating Stephen into her mouth.

She came first, jamming her head down to take his cock deep in her throat and clutching at her welted bottom as shiver after shiver of ecstasy ran through her, making her flesh jiggle and her hair shake. Only when she'd fully finished did she try to lift her head off Stephen's cock, but he had already put a hand in her hair, holding her firmly in place. He took his cock, tilting her head back a little so that we could all see clearly as he masturbated into her mouth, and pulling it free at the last moment to come in her face, first laying a long streamer of semen across one cheek and then squeezing out a thick white blob on to the very tip of her nose.

Maid training continued for the rest of the morning, although most of it consisted of the seven of us doing household tasks with the threat of the cane constantly hanging over us if we failed to work hard enough or to pass Mistress Kimiko's inspections. Having seen how badly she caned I was more determined than ever to avoid punishment, and worked hard at every task I was set, which wasn't made any easier by Sabina and the other dominants.

First I had to scrub the tiles in the hall, on my knees, and with my knickers pulled down at the back after Sabina had adjusted them to rub in my humiliation. Mr Spottiswood also walked right across my wet floor in dirty shoes, although apparently out of sheer indifference rather than as an act of sadism. Once I'd finished and passed inspection I was put to polishing the brass doorknobs, something nobody had done for years, and still with my bottom showing to everybody who went by. By the time I'd finished, Poppy and Sophie had already been told off to start lunch, while the others were gathered in the sitting room to watch Tasanee dance.

To my surprise and relief I managed to pass Mistress Kimiko's inspection a second time and was told to help with the lunch, serving as a maid. I was amazed that I'd escaped the cane, and I was the only maid without a welted bottom. Poppy had been caught sweeping dust under the sofa and had been made to bend over it with her knickers pulled up between her cheeks as she was given six, while Tasanee had failed inspection for her hoovering although I was sure she had been every bit as conscientious as me. Stephen had done her, touching her toes in the hall, six hard strokes perfectly delivered across her trim cheeks. She'd squealed terribly, but still managed to thank him after each one and kiss his shoes afterwards.

The men had also managed to get caught out, and although I didn't see them punished I heard one, as Mr Petherick made more fuss than I would have done and then tried to demand the right to punish Mistress Kimiko in turn. He was turned down flat, and went into a sulk which he came out of only when Stephen ordered Tasanee to take him into the downstairs lavatory and masturbate him.

It was a hot day outside, and we served them a ham salad for lunch, bending and bobbing just as we'd been instructed, although they seemed to have lost interest in punishing us for the time being. I was hoping we would be able to go outside for the afternoon, and that I would be given a chance to take a break from being a maid. Unfortunately all those in charge seemed to like having us in service, so while Sabina ordered a deck chair to be brought out on to the lawn for her I ended up still in my ridiculous uniform, only now outdoors, which made being topless and having my knickers on show stronger still.

To my added chagrin the men were allowed to change, both Mr Petherick and Mr Noyles resuming their ordinary clothes while Mr Greene preferred to be naked while he finished the housework, something I had no desire whatsoever to see. Nor, it seemed, did anyone else, Mistress Kimiko also coming outside to sip cold beer and laze on the lawn, while indoors Stephen continued to put Tasanee through her paces in front of the other men.

As I knelt on the lawn beside Sabina's chair nobody had spoken for a while, both she and

Mistress Kimiko sipping their drinks, while the application of the cane to their bottoms had beaten the cheek out of both Poppy and Sophie, at least for the time being. I was wondering what life would have been like as a real maid and feeling very glad I wasn't one, while also thinking it was about time Sabina stopped lazing about and played with me, when Mistress Kimiko spoke up.

'We should take a bet, Sabina. What do you say we pick a girl from these three and send them into the woods to pick fir cones. If my girl wins, I get to spank you.'

'I am never spanked,' Sabina answered.

'You let me give you a stroke of my tawse, bare,' Mistress Kimiko pointed out.

'That was different,' Sabina insisted, 'and anyway, they'd only cheat to get me dealt with, or maybe you, I'm not sure. Gabby, who would you rather see take a spanking, me or Mistress Kimiko?'

I knew the safe answer to that.

'Neither of you, Mistress. It would not be appropriate.'

It was a lie, because I would happily have watched either of them spanked, although it would have been hard to choose. She laughed, then spoke again.

'It would be more fun to send all three of them into the woods and make the winner spank the loser. That way you can be sure they'd try.'

Kimiko seemed a touch disappointed, but answered quickly enough.

'That would be good. How long shall we give them?'

'Half-an-hour?' Sabina suggested, checking her watch. 'And it should be as many pine cones as they can fit down their knickers, which will be far more fun.'

Mistress Kimiko laughed and nodded to us.

'Go on, girls, off you go.'

We made for the woods, hurrying as fast as we could in our heels, but as soon as we were around the corner of the house Poppy spoke up.

'You ought to take this one, Gabby. We've both been caned.'

'Yes, you should,' Sophie agreed, 'and I'm sure they've been going easy on you.'

'No they haven't,' I protested. 'I've just worked harder, that's all.'

'Yeah, sure. They're letting you off because you can't take it.'

'No. After all, they're letting me be spanked if I lose this game.'

'Big deal!' Sophie scoffed. 'So what, are you going to let me win?'

'Who says you get to win?' Poppy demanded.

'Oh come on,' Sophie protested. 'You get to spank her any time you like.'

'If we get the same amount of cones, maybe they'll let us both do it?' Poppy suggested.

'We do this fairly,' I insisted, 'but if I win I promise I'll be gentle, OK?'

Poppy shrugged. Sophie made a face. We'd reached the edge of the woods, where the grass gave way to a carpet of pine needles spotted with cones from the trees above. I began to pick them up, gathering as many as I could hold in one hand before dropping them down the front of my knickers. Immediately I realised that I should have removed the loose needles first, as the moment I bent to pick up some more cones they began to jab into my flesh, right on my sex lips.

There was no time to stop, with both Poppy and Sophie picking up cones just as fast as I could. Both of them were grimacing as they began to stuff their knickers, but neither of them slowed down. I moved a little to one side, hoping that the needles from a different sort of tree might be less painful, but if anything they were worse. Already my knickers were bulging at the front, and one of the cones had worked its way down to lie directly against the mouth of my sex, but I kept on, determined to avoid what I knew would be a hard spanking.

Soon I had as many cones down the front of my knickers as I could possibly fit, with some even bulging out at the sides around my sex, while walking had become horribly uncomfortable, with every step jabbing what seemed like hundreds of pine needles into my sensitive flesh. I found a particularly rich patch of cones and began to load the back of my knickers. From the moment the very first cone settled into place between my cheeks it was impossible not to react to the sensation of weight and the way my knickers bulged behind, putting a smile on my face and bringing back happy memories of misbehaviour. As my knickers began to stretch and the lump inside them hung gradually lower and heavier I was soon lost in a daydream. I didn't hear Poppy until she spoke from almost directly behind me.

'Let's get her!'

I jerked around, slipped and sat down on the load in my frillies, jabbing needles into my flesh across the full width of my bottom and between my cheeks. My squeak of pain was cut off as something soft was jammed into my mouth, stifling my protests as I was pushed down to the ground and sat on. All I could do was kick and wriggle while they made quick work of gagging me and tying my feet together; then I was hauled upright and pushed against the trunk of a tree. Poppy held me in place, grinning into my face as between them they forced my arms around the back

82

of the trunk. Sophie tied my wrists together and that was that. I was bound and helpless, after just seconds, with both of them giggling as they stood back to see what they'd done. Both of them were bare-legged because they'd tied me up with their stockings.

'That'll teach you not to play fair,' Sophie laughed. 'We're going to leave you there until we've finished, and make sure we have exactly the same number of cones, then, Gabrielle, it's going to be spankies time for you.'

Poppy laughed, then stepped forward to pull open the front of my knickers, peering down them to see how many cones I'd collected. I tried to speak, but all that came out was a muffled grunt.

'Not bad. They prickle, don't they?'

I nodded urgently, trying to plead with my eyes, but both of them were now peering down my knickers and didn't even notice. Somebody's hand closed on the bulge of pine cones over my sex and squeezed, making me wince as the needles pricked at my flesh and I knew there would be no mercy.

'Don't worry,' Poppy assured me, 'it won't be long. OK, let's count our cones.'

They walked back to where they had been collecting, leaving me tied to the tree, completely helpless. The prickle of needles around my sex and bottom was unbearable, but my wriggling only made it worse. I was uncomfortable too, both from my bound arms and because they'd pulled me so tight against the tree that the cones in my panty pouch were pressed to the trunk, forcing my belly into prominence. That left me feeling vulnerable too, so I was praying they wouldn't leave me too long, and wondering what Stephen or perhaps Mr Masham would do if they found me.

It was Mr Spottiswood. He must have been watching from indoors, because no sooner had Poppy and

Sophie disappeared around the corner of the house than he emerged from the service yard. I tried to plead with him, mumbling through my gag and batting my eyelids in what I hoped was mute appeal, but from the leer on his face I already knew I was going to get felt up. Sure enough, his hands went straight to my breasts, cupping them and squeezing them as he feasted his eyes on me.

'Nice titties, very nice,' he drawled, 'small but firm, and don't your nipples pop up nicely?'

I managed an angry grunt in response, but he merely gave a dirty chuckle and carried on fondling me, now rubbing his knuckles over my nipples to bring them fully erect. All I could do was shut my eyes and try to ignore the trembling of my body as I was molested, first my breasts and then my legs, his thick, hard fingers sliding over my skin, gradually higher to where my bulging panty gusset was thrust out towards his face.

'I've been watching you,' he said. 'I like you. I'd like to spank your little bottom . . . over my knee with your panties down. You like to go in a nappy, don't you? That's dirty. I like a dirty girl. What about the game with the pine cones? I bet that's something dirty too.'

His hands had moved to the bulge in my frillies, back and front, pressing the cones to the flesh beneath and jabbing what seemed to be ten thousand needles into my skin. I arched my back against the pain and the agonising frustration of being touched up and completely unable to stop him, but I couldn't stop the moan that rose in my throat. He gave a chuckle of amusement and began to jiggle the front load of pine cones against my sex.

'You like that, don't you?' he said. 'Dirty . . . oh so dirty. Shall we see if I can make you come?'

I shook my head, but he didn't even see, now rubbing the cones firmly against my sex. It was going to happen, there was nothing I could do about it. One of the biggest cones had wedged between my lips, the bumpy surface directly on my clitoris, while the prickle of needles around my bum and pussy had brought the blood to the surface, exciting me despite myself. That didn't stop me wriggling in an agony of shame and frustration as he masturbated me, and as my pleasure rose my emotions only grew stronger. Then I came, wriggling my cunt against the pine cones as he rubbed them into me, utterly disgracing myself.

It wasn't over. He stood up, grinning from ear to ear and squeezing his crotch. I imagined myself being fucked then and there, maybe my ankles untied, my frillies pulled off and my body lifted on to his erect cock to be fucked while I was still tied to the tree, or carefully turned around to stop me escaping and taken from the rear, maybe even up my bottom, or just untied and humped on the ground among the pine needles . . .

'I'll do you a deal,' he said, his voice breaking into my rising panic. 'If I untie you, will you promise to spunk me off?'

My first reaction was relief that he wasn't just going to fuck me then and there, followed by annoyance and frustration at his dirty request, which I knew I was going to accept. The pine cones in my knickers hurt, my arms hurt, but worst of all the itching had grown to a constant, agonising throb, while an unpleasant wriggling sensation between my cheeks suggested that something with too many legs had escaped from among the pine cones. Still I tried to resist, angrily shaking my head, only for the motion to change to a frantic nodding as whatever was between my cheeks slithered into my anus.

'Thought you might,' he chuckled, and ducked down to untie my feet.

I was trying my best to keep still as he struggled with the knot, but whatever horrible little creepy crawly was in my bottom hole seemed to be trying to get up inside me, bringing me close to the edge of panic for all my efforts to stay calm. The moment my legs were free I was kicking out, desperate to get it out of my hole and ease the agonising prickling sensation of the pine needles. Mr Spottiswood looked at me as if I'd gone mad.

'What's the matter?'

All I could do was mumble urgently through my gag. He began to laugh, but my need for relief was simply too strong for me to care how undignified I looked as I pressed my cone-filled panty pouch against the tree and began to rub my bottom on it, desperate for friction. All I got was another million pine needles jabbed into the flesh between my cheeks, that and Mr Spottiswood's derisive laughter, but he had at least gone to work on the knot binding my wrists, speaking as he did so.

'Hold still, love. What's the matter, got ants in your pants?'

I nodded desperately, trying to make him understand, although whatever now seemed to be doing the locomotion in the opening of my bottom hole felt more like a millipede in high heels. He seemed to be taking forever, and tears of sheer frustration had begun to well up in my eyes before he finally got the knot loose and my hands were free. I didn't even bother with the gag, ripping my knickers off to spill their load out on the forest floor and jamming them between my cheeks to wipe myself, completely indifferent to the absurd exhibition I was making of myself until at last my bottom hole felt clean and free of obstruction. I slumped down into a squat, exhausted, the tears streaming down my face as I pulled my gag free to gasp in the sweet, fresh air. When I finally opened my eyes it was to find Mr Spottiswood looking down on me, his homely face full of doubt and concern.

'Don't take on so, love,' he said. 'It's only a blow-job, or you can tug me if you'd rather?'

'Later,' I managed. 'I'll do it, but later . . . that's fair, isn't it?'

He put one finger to the back of his neck, scratching a spot beneath his collar.

'I'm hard now, love.'

'I'm sure you are, but . . .'

'I did you, didn't I?'

I looked up at him, my mouth falling open in disbelief for what he'd said. He'd interfered with me while I was helpless, felt me up and amused himself by rubbing me off, and he felt that meant I should be grateful and suck his cock in return. It was so outrageous I couldn't even find an answer for him.

'Come on, you did say,' he wheedled, apparently oblivious to my reaction. 'I've got girls' knickers on and everything.'

He'd opened his trousers as he spoke, and sure enough, he was wearing women's underwear, a tarty pair of scarlet nylon knickers, see-through, with his cock and balls bulging obscenely in a crotch designed to cover a pussy. I could only stare, mesmerised by the grotesque sight, especially the way one of his balls had escaped the confines of the panties and was sticking out to one side, round and hairy beneath the red lace trim.

'Come on, love,' he urged. 'You can see I need you, and you did promise.'

'Later, please, Mr Spottiswood,' I urged.

'Aw, please, love,' he whined. 'You're so gorgeous, you are. I just love the way those little tits of yours jiggle about when you walk, and you've a lovely bum, and . . . come on, darling, suck me. I know you want it really.'

'I said I would, later.'

'Yes, but I don't want it later, I want it now.'

I hesitated, wondering if it was best to get it over with or spend the rest of the day thinking of what I was going to have to do later. There was only one sensible choice.

'Oh for goodness' sake, OK!'

'I knew you would. How about you start with a panty wank? I love those frilly knickers you were wearing.'

He didn't seem to care that I'd wiped my bottom on them, and put his back to the tree, pushed his trousers down and lifted his shirt, exposing a round little paunch and the full spread of the red nylon panties. I knelt down in the dirt and picked up my discarded knickers, shaking the last few pine cones out of them. He was waiting, and spoke up as I reached out to take down his ridiculous nylon knickers.

'No, don't do that. Leave them up and take it out the side.'

I drew a sigh as I pulled his panty gusset aside, flopping out his cock and balls, which stirred lazily as they were released from constriction. As I took him in hand with my frillies wrapped around his shaft a wet, oily-looking helmet emerged from his foreskin, which quickly peeled back as I began to masturbate him. He was already half hard, and his cock grew so quickly to full erection that I was wondering if I could make him come without having to take him in my mouth.

'Tell me what you're doing,' he grunted. 'Tell me how you're going to spunk me off in your mouth with your panties. Tell me what a dirty bastard I am for wearing girls' knickers.'

'You are,' I assured him, 'a really dirty bastard, both for wearing women's underwear and making me masturbate you like this.'

He broke off with a grunt as I went back to my task, tugging hard on his now rigid shaft, but he spoke up again.

'Go on, tell me how disgusting I am . . . tell me I'm a pervert . . . tell me what a slut you are too.'

I hesitated, but if it was going to get him there quickly it was no doubt for the best. He seemed to like women's underwear, on us or on him, so I concentrated on that.

'You are disgusting. You are a pervert. Imagine putting on women's underwear? That's so dirty, but not as dirty as making me masturbate you with my knickers. You're a dirty old man, a disgusting dirty old man. I suppose you think women like you behaving like this, don't you, you filthy little boy!'

He moaned in ecstasy and I tugged harder still, sure he was about to come as I moved back a little to avoid getting it in my face.

'Keep on,' he demanded, 'keep talking, and suck my cock . . . suck me, you beautiful little slut.'

'I can't do both,' I pointed out, but my resistance was weakening, his demand tempting me to take his cock in and suck on it until he came in my mouth.

I told myself it would be cleaner that way, that it was just that I didn't mind swallowing sperm, but I knew it was a lie. Really I wanted to suck his cock and have him come down my throat while I revelled in the obscene sight of his erect cock and great fat ball sack bulging out around the side of the tiny scarlet panties.

'OK, I'll suck,' I told him, and I did it, thoroughly ashamed of myself even as I took him in my mouth.

He gave another moan, deeper and more urgent still, now staring down to watch as my mouth worked on his big, ugly penis. I began to rub his balls with my frillies and pushed my bottom out to let him enjoy the view of my cheeks sticking out from under my maid's skirt as well as my bare breasts.

'You juicy little slut,' he breathed. 'That's right, show it all off . . . show it all off while you suck my dirty cock. I'm going to come . . . you're going to like this, I take these pills that . . . oh God!'

He came, my cheeks bulging as spunk filled my mouth, an enormous quantity. I tried to swallow, but started to choke, coughing up spunk all over his balls and the red nylon panties as he whipped his cock free. Spunk exploded from my nose and I tried to twist my head away, but he had me by the hair, wanking in my face to lay long, thick streamers and fat, glistening blobs of it over my cheeks and nose, in my hair and over my glasses, then in my mouth once more as he thrust himself deep when I tried to gulp in a mouthful of air.

'. . . thicken my spunk,' he said, finishing his earlier sentence as he held his cock deep in my mouth.

I finally managed to push him away, still gagging on his spunk, with two thick streamers of it dangling from my nose and a curtain mixed with spittle hanging from my chin as I coughed my mouthful out on to the carpet of pine needles between my knees, also down my cleavage and the front of my uniform. He squeezed out a last blob into my hair as I rocked back on my heels, still spitting come and barely able to see for the mess he'd made on both lenses of my glasses.

'You look great,' he breathed. 'I wish I had a camera. That was a good one too, thanks.'

'You really are disgusting,' I told him. 'Look at me!'

'You should have swallowed, love,' he laughed.

I didn't want to admit that I'd tried, or how much I'd been enjoying it by the end, let alone that I now wanted to come again. He began to tidy up, and so did I, in silence, using my already ruined frillies to wipe my glasses, but only succeeding in smearing the spunk all over the lens. Obviously I needed to shower, but no sooner had I started towards the house than Sabina appeared around the side, dragging Poppy by the ear. Mistress Kimiko and Sophie were behind, and all four stopped as they saw the state I was in.

'What happened to you?' Sabina demanded.

'Mr Spottiswood made me suck him off,' I admitted.

'Without my permission?' she retorted. 'Right, where is he?'

I looked around, but he'd gone, leaving just a little pile of fir cones to mark the spot where he'd had me.

Four

The rest of Sunday was mercifully uneventful. While I'd been sucking Mr Spottiswood's cock I'd been vaguely aware of slaps and the occasional squeal in the background, which had been Poppy and Sophie getting spanked for the trick they'd played on me. I'd been let off, and I'd had enough anyway, retiring to the house for a long, hot bath, although I couldn't resist masturbating over what I'd done.

By the time I'd got out, washed my hair, dried, shaved, powdered and generally done all the things that make me feel good in myself, Kimiko was on the prowl for us to help prepare a Sunday roast. My maid's uniform was filthy, so I put my baby-doll dress back on, without knickers, and stayed that way for the rest of the evening, cooking and serving, then cuddled up on Sabina's lap as Sophie and Poppy were first spanked and then made to suck off four of the men for their general bad behaviour. This time I had no sympathy.

I woke on the Monday morning to the promise of a genuinely hot day. There was a faintly baked smell in the air even with the sun only up for a couple of hours, and not a breath of wind. I was the first one up again, and this time sneaked down by the old servants' stairs next to Stephen's room to make myself a coffee before Mistress Kimiko could catch me, only to find Mr Greene already there. He was in his maid's uniform, and addressed me as Mistress, offering coffee or tea. I took a coffee, sipping it as I watched him complete his task and disappear with the heavy tray.

As I drank I thought of how easily I had slipped into the routine of the Institute, behaving in ways that would have horrified my clients and my ordinary friends. It wasn't just that I enjoyed doing so either, but that I find it's always easy to do what is expected of me. In London I drank white wine spritzers at the Café Eperney and discussed art or the latest films with my friends. At the Institute I drank coffee served by a middle-aged man in a blue-nylon maid's uniform and watched my friends given bare-bottom spankings.

I had no moral objections to my situation, far from it, but I knew that in London I would never have given in to Mr Spottiswood's demands, and part of the reason would have been social pressure operating at rather less than the conscious level. As it said in the brochure, at the Institute the normal rules didn't apply. It was all right to suck off dirty old men in the garden, because everybody approved of it, and while they would all call me a slut, it was a genuine compliment. That was immensely liberating.

My little piece of moral philosophy was interrupted by Mistress Kimiko just as I was finishing my coffee. She was in her leathers as usual, her tawse swinging at her hip, and I automatically straightened up as I saw who it was.

'Why aren't you in uniform?' she snapped.

'Sorry, Mistress,' I answered, 'but it had to go in the wash.'

'Yes it did,' she agreed. 'You will go in the nude to do your work this morning. Give me your gown.'

94

I obeyed, slipping off my robe and handing it to her to leave myself stark naked.

'You will need to be nude later anyway,' she remarked. 'Start the breakfast.'

She left as abruptly as she'd come, taking my robe with her. I began to put the breakfast things together, feeling rather sorry for myself for having to go nude, but enjoying that very sensation and the casual way she'd made me strip. It hadn't even occurred to me to refuse.

Sophie and Poppy were soon down, both in their uniforms, teasing me as we served breakfast and making sure that I had to go out to the dining room as often as possible so that all six of the men got a good eyeful. I didn't mind, and even ate at the main table, acutely aware of the eyes lingering on my bare breasts. Tasanee was also naked, kneeling beside Stephen's chair in her collar as usual, and I even found myself biting down a touch of irritation because she was taking some of the attention away from me.

Mistress Kimiko had her clipboard with her, resting on the table beside her plate, which made me a little nervous for the prospect of the punishment I'd so far managed to avoid. For all my care I knew that if she wanted to find an excuse for me to be caned or tawsed she could do so. They always can. When she finally dabbed her mouth with her napkin and picked up the clipboard my stomach was fluttering, and the fact that she was smiling and in an unusually happy mood did nothing to help.

'Each day,' she said, 'of the next three, will be a special day for one of the unattached girls. On Thursday it will be the Master's day, and you may have a choice of serving him unconditionally or adopting a dominant role over those men who enjoy submission. Today, it is Poppy's day, and as Poppy

95

likes so very much to be a pig-girl, today is pig-sticking day.'

'I'll kill Jeff,' Poppy muttered.

'Quiet!'

'Sorry, Mistress Kimiko.'

'Pig-sticking day,' Kimiko repeated, examining her clipboard, then beginning to read from it as if recommending a cruise or a tour of a château. 'Wyddon Manor is ideal for the game of pig-sticking. The extensive, private woods give the perfect cover, both from the eyes of inquisitive strangers and to provide concealment for the pigs, so increasing the excitement of the chase for the hunters. The rules of pig-sticking are simple. The pigs – or rather, pig-girls – are released into the woods with a ten-minute start. The hunters then follow, their task being to catch as many pigs as possible. They have nets, but naturally they do not use real spears to stick their pigs. Their sticks are their cocks. Each hunter will carry a pen of a distinctive colour, with which he will mark the pig on her bottom once she has been successfully stuck. Cocks must be erect but a pig may be stuck in her cunt, mouth or bottom . . .'

'Um . . .,' I put in, raising a finger. 'I don't really think I could cope with anal sex at this point.'

'You have a stop word, Gabrielle. You can use it for your bum . . . and your cunt if you want, but you must suck.'

I nodded weakly. Sometimes it's easier to take a cock in my sex than to suck, but I was already imagining myself down in the dirt with a cock in me from either end and sure one of the men would get carried away and try to bugger me. I'd heard of the pig-sticking game before, although I couldn't remember when, and I knew the sort of thing that was likely to happen. Mistress Kimiko continued.

'The aim of the pigs is to avoid being stuck, by any means, but once caught they must go on their knees to be stuck. To ensure they try their hardest a severe punishment should be awarded to the one most often caught, to be administered by the victorious hunter, who is the one who has marked the most pigs. The game is over when the first pig has been marked by all the hunters. Is that all clear?'

Mr Noyles spoke up.

'Er ... I hope I speak for everybody when I say this, but what if we catch a pig and come in her, then can't get it up for the next one?'

'You'll have to learn to restrain yourself, won't you?' Sophie answered him while Mistress Kimiko was still trying to digest the question.

'Mind your place,' Mistress Kimiko warned Sophie. 'Yes. An eager man will not do well.'

'Are all of you girls being pigs?' Mr Spottiswood asked hopefully.

'No we are not,' Sabina answered immediately. 'Kimiko and I are hunting, with strap-ons.'

'I think that gives you a bit of an unfair advantage,' Mr Noyles put in.

'Yes,' Mr Petherick agreed, 'and I think we should have some sort of handicap as well. I don't run very fast, you know. The older and heavier gentlemen should have at least two free pigs, which they can enjoy before we start ...'

'You're making it too complicated,' Sabina cut in, 'and it's not my fault you're a fat bastard, is it? A few less pies, and maybe ...'

'Please,' Mistress Kimiko interrupted as Mr Petherick began to go slowly purple, 'let us have no disagreement.'

'It is a little unfair though,' Stephen put in. 'Perhaps we should say that if Mr Petherick wins, the losing pig gets a lighter punishment. That way the girls . . . I mean the pigs, will be encouraged to let him catch them.'

I thought of how it would feel to have Mr Petherick mounted on my back with his cock up me and I wasn't so sure, but it did rather depend on the punishment. It was easy to imagine myself bending for the cane with three burning lines across my bottom and wishing I'd let myself be fucked rather than have to take another three. I saw Tasanee whisper into Stephen's ear. He nodded then spoke up.

'What will the punishment be?'

'That is for us to choose,' Kimiko told him, 'but it must be severe so the pigs do their best.'

'It should be something we can vary for the handicap then, I suppose.'

'We should simply give the losing pig to the winning hunter,' Mr Masham suggested, 'to do with as he pleases.'

'That sounds good,' Mr Noyles agreed, 'and if anyone wants a handicap, they can choose their own proportion of the maximum time they get to have the girl.'

'Good idea,' Mr Spottiswood added.

Stephen nodded. Kimiko exchanged a glance with Sabina, then spoke up.

'This is good. Two hours for the winner with the loser, and you slower men will choose your own . . . what is it, handicap?'

'Yes,' Mr Spottiswood responded, 'rather like golf, really, only with different-shaped balls. I'll take one hour. How's that, girls, let off your punishment by half for a trip on the old John Thomas, good, eh?'

I wasn't so sure. It seemed to be more a question of who would do what with us. Mr Masham looked as if he liked to inflict pain, while Mr Spottiswood and Mr Petherick might like to dish out spankings but were basically more dirty than cruel. Mr Noyles was an unknown, but something about his large, clammy hands incited a crawling feeling in my stomach. Then there was Mr Greene, who wouldn't do anything, but he spoke up even as I was considering my tactics.

'What about me, Mistress? I couldn't hunt, not possibly, but I wouldn't mind being a pig, just for you and Mistress Sabina of course.'

'That wouldn't work at all,' Sabina answered him, 'and do you really think the girls are flattered because you won't fuck them? Get a life.'

'Sorry, Mistress,' he said meekly, but his face looked more than a little sulky as he hung his head. 'May I be maid, please? I'll carry water, and . . .'

'Yeah, yeah, whatever,' Sabina cut in, dismissing him.

I drew a sigh, but it wasn't going to make that much difference anyway. It didn't take Einstein to work out the maths. The way the game was structured, and with seven hunters and four pigs, the losing pig was going to have been had at least seven times, so even if I didn't lose I could expect to be fucked repeatedly. Worse, as the game wouldn't be over until one of us had been caught by all seven of them, it meant at least one of us would have to let herself be caught by the slower hunters or we'd just end up getting continuously used by the faster ones, presumably until it was too dark to play. Whoever had worked out the rules was a true sadist.

Mistress Kimiko clapped her hands.

'Girls, pig up, chop chop!'

The four of us went upstairs. I could already feel my adrenaline building up, and a lot of nervous tension, while my sex had begun to juice so strongly I was wet between the thighs. Our gear was already

in the dormitory, the same humiliating outfit Sophie
had worn on the first day; pig snout, curly tail and
trotters, without a scrap of clothing to cover so much
as an inch of our bodies.

'We'll need sun block,' Sophie pointed out, 'even in
the woods.'

'Yes,' Poppy responded, 'but put your snout and
tail on first or the gum won't stick properly.'

'Oh, right, thanks. I suppose we'd better lube up
our bumholes too. There's always one dirty bastard.'

'More like seven.'

Sophie laughed.

'Can I borrow some of that cream you use,
Gabby?' Poppy asked.

'Do you think cream, or jelly?' Sophie queried.

'Jelly,' I told her, 'the cream won't last.'

It was the most bizarre conversation, casually
discussing how best to prepare ourselves to be made
up as human pigs, hunted down and buggered, but
without getting sunburn. Yet there, at the Institute, it
seemed completely reasonable, with only a small and
detached part of my mind telling me just how utterly
unacceptable it was according to the normal rules.

I reached into my bedside cupboard for my anal
jelly, wondering if I should use some myself. It was a
tricky decision, because I had to go on my knees for
my sticking so I would be showing my bottom hole.
If one tried to stick his cock up without bothering to
ask it would hurt, but if they saw I had lubricated
myself, it was sure to encourage them. I could refuse,
but once I was on my knees and probably in a net
they might be tempted just to stuff it up anyway . . .

'Do me, would you?' Poppy asked, breaking into
my increasingly worrying line of thought.

She bent over her bed, her bottom thrust out to
make her full cheeks part and show off the soft pink

dimple of her anus. I applied a worm of jelly and rubbed it in with my finger, around her star and a little way up her hole, making her purr. Sophie had adopted the same rude pose and I did her as well, then rolled my legs up and applied a little jelly between my own cheeks, telling myself that if there was even a chance of me being buggered it was better to be prepared. I spent a moment with my finger in too, opening myself just a little, both to make myself ready and to turn myself on to the thought of anal play. After all, it might be Sabina who caught me, and she might well want to put her strap-on up my bottom just to humiliate me.

'The gum takes ages to dry,' Poppy warned, picking up her snout. 'You have to hold it on.'

We followed her instructions, painting the gum on to our snouts and tails one at a time before applying them to our faces and above our bottoms. The snouts were turned up at the end, and had nostrils, so I could still breathe through my real nose, which I imagined might make life a lot easier for me if any of them wanted to fuck in my throat. Once the gum was dry the three of us lined up to admire ourselves in the big wardrobe mirror, three little pigs, as pink and bare as the day we were born, an image at once sexual and comical. Poppy looked best, or most ridiculous according to perspective, with her big bottom and heavy breasts, so that it was easy to think of her being made to go as a pig to punish her. It also worked well for Sophie, with her petite figure, but I was more critical of myself, too tall and too skinny to make a good pig.

Once our snouts and tails were fixed and we'd given each other a liberal coating of sun block we trotted downstairs. The others were already out in the garden, Tasanee as a pig, complete with snout and tail in a yellow-brown rubber to match her skin, Mr Greene still in his maid's uniform but carrying several bottles of water and a wickerwork picnic hamper, the rest as hunters. As usual, the men hadn't gone to any real effort with their looks, all five dressed in their normal clothes, with Mr Masham's leather jeans and a rakish bush hat worn by Stephen as the sole contributions to anything even remotely fetishistic. Sabina and Kimiko were a different matter, both in full leathers, including relatively sensible boots, a riding crop and a tawse at their belts respectively, and large strap-on dildoes harnessed to their crotches to create an image equally terrifying and desirable.

'About time too,' Sabina remarked, looking us up and down. 'Very sweet. Turn around.'

We showed her our bottoms, my self-consciousness now rising and my heart hammering under the lewd stares of the men. I was definitely going to try my best, and I knew I could easily outrun both Poppy and Sophie, probably Tasanee too, yet I was still far from confident.

'Five minutes!' Mistress Kimiko called out, tapping her watch.

I began to warm up, running on the spot, but stopped as all six men began to watch the way my breasts jiggled. There was no point in encouraging them to single me out. Touching my toes was no better, so I spoke to Sophie instead.

'Sophie, who did you play pig-sticking with before?'

'It was up at Amber Oakley's place,' she told me. 'I think she organised it, but it might have been Gavin and that mob.'

'Stephen wasn't there, was he?'

'No, it was before we met him, quite a bit before. Why?'

'I was just wondering who Kimiko's mysterious Master is.'

'It wouldn't be Amber, or Gavin. They'd be down here. Do you think it's Stephen?'

'I don't see what he gains from being secretive, but Kimiko does seem to defer to him and who else would know what colour to make Tasanee's nose and tail? They match her skin almost perfectly.'

'Could be, but he might just have given her details,' she said, as Mistress Kimiko again tapped her watch.

'One minute!'

I began to walk towards the edge of the lawn, along with the others. There was a tight knot in my stomach, and the dim space beneath the otherwise sunlit pines looked sinister and yet alarmingly open, with nowhere to hide, nowhere I could keep myself from being caught in a net and put on my knees to have either a man's erection or a strap-on dildo inserted into my jelly-smeared anus . . .

'Go!' Mistress Kimiko called out. 'We follow after ten minutes.'

'Run, piggies, run!' Mr Masham added, clapping his hands as if to scare a group of timid animals.

He didn't need to make the point. I was already running, down the side of the house and in among the trees, as fast as I could in my awkward trotters, which I now realised were going to be a serious handicap. The girls had boots, some of the men even had trainers, and the only one I had any confidence in outrunning was the grossly fat Mr Petherick. I'd been meaning to keep a careful watch somewhere fairly open and run for it if anyone saw me, relying on speed to get away, but changed my tactics. There had to be somewhere to hide.

There was, right at the fringe of the woods, where bushes and thick undergrowth had grown up between

103

the pines and the stone wall that marked the boundary with the open hillside. I quickly made myself a little hide, curling up on the dry, warm grass with just a peephole to allow me to see into the wood, silent and alert for the slightest sound.

Nothing happened, at first, beyond the occasional distant shout or the snap of a twig, and once a despairing scream. I stayed put, trying to ignore the buzzing flies and the sweat that had begun to trickle from my body in the heat. As my nerves subsided I began to feel bad about what I was doing, only to think again as Tasanee flashed past me on the path that bordered the wood. Mr Masham was after her, panting as he ran, with his face twisting into an expression of such lewd aggression that I found myself feeling faintly sick as I listened to their retreating footsteps.

I didn't discover if she escaped or not, but with the wood quiet once more the feeling that I was being unfair returned, creeping slowly back into my mind despite my best efforts to stave it off. Soon I would begin to feel that I was being silly too, and that I'd only regret it afterwards when Poppy and Sophie were comparing notes and delighting in how dirty the hunters had been with them.

Finally I decided to revert to my original tactics and at least take a chance, maybe let Sabina catch me so she could fuck me with her dildo and make me suck my own juices from the shaft, always a favourite of hers. I climbed out from my hiding place, very cautiously, my every sense alert for the hunters. The paths were too obvious, and I set off between the trees, but my trotters were sinking deep into the soft ground, which was going to make it harder still to run. I began to sneak along the edge of a path instead, but I hadn't gone twenty metres before Mr

Spottiswood stepped out from where he appeared to have been urinating against a tree.

For a moment we just stood there, staring at each other, both equally surprised, before I'd darted away down a narrow track between close-set pines, straight into a net as it was jerked across the path in front of me. I went down, sprawling in a patch of bracken, shock and fear welling up inside me as I struggled to break free, a moment of hope as I shook the net off my shoulders, then despair and consternation as I was brought down hard on the ground with a man's arms wrapped hard around my legs.

I fought, kicking out in blind panic, no longer playing a game but really trying to get away. My foot hit something hard, drawing a grunt of pain, then an all too familiar voice, Mr Noyles.

'Ow! Gabrielle, be careful, that was right in my eye!'

All my animal panic, and all my fight, just disappeared at his words. I was actually apologising as I rolled over, still stuck in the net, to find Mr Spottiswood panting up to us, his face splitting into a huge and dirty grin as he saw that I was caught. His cock was still hanging limp from his fly, with a single drop of urine at the very tip of his foreskin.

'Well done, Clive,' he puffed. 'Nice tactics.'

'She kicked me in the face!' Noyles complained.

'I'm sorry,' I said again. 'I . . . I panicked a bit.'

'So what's it going to be?' Mr Spottiswood addressed me. 'I fancy a suck and a fuck if you're up for it.'

'That's the least I expect,' Mr Noyles agreed, still rubbing his eye.

'Let's spit-roast her then,' Mr Spottiswood suggested. 'That's how you do a pig, isn't it? Arse in the air, Gabby, and let's see you shake that tail.'

His hand had gone to his cock, and he licked his lips as he began to tug at it. I gave a single, helpless shrug, the consternation once more boiling up in my head as I turned over on to all fours. He gave a deep, satisfied sigh as he got down behind me, rubbing his cock on my bottom and between my cheeks. Mr Noyles got up too, shuffling around to my head and unzipping himself in my face without the slightest ceremony. Out came his cock, he fed it into my mouth and I'd been pig-stuck, a prick in one end of me and about to get a second in the other.

Mr Noyles's cock was as long and thin as his body, also bent, making it difficult to suck on properly as he grew quickly hard. I'd thought he'd be dirty and he wasn't, but it was no great relief because he tasted of soap and some particularly revolting after-shave. All I could do was suck as best I could, hoping to make enough spit to get rid of the taste. He had me by the head anyway, with his big, clammy hands gripping me by my ears, so there was nothing I could do about it.

Mr Spottiswood was making a meal out of getting himself erect between my bottom cheeks, but mercifully he was pushed up close and didn't seem to have realised that I was lubricated and ready for a buggering. He'd taken hold of my hips, grunting and muttering to himself as his cock grew slowly fatter and stiffer in my crease, until at last he was hard enough to slide it in up my sex.

I expected a proper fucking, and as I felt myself fill I was resigned to a full spit-roasting, having them swap ends, being made to suck up my own juices and being spunked in at the end. All I got was the swap, Mr Spottiswood's sticky cock pushed into my mouth as Mr Noyles took me from behind, but after rocking me back and forwards on their erections for a bit the motion in my vagina stopped.

106

'That's enough for now,' Mr Noyles breathed, 'or I'll come. I want to try to win this.'

'Tempting though,' Mr Spottiswood sighed. 'I'd love to spunk right down the little slut's throat.'

He finished with a grunt, jamming himself deep, so that for a moment I was gagging on his cock, and I was left gasping for air as they pulled out of my body. I was going to move, but Mr Noyles spoke again.

'Stay still, I haven't marked you yet. Keep that bum stuck out.'

I did as I was told, holding my rude pose as he marked a cross on one bottom cheek. He was using a blue large marker with the word 'Indelible' written on the side, and I wondered how long it would be before I could get the ink off my bottom. Mr Spottiswood had come around behind me, and I stayed still while he made his own cross, in brown and at the crest of one cheek, only to squeak in alarm as I felt the tip of the pen touch between them.

'What are you . . .,' I began, and stopped, realising he was drawing a brown area around my anus. 'Do you have to be so disgusting?'

'You love it!' he chortled. 'There, that looks good, like you haven't wiped properly.'

They both laughed and he gave my bottom a firm slap, then stood up, pulling the net off my body without warning so that I rolled over in the dirt, my open, sticky sex spread to him for one moment before I could scramble around. Mr Noyles gave a last dirty chuckle and they left, not even bothering to look back, but discussing the trap they'd used and how it could be improved.

I walked away in the opposite direction, feeling thoroughly used, a little dazed and not sure how long they'd wait before trying to catch me again. According to the rules I had a ten-minute start, at least at the beginning, but I wasn't taking any chances. They'd got me ready for more too, but that didn't mean I would be giving myself up without a fight. As soon as I was sure they couldn't see me I looped back towards the edge of the wood, where I spent a few minutes in my hidey-hole until I was ready to go out again.

There were noises in the distance, laughter followed by a feminine squeal, and I froze to listen, right on the path, just as Stephen appeared around the corner. I ran, but I knew I was lost from the first step. He was taller than me, stronger than me, and more importantly properly dressed and in sensible shoes. I still tried, running until my legs were burning and my heart was hammering in my chest, but it was no good. He drew closer, his boots thumping on the hard-packed earth of the path, ever nearer, with my sense of hope fading and finally giving way to despair as his hand closed on my arm.

'Got you, Gabrielle!'

I stopped, to stand panting for breath with my hands on my knees. Stephen knew I wouldn't try to run again and let go, leaning on a tree until he too had got his breath back, then casually unzipping and flopping his cock out.

'Suck me erect,' he demanded, 'when you're good and ready, Miss Piggy.'

He was smiling, and I nodded, waiting a moment more before going down on my knees and taking him in my mouth. It seemed the most natural thing in the world to be sucking a friend hard in some remote wood, and I took my time, enjoying his cock but still playing the game by trying to make him come so he'd be spoiled for a while. He wasn't having it, laughing as he pulled me back by the hair.

'Oh no you don't, young lady. Come on, show me your bum.'

I turned around, sticking out my bottom to have his mark put on me, in orange. He chuckled at the way Mr Spottiswood had coloured my anus, gave me a couple of slaps to set my cheeks tingling, and left. I stepped in among the trees to recover for a minute, then continued, only to find him hiding behind a tree just a few metres along the path. When his hand closed on my wrist I nearly jumped out of my skin, but accepted my second capture with a shrug. He gave a pleased grin, then spoke.

'On your knees, I'm going to fuck you.'

I obeyed, responding to his command as much by instinct as desire. With my bottom lifted to him he gave me a couple of gentle slaps, wobbled my tail and slid himself up me. My fucking was brief and casual, just a few firm thrusts, but we both knew it meant more than that. He'd fucked me, however briefly, just as Mr Noyles and Mr Spottiswood had fucked me, three men within less than an hour.

A second orange cross was applied to my bottom and he left. This time I was more careful, moving slowly off among the trees until I was sure I was clear, and then starting off towards the south as all the noises seemed to be coming from the other direction and I could at least hope nobody was in the area. I seemed to be right, soon reaching a different part of the wood, with older, deciduous trees and a lot more cover, but I was just climbing an ancient moss-covered wall when I caught a movement among the trees.

I froze, but it was only Sophie. She looked exhausted, her normally beautiful blonde hair hanging around her face in sodden rat-tails, her skin glistening with sweat and heavily marked with scratches, both filthy with spunk and earth and pine needles. Her breathing was harsh and deep as she flopped down on a tussock of moss and leaves.

'How many?' she panted.

'Three men, but I've been caught four times,' I told her, twisting to show her the crosses on my bottom. 'Mr Spottiswood, Mr Noyles and Stephen twice.'

'I'm on six,' she responded, 'more than once, some of them. Masham's the worst. He stuck his prick up my bum and made me suck it afterwards. Sabina got me too, with that fucking dildo. It's huge!'

She shifted uncomfortably on the moss as she spoke. I found myself grimacing in sympathy.

'Who hasn't caught you?'

'Petherick, of course, same for Poppy. The other six have had her too. Noyles and Spottiswood made a sort of trap with their nets and took turns with her, end to end.'

'They did that to me too,' I admitted.

'She made them spunk though, both of them, and Stephen did it in my face. God, I'm knackered.'

'One of you is going to have to let Mr Petherick catch you.'

'Not me. Masham's in the lead, and he's still running around with a hard-on. Let's see.'

She rose, twisting around in an attempt to look at her bum, but failing and sticking it out to me instead. Her lower back and most of her cheeks were covered with crosses, six different colours, nine in all, with three in Mr Masham's purple.

'Poppy's worse,' she told me, 'with four from Masham, I think. All the other men except Petherick have come, at least once, so the only way anyone else is going to win is if we make it easy for Kimiko. If it's Sabina they'll just say we cheated.'

'What about Tasanee?'

'I haven't seen her, which is all the more reason to make sure Kimiko gets us often.'

'I don't know, after the way she caned you so badly.'

'Come on, Gabby, you've only been had four times, and she'll be gentle with you if it means she gets to win.'

'Will she? I'm not so sure.'

'It's that or Poppy or me get given to Mr Masham! Please, Gabby, apparently he does some really weird things, creepy things. He likes to use needles, apparently.'

'Um . . . OK. I'll try to find Mistress Kimiko.'

'Thanks.'

We kissed, holding on to each other for a few seconds, then moving back among the trees. It wasn't going to be easy, given the size of the woods and that I had no idea where anyone else was. I still moved cautiously, hoping to hide if I came across anyone except Kimiko, but the first person I saw was Mr Masham himself, and Poppy. He had her on the ground, kneeling on all fours, her body wrapped in his net, with the mesh pulled tight around her bottom to make the soft, pale flesh bulge out in rough squares, while her piggy tail projected straight up in the air through one hole and her breasts dangled down beneath her chest through two more. She looked as exhausted and dirty as Sophie, her face and buttocks both smeared with spunk, while some had dried in her hair. Mr Masham obviously didn't care what state she was in, kneeling behind her to masturbate himself erect over the sight of her well-spread bottom.

I was almost directly behind them, and drew back a little into the shelter of the trees as I watched. Poppy's bottom was fully open to me, her sex puffy and wet, her anus glistening with jelly. She was being very passive about it, obviously turned on, and as Mr

111

Masham touched his now erect cock between her sex lips she responded with a low moan. I saw his cock go in, but he only gave a couple of brief shoves before pulling it free, then moved close once more, this time aiming higher, his knob pressing to her slippery anal mouth.

'No not that, you bastard,' Poppy sighed, but she made no move to stop him as he eased his cock slowly in up her back passage.

Soon he was up, her bottom hole perhaps already made loose and juicy by him or somebody else. As the buggering began her tits started to swing and he reached under her chest, letting his fingers brush her nipples as the fat pink globes wobbled and shook to his thrusts. He was also laughing as he used her, almost disturbed, and watching her ring pull in and out on his cock shaft, but he never once lost control, giving her a good solid buggering and then pulling his cock free.

Her anus was left a gaping black hole into her body, which slowly closed, oozing fluid. I'd guessed what he was going to do, and found myself unable to turn my eyes away as he moved to the side, took her firmly by the hair and inserted the cock he'd just that instant withdrawn from her rectum into her mouth. Poppy's face screwed up as she tasted herself, but she was too far gone to stop, sucking him deep as he once more began his wild laughter.

I was wondering if he was truly sane, when Poppy drew back and suddenly plunged her head down on his cock, deliberately jamming the full length down her throat. He cried out, in shock, and in something halfway between ecstasy and pain, then swore. I realised she'd made him come in her mouth, and as she pulled off him she was laughing, only suddenly to sick up a mass of come and spittle on to the ground.

'You wicked bitch!' he rasped.

'Me?' Poppy answered, gasping. 'You're one to talk.'

'Show me your bum then,' he demanded. 'I'm still going to win.'

Poppy turned her bottom to him, and I watched as he added a purple cross to the collection already marking her skin. I could see ten, and the thought of her being given over to him for his amusement set my stomach tight. She could take care of herself, but there was something almost demented about his behaviour, and not so much what he did, but the way he did it. Jeff would happily put his cock up a girl's bottom then make her suck it, but he was like a dirty schoolboy. When Mr Masham did it he was being deliberately cruel.

I moved back before he could see me. She'd made him come, which meant he was out of the game for a while. He'd caught at least seven pigs, even without Tasanee, but Stephen hadn't done badly either, or Mr Noyles and Mr Spottiswood with their team work. I still wanted to make sure, and was scanning the woods for Tasanee as I went, a little more confident now that I knew every man except Mr Petherick had been given an orgasm.

The next person I came across was Mr Greene, and I paused to drink the best part of a litre of water and clean myself up a bit. He also told me where he thought Kimiko was, in the central part of the wood, which I'd so far only passed through briefly. There were other people around too, Stephen, who I narrowly avoided by ducking down among some ferns, and Mr Petherick, seated on a stump mopping at his round red face with a handkerchief and looking sorry for himself.

I'm always told I'm too soft hearted, and my immediate reaction was to feel sorry for him. He had a green marker in one hand, toying with it dejectedly. There had been no green crosses on Poppy's bottom, and I knew he hadn't caught Sophie either. Unless he'd caught Tasanee, who seemed quite fit, he'd had no luck at all. He also had rather a nice cock. I hcsitatcd, telling myself I ought to be looking for Kimiko, but decided to be charitable. He wasn't even looking as I walked up behind him, and turned around with a start when I put my hand on his shoulder.

'I suppose you've caught me,' I told him.

For a moment he just looked puzzled, before the fat red globe of his head split into a grin. I gave him a friendly pat on the back, which seemed the right sort of thing to do, and got down on my knees. He hurriedly adjusted himself, unzipping to pull out the full mass of his cock and balls, which I took in hand, stroking the bulbous sack of his scrotum and kissing at the tip of his cock. It felt good and pleasantly dirty.

He threw his net over my back as I took him properly in, still kneading his balls as I mouthed on his rapidly thickening shaft. Soon my jaw was wide around his stubby, solid erection and I could feel myself getting eager, with a dozen fantasies flickering through my head. Just to picture myself as I was felt exquisite, naked and done up as a pig, caught in a net as I sucked penis for a fat old man, a fate so deliciously undignified it made me want to come. Or there was the idea of offering to suck cock as an act of charity, deliberately allowing the least attractive man around to use my mouth and enjoying every moment of it. Or there was the simple pleasure of being naked in a sunlit wood with a big cock in my mouth, showing off outdoors in the nude and being purposefully dirty.

I got up into a crawling position to better enjoy the feel of being naked, now with my sex flaunted behind, nothing hidden, and all of me available to the man I was sucking. Soon I was going to get a mouthful, unless he chose to fuck me, and if he did there would be no resistance. I'd stick my little piggy bum up and let him enter me, enjoying every lewd detail, the weight of his belly on my cheeks, the grip of his podgy hands on my hips, the feel of his fat cock pushing up inside me ...

It wasn't his cock I got inside me, it was Sabina's dildo. I'd never heard her, too lost in my dirty thoughts, and Mr Petherick must have had his eyes shut. I didn't even realise anybody was behind me until I felt something rubbery press to my sex, and before I could react she was up me, laughing as she drove the thick dildo shaft into my body and began to fuck in my hole. I'd jerked in shock, but that was the limit of my resistance. Now my Mistress was in me, fucking me as I sucked a dirty old man's cock.

'You dirty bitch, Gabrielle,' she taunted. 'Just look at you!'

I just nodded and began to masturbate Mr Petherick into my mouth, deliberately showing off for her. She laughed again and began to slap my bottom, still easing the dildo in and out as she spanked me and chided me for being so dirty. I wanted to come, right there, down on my knees in the dirt with Mr Petherick's cock in my mouth and Sabina up my pussy. My hand went back, to touch my breasts and feel the way they moved to Sabina's thrusts, and further, to the hot, wet crease of my sex, to touch the thick rubber shaft stuck so deep inside me.

'Filthy pig!' Sabina laughed as she realised I was masturbating. 'That's right, Gabby, rub your cunt while we use you, you dirty little slut, you tart ...

that's what you are, Gabrielle, a fat man's tart! No offence, Mr Petherick.'

Mr Petherick tried to speak, but all that came out was a grunt and his fat, soft hands had closed on my head. He began to jam his cock deeper, fucking my mouth with ever faster strokes, jamming the head into the back of my throat until I began to choke. I'd been rubbing at myself, near to orgasm for Sabina's words and what was being done to me, but I lost control, now batting pathetically at Mr Petherick's thighs as he fucked deeper, and harder, and came.

Spunk exploded out of my mouth and nose at the same time, filling my snout and erupting all over Mr Petherick's balls and the front of his trousers, his belly too. I came up choking, only to receive a second ejaculation full in my face, on my glasses and in my open mouth. He was still holding my head, and stuck his cock back in before I could stop him, finishing his orgasm down my throat with a long sigh of content-ment and holding himself in as his spunk began to dribble slowly down my face and from the nostrils of my piggy snout.

'Nice one!' Sabina laughed. 'You are a dirty bastard, Mr Petherick. OK, so who's next?'

As he'd begun to work my mouth I'd been vaguely aware of new voices behind me, but even with the shock of realising I'd been watched I was too busy retching come and mucus on to the ground to look back. I heard Stephen's voice, claiming me for a fuck, and before I could react one way or the other Sabina had vacated my cunt and he had replaced her.

'Form an orderly queue, boys,' Sabina said from behind me, and as Stephen began to pump himself into me I finally managed to turn around.

'Hang on a second, I . . .'

116

I stopped. A thick blob of Mr Petherick's spunk on one lens of my glasses made it difficult to see, while my pig's snout was full of it too, distracting me as I tried to blow it out through my nose. There were four men beyond Stephen and Sabina, and two at least had their cocks in their hands. I still wanted to come, my arousal gradually building again as Stephen fucked me and now that I could breathe properly again. Yet I was still aware of the game, and trying to count as I struggled to stand up and get Stephen's cock out of me.

'Hold on . . . let me up for a second, please?'

They just laughed at me, only one bothering to reply at all, and not to me.

'Hold her still, Alan. Tread on the net.'

It was Mr Spottiswood, and Mr Petherick responded immediately, pulling the net up over my head and pushing his feet into the mesh at the same time, to trap me, forcing my head low even as Stephen lifted my hips to get my bottom into greater prominence and make it easier to fuck me. I couldn't even look up, or get my hands to my pussy without going face down in the dirt, while my arousal was warring with confusion and self-pity as I realised I was just going to be held there and fucked and fucked and fucked whether I liked it or not, until they'd all had me, until I lost the game and got given to Mr Masham to be tortured, to have needles stuck in my breasts or whatever horrid thing he liked to do to girls.

'Please . . . please, Mr Petherick,' I managed, speaking between grunts as Stephen took up a slow but firm rhythm in my cunt. 'Let me go . . . I was nice to you . . . wasn't I . . . wasn't I?'

'And I'm going to be nice to you,' he responded. 'I'm going to hold you down until you've got your rocks off. That's what you really want, isn't it?'

'Not like this!' I whined. 'Please, Mr Petherick . . . Alan, let me go! I sucked your cock!'

'Just you stay where you are, Miss Piggy,' he chuckled. 'You know it's what you really want.'

My answer was a sob, and they were both laughing as Stephen quickened his pace in my cunt, setting me gasping and clutching at the wet earth beneath me and the net too. It was tight now, and I could feel the mesh cutting into the flesh of my bottom as his cock worked in my hole. They were going to take turns with me, and there was nothing I could do about it, caught and stuck, penetrated over and over until each and every one of them had had his fun with me.

'I'll give you what you need, Gabby,' Sabina offered, and her arm came around me.

She held me, tight around my waist, her hand up under my belly to rub me as my fucking continued. The moment she touched between my lips I was lost, the final shred of dignity that was my resistance gone. I was wriggling in her grip, my mouth wide in the hope that somebody would stick a cock in it, even Mr Petherick's now limp tool. When Stephen pulled out I was begging for him to put it back, only to have my bottom spattered with hot drops of come as he jerked himself off on my cheeks.

He was replaced almost immediately. I didn't know who by, Mr Noyles maybe, or Mr Spottiswood, and nor did I care, just as long as there was a cock in my cunt. They filled my mouth too, Mr Masham twisting my head around and squeezing my jaw to make me take him in through the mesh. He didn't need to force me. I'd have sucked anyway, my orgasm rising as I was worked from either end, a netted pig, fucked for their sport and their amusement, and in ecstasy for it.

I came, a blinding, red-hot orgasm beneath Sabina's fingers, sending my body into powerful spasms over which I had no control whatsoever. It seemed to last forever, and just at the perfect moment Mr Masham came in my mouth, adding one last glorious detail to my exquisitely filthy experience.

They fucked me, all seven of them, holding me trapped in the net as cock after cock was inserted up my wide-open hole. Mr Spottiswood had been handing out pills to keep the men up to scratch, and both he and Mr Noyles came over my bottom, leaving me slippery with spunk as well as sweat. Mistress Kimiko had me too, laughing and slapping my bottom as she eased her dildo in and out. Every time they marked a cross, until I knew that seven different colours and eleven crosses marked my filthy bottom. The pig-sticking was over, and I'd lost.

By the time Sabina had taken me to the tap in the service yard and washed me down, the others were gathered on the lawn, with Poppy, Sophie and Tasanee lined up with their bums in the air for their crosses to be counted. My heart sank as I joined the line, now sure that I'd lost. Neither Poppy nor Sophie seemed to have been caught again, while Tasanee had only three crosses in total, one in Kimiko's black and two in Stephen's orange. My mind didn't seem to want to clear, my thinking too fuzzy for me to remember who'd caught who, let alone count, but I could hear Mistress Kimiko talking behind us as we held our bottoms out for inspection and she marked the results off on her clipboard.

'. . . for Mr Masham, three on Sophie, four on Poppy and one on Gabrielle. Mr Masham has a score of eight. For Mr Stanbrook, two on Sophie, two on Poppy, three on Gabrielle and two on Tasanee. Mr Stanbrook has a score of nine. I declare that Mr Stephen Stanbrook is our winner!'

Relief flooded through me, only to die as I remembered some of the things he was capable of, and his love of the cane and strap.

'Our losing pig, with eleven crosses,' Mistress Kimiko was saying, 'is Gabrielle. Stephen, Gabrielle is yours for two hours.'

'Thank you, Kimiko,' Stephen responded. 'Right, come along you, and you too, Tasanee.'

I got up, feeling nervous and extremely sorry for myself as he collared me and clipped a lead to the ring in front. It was completely unfair, after I'd only offered to take Mr Petherick in my mouth so that he wouldn't feel left out. In return he'd not only made me gag on his cock but held me down while the rest of them took turns with me. For my generosity I was going to spend the afternoon being used by Stephen Stanbrook, who'd been known to make girls eat dog food and loved nothing better than dishing out the cane to some helpless female's bottom.

The rest of them were clapping as Tasanee and I were led away, even Mr Greene. Tasanee's head was hung down in her usual meek acceptance, but I was trying not to make faces. I badly wanted to hide my resentment and apprehension, but it was a wasted effort, Stephen not even bothering to look back, but with our leads slung casually over his shoulder as we were taken indoors and up to his room. Only there did he bother to acknowledge me at all, clipping my lead to the hook on the back of the door and sitting down on the bed with Tasanee at his feet.

'This is an unexpected pleasure,' he said. 'I was sure Poppy was going to lose.'

I just shrugged, not wanting to make myself look ridiculous by trying to explain. He lay back on the bed, propping his head and shoulders up with the pillows and folding his hands across his stomach, his mouth set in a complacent smile as he admired my naked body.

'What are you going to do with me?' I asked, no longer able to keep my feelings in check.

'I'm not actually sure,' he replied. 'You see, even with Ken Spottiswood's little blue pills there is only so much a man can do. I couldn't resist doing it over your bum just now, but that was my third orgasm in a couple of hours and I'm not as young as I was. Still, there's plenty of time . . .'

He trailed off, smiling to himself, then gave an abrupt nod and swung his legs off the bed. As he rose he snapped his fingers at Tasanee, who followed him, crawling into the bathroom. My stomach had already gone tight, and grew worse as Stephen came out to collect a large black bag from beneath the bed. He gave me a smile as he once again disappeared into the bathroom, but said nothing.

I stayed as I was, listening to the occasional chink and Stephen's muttered commands. All I had to do was slip my lead from the coat hook and I could run, but I knew I wasn't going to do it. When Stephen came out again I let him take my lead and followed meekly into the bathroom, the churning in my stomach rising sharply as I saw Tasanee.

She was in the shower, her hands above her head and fixed to the curtain rail with a pair of leather wrist cuffs, while her feet were braced on either side of the trough and also cuffed in place, one to the towel rail and the other to a pipe. My eyes were drawn to her smooth, yellow-brown sex, open and poised directly above the trough, because I'd already guessed Stephen's intentions. Sure enough, he snapped his fingers, pointing to the trough.

'In there, Gabrielle. Make yourself comfortable.'

I climbed in, curling up in the trough directly

beneath Tasanee's open legs. She was looking down, her huge brown eyes full of mute apology as Stephen made quick work of fixing a system of ropes between my collar and various pipes. With the last knot tied I couldn't move my head more than a few inches in any direction, although my body was free. Tasanee's pussy was just inches above my head, so close I could smell her.

'I've always wanted to do this,' Stephen said, smiling widely as he stepped away. 'You had quite a bit of water, after the game, didn't you, Tasanee?'

'Yes, Master,' she answered.

'Yes, you did,' he agreed, 'at least a litre, much of which you will in due course empty on Gabrielle's head, only in rather different form. However, I find that pig-sticking works up an appetite, and it's time for lunch. If you let go before I get back, Tasanee, I'm going to cane you, understood?'

'Yes, Master,' she repeated, bowing her head.

'Good,' Stephen said happily, 'and of course, should Tasanee manage to hold herself for two hours, you go free, Gabrielle. I consider that extremely unlikely.'

He was laughing as he walked away, leaving us fixed in place to suffer the inevitable consequences of his sadism. I didn't really know what to say. What do you say to a woman who is shortly going to urinate on your head and can do nothing about it? It's not really a good time for small talk. She was less reticent.

'I am sorry,' she said as soon as the door had banged closed behind Stephen. 'He is a good Master, but often cruel.'

'I know,' I told her, forcing a smile. 'I helped teach him, and now I end up like this!'

She returned my smile, briefly, but when she spoke again her voice was serious.

'You do not deserve to be punished. You work hard and always obey, as a good slave should. It is Poppy or Sophie who should be punished.'

I was going to say I wasn't a slave, but I'd just let seven men and women use me and was now tied naked in a shower stall waiting to be urinated on for a man's amusement. Somehow it didn't seem that my denial would carry very much weight. We began to talk instead, swapping our stories of how we'd come to end up in our current situation. As I had guessed, she was a Thai bride, but Stephen had no more taken advantage of her than she of him. She had been sexually submissive for as long as she could remember, always wanting a man to serve as her Master, with her ideas and needs developing as she learned English and read both Western and Oriental texts. I quickly realised how intelligent she was, and the last of my qualms had soon faded.

As she spoke she kept breaking off to apologise for what she was about to do on me. She obviously considered it extreme, which made it harder to take, much less to admit my real feelings about being peed on. I decided to take it in silence, pretending I was ashamed to have it done on me as she obviously was to do it, but I badly wanted to come when it happened and felt I needed an excuse. When she began to bite her lip I decided I couldn't wait any longer, although I was blushing as I pushed the words out.

'Tasanee, would you mind if I touched myself, only it will make it easier to accept.'

She looked shocked, but only for a moment, then nodded. I was feeling deeply embarrassed as I set my knees apart and began gently to massage my sex, but I knew that would make it all the better when the moment finally came.

'Thank you,' I told her, hanging my head. 'Just do it, if you have to. I won't blame you.'

'No, I will hold on, and I understand your need. To touch always makes it easier when you are punished.'

I didn't answer, trying not to feel too ashamed of myself as I masturbated. After a while I looked up, my arousal now high enough to make me want to watch. She was looking down at me, her mouth a little open, showing the strain both of being tied and of holding herself in, but she managed a smile, which I returned. As I began to rub a little harder she gave a sudden grunt and I saw the muscles of her sex tighten. I shut my eyes, expecting a faceful of piddle, but she managed to control herself, her breathing just a little tense as she spoke again.

'It is getting hard to hold, Gabrielle. Soon I must let go.'

'I know.'

'I am sorry . . .'

'You don't have to apologise,' I told her, 'but do try to hold on until Stephen gets back.'

'I'm not sure I can,' she answered, 'and anyway, I deserve to be caned. In the game, I climbed a tree and hid for a long while.'

She forced a laugh as she spoke, but I could see the tension in her muscles and knew she was having to try hard to keep it in.

'No, Stephen is my Master and I must try to obey,' she said, 'but I don't know if I can, Gabrielle, I don't know . . .'

Again I braced myself for my faceful, but she held on, her breathing now slow and even, with gentle contractions running through the muscles of her belly and her hairless sex. Her bottom had begun to squeeze too, and I started to wonder if I wasn't going to get more than I'd bargained for. She gave a little

124

gasp, her muscles started to tighten again, she said something I didn't understand, then gasped again, obviously in pain.

'If it's hurting just do it,' I said, 'never mind Stephen. I don't mind, really, and he'll untie us until you've done it anyway.'

'I know,' she grunted, and she began to shake her head in her desperation, 'and you are brave to say you do not mind, but you do, I know. I must try to hold it . . . ow . . . I can't Gabrielle, I'm sorry . . . I am so sorry . . .'

She was going to do it, a single golden drop trickling from between her lips despite her tightly clamped muscles, then exploding, full in my face, hot and pungent, splashing in my hair and over my glasses, and in my open mouth as I gave in to the inevitable and stopped trying to pretend I didn't like it. I splayed my legs, already rubbing hard at myself as her pee filled my mouth and began to bubble out at the sides, trickling down over my breasts to drip from my suddenly rock-hard nipples and run down between my thighs. I felt the warmth on my cunt as I masturbated, and opened my mouth to her, swallowing down one mouthful and a second, now in ecstasy.

I got it all, in my face and in my mouth, down my back and down my front, over my head and over my bottom, until I was sodden and sticky, and all the while with my fingers busy between my legs. Tasanee was still babbling apologies, her head thrown back in an agony of despair for what she'd done, until my tongue found her sex as I rose on my knees, licking urgently as her pee gushed out straight into my mouth with my orgasm rising, and breaking as she gave in completely and did it all over me, soiling my breasts and belly as I fed from her cunt with my body shuddering to peak after exquisite peak.

Five

As I sat watching Tasanee given a dozen hard strokes of the cane after yet another dinner of bangers and mash that evening it was hard not to feel guilty. I had lost the game, and all I'd got was one of my favourite treats, while she'd won and ended up being caned in public. Not that it was either of our faults really, because it had been nearly an hour from when Stephen went downstairs for lunch until Tasanee finally lost control, but as always there was no point in trying to argue. The Master, or Mistress, is always right.

He didn't even make a proper job of me afterwards, because his cock was too sore after all the sex that morning. That had him complaining bitterly about the game, which he claimed must have been designed by a woman. At that I asked him straight out if he was behind the Institute, but he denied it flatly, pointing out that if he had been he would have organised the pig-sticking so that the winner got to take his prize the following day.

I was exhausted, and slept like a log, waking only when Poppy shook me by the shoulder, to find Mr Greene hovering with his tray. The sight of him in his uniform was a bit much when I'd only just woken up, but I was grateful for the coffee. Poppy was already dressed, and Sophie was just doing so, both in the same uniforms; white blouses and red tartan mini-skirts, knee socks and big cotton knickers, plain black shoes and red-and-white-striped ties.

'School day today,' Sophie said happily, 'less cock, but lots and lots of spanking, with any luck.'

'There's sure to be,' Poppy agreed, 'but I don't know how they're going to work it with only four girls.'

'Begging your pardon, Miss Poppy,' Mr Greene put in, 'but boys can go to school too, and some of us have been made honorary girls for the day.'

Sophie giggled.

'That'll be a sight worth seeing! Who's doing what?'

'Ken Spottiswood, Alan Petherick and myself are girls,' he told us. 'Clive and Derreck are the boys, and prefects.'

I took a sip of coffee, trying not to think of Mr Petherick dressed as a schoolgirl. It was impossible, the vision simply too grotesque to ignore, while the others were little better and the prospect of Mr Noyles and Mr Masham as prefects was alarming, to say the least. My cheeks tightened at the thought of what seemed to be inevitable spankings and the possibility of the cane. I was going to be extremely well behaved and stick close to Sabina, even if that was only likely to mean that she was the one who got to beat me.

'I can't wait!' Poppy laughed. 'Come on, Gabby, get up, lazy bones.'

She wrenched my bedclothes back as she spoke. I was nude, and instinctively covered myself as Mr Greene turned to take a sneaky peek, despite the fact that they'd all seen every tiny detail of my body and penetrated at that. As Poppy turned her skirt rose up, showing off the seat of her school knickers, but I was too slow in putting my coffee down to take my revenge.

'You can get out now,' I told Mr Greene, who was lingering to watch Sophie and me dress.

He left with an apology and I began to sort out the clothes I'd been brought. My uniform was identical to the others, but as with the maid's outfit, while they needed to bend a little to show their knickers, mine were permanently on show. On the other hand my blouse was a reasonable fit and having no bra only meant that my nipples were rather prominent, while Poppy was bursting out of hers even with the top three buttons undone. I was at least covered, although it's not much consolation to have knickers on when you know that the only reason you've been allowed them is so that they can be pulled down.

We trooped downstairs to do breakfast, during which I was rewarded with the sight of Mr Spottiswood, Mr Petherick and Mr Greene dressed as schoolgirls. I'd begun to get used to seeing Mr Greene in women's clothes, and Mr Spottiswood had looked equally ridiculous as a maid, but Mr Petherick really was something else again. His skirt entirely failed to cover his monstrous buttocks, or his crotch for that matter, leaving the very sizeable bulge of his cock and balls constantly on view within his white cotton panties.

Both Poppy and Sophie just thought it was funny, leading to the first spanking of the day, with the pair of them put over the knee by Mr Masham and Mr Noyles and spanked face to face so that they could watch each other's expressions as their knickers were taken down and their cheeks smacked up to a rosy pink. Mistress Kimiko looked on with amusement, seated at the head of the table as usual, but dressed in a beautiful yellow silk kimono instead of her normal leather. She also had a school cane, as did Sabina and Stephen.

'Are you finished?' she asked when the men finally paused in their spanking.

'Just about, thank you,' Mr Masham responded, and Mr Noyles nodded agreement.

Neither man let his girl up, and Mr Masham began to fondle Sophie's buttocks as Mistress Kimiko consulted her clipboard.

'Um . . . excuse me,' Poppy ventured as Mr Noyles began to explore her bottom in turn, 'but could I get up now, please?'

'Shut up,' Sabina told her.

'Yes,' Mistress Kimiko agreed. 'Show some respect.'

Poppy opened her mouth to protest further, but thought better of it and let herself go limp across Mr Noyles's legs as he continued to molest her. I sat up very straight, imagining his long, clammy fingers wandering across and between the cheeks of my bottom, making me more determined than ever that my behaviour should be immaculate, as Mistress Kimiko began to read.

'Today is Tuesday, Sophie's special day. We will be at school all day and rules are to be strictly enforced, with appropriate punishments for naughty girls, including special girls . . . and boys.'

She had added the last bit, glancing at the two male prefects. Mr Masham was tickling Sophie's bottom to make her wriggle and kick, while Mr Noyles had pulled Poppy's cheeks apart to inspect her anus.

'Prefects,' Mistress Kimiko pointed out, 'are not exempt. Put them down, or you will both be caned.'

Mr Noyles obeyed but raised his hand. Mr Masham kept Sophie firmly in place but did stop tickling her.

'I understand that I'm subject to the rules,' Mr Noyles said, 'but I must insist that if I am punished I have the right to punish whoever does it in turn.'

'I agree with that,' Mr Masham put in.

'I am a Mistress,' Kimiko answered, with genuine outrage. 'I am not punished.'

'Nor am I,' Sabina agreed, 'but there's a simple way to get around the problem. If either of them needs to be beaten we get one of the girls to do it, then they can take their revenge whenever they like.'

'That suits me,' Mr Noyles responded.

'I agree,' Mr Masham added, finally releasing Sophie, who promptly stuck out her tongue at him.

'Attention please!' Mistress Kimiko snapped. 'For just a moment. This morning we have classes. I will be teaching deportment. Mistress Sabina will take French, and Master Stephen will take Maths.'

I allowed myself to relax a little, confident in my ability to behave for Mistress Kimiko and certain that I knew far more about their chosen subjects than either Sabina or Stephen, especially French. The same was not true of Poppy or Sophie, who were also bound to misbehave, so with luck I could avoid punishment.

'Classes are followed by lunch,' Mistress Kimiko was saying. 'In the afternoon there will be games. First lesson starts in ten minutes, in the old library.'

We hurried to get the washing-up done before the start of class and made it just on time. The old library had previously been locked, and was a fairly bare room, with shelves and oak panelling on the walls but only a handful of books. To make it a classroom Mistress Kimiko had moved in an assortment of tables and chairs, also an easel with a blackboard propped up on it. I took my seat next to Tasanee in the front row, sure that was the best way to stay out

131

of trouble, while Poppy sat with Sophie behind us. The two prefects were to our right and two of the 'special' girls behind them, with the unfortunate Mr Greene on his own in the window seat. Mistress Kimiko came in, clipboard in hand, and we managed a chorus of greetings which she acknowledged with a severe look before speaking.

'Deportment class. If a girl is to become a young lady she must have deportment. Sophie, what is deportment?'

'Search me, Miss,' Sophie answered.

'Stand up,' Mistress Kimiko ordered.

Sophie stood, clearly expecting to be spanked on the spot, but Mistress Kimiko had other ideas. Taking a book from the shelves, she balanced it carefully on Sophie's head.

'Drop the book and your bottom will be smacked,' Mistress Kimiko stated. 'An upright stance is an important aspect of deportment. A lady does not slouch. Now who will tell me what deportment is?'

I raised my hand, hoping that if I answered a question correctly so early on I would be spared her attention later.

'Gabrielle?' she asked.

'Deportment is the physical aspect of social grace, Miss,' I told her.

'Very good, Gabrielle,' she answered.

'Swot,' Mr Spottiswood hissed.

'Stand up, that girl,' Mistress Kimiko said immediately, and he too was left with a book balanced precariously on his head.

She came back to the front of the class, looking us over with an expression of disdain. I was amazed that Sophie had bothered to keep the book on her head so long, but she seemed to have decided it was part of the game. One of us was going to get spanked anyway, and soon, it was just a question of who. Mistress Kimiko seemed to prefer punishing her own sex, while I was sure the men would all be looking forward to seeing a girl's knickers come down, so I remained on best behaviour while more questions were asked. Both Mr Greene and Mr Petherick were standing with books on their heads before Mistress Kimiko once more turned her attention to me.

'Gabrielle, in what circumstances can a lady refuse the invitation of a gentleman to dance?'

I had no idea even which culture she was referring to, but tried what seemed a commonsense answer.

'When she is otherwise engaged, Miss.'

'No,' she answered. 'A lady can only refuse a gentleman's invitation to dance if she has already accepted an invitation from another gentleman. Stand up.'

It was what I'd said, more or less, but I knew better than to refuse, which would mean my knickers coming down immediately instead of taking my chances with the book. I stood up, trying not to pout as she balanced a thick volume on my head.

'Drop the book and your bottom will be smacked,' she said, unnecessarily. 'Now then, who can tell me the appropriate uses of a fan?'

She seemed to have picked up her ideas from all over the place, mixing Japanese and Western culture, which made the questions very difficult to answer. Nobody knew about fans, which left Mr Masham and Mr Noyles in the same precarious position. I was quite hoping one of them would get spanked, not for the erotic pleasure, but to see them get what they were so happy to dish out. Mr Spottiswood would have been equally good, and Mr Petherick better still after what he'd done to me the day before. With only two of us seated it couldn't be long.

'You stand very well,' Mistress Kimiko remarked as she returned to the front, 'but I suspect it is only the fear of spanking. Now . . .'

Something hit my leg, hard enough to sting, and to make me jerk in surprise. I heard Poppy's giggle as my book started to slide, but by some miracle I managed to balance it again, too late. Mistress Kimiko was looking at me, one eyebrow raised. I thought I'd had it, but she didn't say anything, turning to the class once more, just as I caught another stinging pain in my leg. This time I was ready, and held still, biting my lip against the urge to scratch where I'd been hit.

Mistress Kimiko began to talk again, with me standing stock-still except for the helpless twitching of my thigh muscles in anticipation of another hit from whatever Poppy was flicking at me. It never came. Instead I felt something soft touch the back of my legs, between my calves and moving slowly up, tracing a slowly and agonisingly ticklish line all the way to where the seat of my knickers showed beneath my abbreviated skirt. I struggled to ignore it, telling myself that the tickling sensation was all in my mind, but my muscles were jumping despite myself.

Still I kept the book as it was, not daring to move, not daring to speak. At last Poppy stopped, and with Mistress Kimiko facing the prefects I risked a careful glance backwards, to find her leaning forward across her desk with a long ruler in her hand, just as she brought it down hard across my cheeks. I jumped and squeaked as the ruler caught me, clutching at my bottom and snatching for my book as it began to slide, too late again. Mistress Kimiko had turned to me and was nodding thoughtfully. I had to speak.

'Sorry, Miss. Poppy flicked something at my leg, Miss.'

She knew perfectly well, because she'd had a clear view of Poppy all the time, and I had to fight down the urge to protest that it wasn't fair. I knew they'd just laugh at me, that I was trapped. I was finally going to get my spanking, the same painful and humiliating treatment Poppy and Sophie had suffered, in front of the men and bare bottom. It was always bare bottom.

Mistress Kimiko nodded once more, then lifted a single finger, beckoning to me. My stomach went tight, my pathetic protest still trembling on my lips, but she spoke before it came out.

'Come across my knee, Gabrielle,' Mistress Kimiko ordered. 'It's time you had that bottom smacked.'

I waited as she pulled out my own chair and sat down on it, making a lap for me to bend over and positioned so that the class got the best possible view of my bottom. My heart seemed to have come up into my throat as I laid myself down across her knees, full of apprehension and self-pity, which grew abruptly stronger as my school skirt was lifted to show off my white cotton knickers. I waited as Mistress Kimiko took a safety pin and fastened my skirt so that it would stay up, with Poppy and Sophie giggling together over my humiliation. There was an odd shuffling noise that suggested one of the men was playing with his cock, which sent my cheeks red as Mistress Kimiko took hold of my knicker elastic.

'And down come your panties,' she said.

My bottom was exposed, my knickers peeled casually away to lay me bare, not just my cheeks either, but my sex, peeping out between my thighs, and even a hint of my anus. I wished I had a big, fleshy bottom like Poppy's so that I didn't look quite so rude from the rear. Now they could see, the men passing whispered comments and Poppy and Sophie laughing openly at my plight.

'A little decorum, please,' Mistress Kimiko said, and she began to spank me.

From the first stinging slap I knew I was lost. I tried to fight, but I couldn't. It hurt, and I was feeling sensitive, exposed and pathetically sorry for myself. My failure to avoid punishment was running over and over through my head, worse even than having my knickers down in front of a load of men, leering, gloating men, men laughing at my plight and admiring every rude detail between my pumping thighs as I began to kick.

They'd seen it all before, my sex, my bottom, my anus, but not while I was spanked, not with my cheeks bouncing to Mistress Kimiko's slaps, not with my legs kicking stupidly up and down, not with tears running down my face and snot bubbling out of my nose.

I heard Mr Spottiswood call me a cry-baby and I lost the last of my control, surrendering myself to the pain and the humiliation in a full-blown spanking tantrum, kicking wildly in my lowered panties and bawling my eyes out, full of shame and consternation for the way I'd been picked on and singled out for spanking, just because I hated it, just because it made me cry and made me wet at the same time. It had indeed, my sex hot and wet between my thighs even with my cheeks still bouncing to the stinging slaps and the tears running freely down my face.

'See how wet she is?' Mr Noyles remarked from directly behind me, drawing fresh tears from my eyes. 'What a little tart.'

'Quiet!' Mistress Kimiko snapped. 'Right, that should do.'

She finished me off with a final salvo of slaps and I was let up, snivelling badly, half blind with tears and snotty nosed. Her eyes were full of contempt as she looked up.

'I'd heard you made a fuss, but I didn't realise you were quite such a big baby. In the corner with you then, hands on your head, and you're to leave your panties down so everybody can see what happens to naughty girls.'

I went, quickly wiping my nose on my sleeve before putting my hands on top of my head. With my skirt pinned up and my knickers down, my red bottom was on full show, and while I didn't dare turn around the funny noises had started again. At least one of the men was wanking over me, but Mistress Kimiko just went back to talking about deportment, obviously quite happy to let her pupils masturbate over the sight of my smacked bottom. It was so grossly unfair I began to cry again, at which whoever it was gave a final, orgasmic grunt and a long sigh of satisfaction.

'If you've quite finished, Noyles?' Mistress Kimiko queried, her voice dripping sarcasm.

'Yes, thanks, Miss,' he answered. 'Sorry, but I couldn't resist that perky little bum.'

'Quite understandable,' Mistress Kimiko answered. 'As I was saying . . .'

She went on and I was left standing there in the corner, on show to all of them, until she was finally done. Even then I was told to keep my knickers down and sent to sit on my hot, bare bottom as we waited for the next class. Mistress Kimiko had left, and there was a moment of expectant silence before everybody started to talk at once.

'That was good, Gabby,' Poppy said happily. 'Did you look a sight! Let me feel how hot you are.'

She came round to my desk and I lifted my bottom to let her touch, my eyes closed as she felt my hot cheeks, all the while making little purring noises in her throat for the pleasure of touching my smacked bottom. I couldn't resist, closing my eyes as she caressed me and sighing as she slipped two fingers between my sex lips and in up my hole, feeling how wet I was. She'd begun to ease me over the table, and I was wondering how far she'd go and if I should give in with all the men watching when she stopped abruptly at the sound of a cough.

Sabina was standing in the doorway, her arms folded across her chest, her face set in very obviously mock exasperation. Her cane was dangling from one hand.

'Right you two,' she sighed, 'get up here.'

'But, Miss ...' Poppy began, and stopped as Sabina started forward.

I'd stood up, and watched, biting my lip as Sabina caught Poppy by the ear and dragged her squealing to the front. She was flipped up, bottom high across Sabina's knee, her school skirt quickly tucked into its own waistband and her knickers whipped down. With her big pink bottom bare to the room she was given several dozen hard slaps, far harder than those Mistress Kimiko had given me. It left her whole bottom rosy and her face downcast when she finally got up. Like me she was sent into the corner to stand with her hands on her head and her bottom on show to the class, and then Sabina snapped her fingers.

'Now you, Gabrielle, you little slut.'

'Please, Sabina, not too hard ...'

'Shut up!' she snapped. 'I'll decide how hard you get it, now bend over!'

She grabbed my wrist and jerked me towards her. I was caught off balance and sprawled across her lap, my legs wide open, and before I could recover myself she had hooked her foot around my calf, spreading my sex open to the laughing audience with my already lowered panties stretched tight between my thighs. All I could manage was a squeal of alarm and a few babbled pleas before my spanking began.

I'd thought it had hurt from Mistress Kimiko, but Sabina was far worse, using the full strength of her arm to rain furious slaps on my poor bare bottom without giving me a chance to catch my breath. From the moment it started I was out of control, making a truly pathetic display of myself with my fists beating on the hard wooden floor, my free leg kicking wildly in the air and my thighs and bottom spread wide to show off not just my wet cunt but my anus too.

Even while Poppy was fingering me I'd been snivelling a bit, too emotional to stop myself, and I burst into tears again immediately. That brought laughter and catcalls from my audience, Mr Spottiswood clapping his hands in delight and calling me a cry-baby over and over again, Mr Masham urging Sabina to spank me harder, and Sophie . . . Sophie coming up behind me and giving Sabina her shoe.

I'd forgotten how much a proper punishment could hurt. The first smack of the shoe had me screaming and thrashing in Sabina's grip, and then my whole body was writhing as she laid in, beating me hard and purposefully, until I'd been reduced to a bawling, tear-stained mess, my bottom ablaze with pain, my face and my glasses covered in snot and spittle, my cunt an open, aching hole between my thighs. She didn't let me up, either, but held me firmly in place once she'd dropped Sophie's shoe, my thighs still held wide.

'OK,' she said, 'as you like things up your dirty little cunt so much I'm going to have one of the men fuck you.'

'Me please, Miss,' Mr Masham said immediately, a fraction ahead of both Mr Spottiswood and Mr Petherick.

I was still struggling as Mr Masham got up, an upside-down blur from my viewpoint back beneath the chair and between my own wide-open legs. My heart wasn't in it though, the burning shame of being fucked in public doing more to make me want to stick my bottom up than stop me. He got behind and flopped his cock out, alternately smacking it on my bottom and tugging on it to get himself erect before sliding it deep up my all too ready hole.

Sabina kept a firm grip on me as I was fucked, but she didn't need to. I'd given in, brought on heat by my humiliating double punishment and willing to accept the final, dirty detail. He was holding me by my hips too, with his thumbs on my bottom to splay my cheeks, showing off my anus and the junction between cock and penetrated cunt hole.

Soon I was gasping and panting, my resistance quite gone as he pumped into me, and I'd begun to try to rub myself on Sabina's leg when he suddenly picked up his pace, only to whip his cock free at the last instant and spunk all over my bottom and the back of my upturned school skirt, which he also wiped himself on before returning to his desk with a word of thanks to Sabina.

'Let that be a lesson to you,' she said as she released me.

I slumped on the floor, too far gone to stand. Everybody was watching me as my thighs came up and my hand went to my sex, masturbating with my rolled-up bottom on show to everyone, my hot spanked cheeks wide to show my bumhole, my newly fucked cunt open and slippery as my fingers worked on my sopping flesh . . .

'Why, you filthy little tart!' Sabina snapped. 'Well, we know what to do about that sort of behaviour, don't we?'

She reached down, first to slap my hands away from my sex, then to pull off my tie. I was rolled on my face, my bottom slapped, my wrists lashed together, my bottom slapped a few more times for good measure and Mr Masham's spunk rubbed into my face. Only then was I helped up, too dizzy to stand easily, and sent into the corner next to Poppy.

We stayed like that for the entire class, only occasionally sneaking crafty looks over our shoulders while Sabina was otherwise engaged. I felt dirty and eager, with the juice running down my legs and my face covered in Mr Masham's mess, while Poppy wasn't much better. We just got ignored, while Sabina made a point of dealing with the rest of the class. Sophie was misbehaving from the start and quickly ended up over Sabina's knee. Mr Spottiswood began to masturbate as he watched, and Sophie was made to crawl to him and suck his cock once she'd been dealt with.

After Sophie had been given a mouthful and made to swallow it in front of everybody, Sabina caned Mr Spottiswood for masturbating in class, then Mr Petherick and Mr Greene for the sake of it. When she managed to catch out both Mr Noyles and Mr Masham at the same time she had Sophie spank them before getting hers in turn, after which she was finally sent to join Poppy and me in the corner. Tasanee came last, her spanking carefully timed so that when Stephen came in to take the next lesson he found his wife across Sabina's lap with her bum the colour of a ripe cherry and her school knickers stuffed in her mouth.

By then my need had given way to a nagging sense of frustration, but my emotions were quickly brought back to the boil as Stephen addressed me.

'What have we here then? Been a naughty girl have we, Gabrielle? That's not like you.'

'No, sir,' I managed as his hand found my bottom.

'Nice and hot,' he remarked, 'and you'll have one or two bruises later, unless I'm greatly mistaken. I wonder if you're ready for the cane?'

'No, sir, not the cane, please,' I begged, and I meant it for all my arousal. 'Spank me, if you think I deserve it, but . . .'

'Now that's not an offer I hear you make very often,' he went on, slipping a finger between my bottom cheeks. 'Is it?'

'No, sir,' I answered, my words coming out in a gasp.

He'd found my bottom hole, already wet and ticklish with juice and sweat, the top joint of his finger slipping in. My mouth had come wide as he began to wiggle his finger in my anal ring, until I was wriggling my toes in reaction, only for him to pop it out and offer it to my mouth. I sucked, unable to stop myself for all my shame at being so dirty and the noises of disgust from the watching men. Stephen laughed and leant close to whisper in my ear.

'Yesterday wasn't entirely satisfactory for me, Gabrielle. You should have waited.'

'I . . . Tasanee couldn't hold on any longer, sir,' I answered, also whispering, because none of the other men knew just how filthy my after-game punishment had been.

'Maybe I should finish you off now?' he suggested.

'How do you mean, sir?' I asked, genuinely worried. 'Not the same, not in front of the men?'

Poppy had heard, and giggled, then squeaked as he landed a meaty slap on her bottom.

'No,' Stephen said, 'not that, but perhaps something similar.'

He stepped away, leaving me both aroused and scared.

'Sit down then,' he said, addressing the three of us, 'but leave your knickers down. I want your bare bums on the wood.'

I didn't get the option, with my hands tied, and sat down, still acutely aware of my naked bottom and lowered knickers. He was supposed to be teaching Maths, and spent a moment drawing sums on the blackboard. We were given one each and got them all right, leaving him frowning.

'Hmm, something a little harder perhaps. Petherick, what is the cube root of twenty-seven?'

'Three,' Mr Petherick answered without hesitation.

'Very good,' Stephen said. 'Noyles, what is four to the fourth power?'

'Two-hundred and fifty-six,' Mr Noyles said smugly.

'Good. Cherwell, what is one-hundred and four divided by four?'

'Twenty-six,' Sophie replied and stifled a yawn.

He gave her a warning look but no more, then turned to me.

'Salinger, what is the answer to Einstein's riddle.'

'The German with the fish, sir,' I told him.

He looked unhappy for an instant, then spoke again.

'OK, Miss Smarty-Pants. If Billy has six doughnuts each weighing four ounces and he divides them evenly between thirteen friends, how much doughnut does each friend have, by weight and as a fraction?'

I began to try to work it out, wishing I had a pencil and paper, not that it would have done me any good with my hands tied behind my back. The smile grew slowly broader on Stephen's face, and then he'd begun to count backwards, immediately making me far too flustered to think straight at all.

'Zero,' he said, 'oh dear, oh dear, oh dear.'

'What's the answer then, sir,' I asked, crestfallen.

'I have no idea,' he told me, 'but that's not really the point, is it?'

He crooked a finger at me. I got up, half reluctant, half wanting it, but hoping me wouldn't spank me too hard before getting down to business, and praying he wouldn't use the cane.

'Tut, tut,' he said, grinning like a wolf as I came to stand in front of him. 'Touch your toes, Gabrielle.'

'Not the cane, sir, please?' I begged. 'Anything else, but not that!'

'Anything?' he asked, his eyebrows rising a trifle.

'Not an implement,' I asked, really pleading. 'I'm already going to be bruised, and . . .'

'Fair enough,' he interrupted. 'Over my knee then.'

I went almost willingly, allowing him to take my body across his lap and bracing my feet on the floor to lift my bottom into a good spanking position. Everybody was watching me, filling my head with strong and erotic shame as he began to spank me, just gently, and pausing between slaps to caress my bottom, stroking my hot skin, teasing my cunt, pulling my cheeks wide to show off my anus, with every new intrusion and humiliation bringing me higher still. Even when he began to touch between my cheeks I couldn't bring myself to feel more than a little resentment, until I felt something smooth, cold and hard press to my anus. My eyes had been closed in submissive bliss, but came abruptly open as my bottom hole began to spread to the pressure and I realised he was about to put something up me.

'What's that?' I asked, trying to look back from underneath the chair. 'What are you doing?'

'You said anything, Gabrielle,' he reminded me, 'so it's this or the cane. Anyway, it's just a little plug. I think it adds rather a nice touch for a girl's bottom to be plugged while she's spanked, don't you?'

'Yes, but . . .'

'No buts, Gabrielle, except this little round pink one I'm about to stick a plug up.'

He chuckled at his own humour and pushed once again. I gave in, letting my already slippery anus spread to the pressure, opening gradually until I was gasping with reaction, but the plug was in, properly up my bottom with my ring held wide by the neck. I could just imagine how I'd look from behind, with the end of the plug showing between my cheeks, quite obviously stuck up my bottom, which as Stephen said, made a very effective addition to any girl's punishment.

I was sobbing as he began to spank me again, overcome by the sheer dirtiness of my situation. It was harder now, making me gasp and bite my lips, then start to kick. I could feel the plug too, jammed in up my rectum with every smack and keeping my hole agape all the while. My cunt was juicing, my inner thighs sticky with it, and after a while Stephen paused to stick two fingers in and feed them to me, filling my mouth with the taste of my own sex as he went back to my spanking.

He was getting clumsy, hard and urgent, slapping the back of my thighs as well as my bum, and constantly breaking off to push the plug in and out of my bottom hole. I wanted to come, and would have been rubbing if I'd been able to get at my cunt, and when he finally stopped and began to lift me from his lap I was completely surrendered to the fucking I knew I was about to get.

I let him manipulate me, placed across the chair with my red bottom still stuck out towards my now silent audience and the plug clearly in place up my bum. He settled me down, stroking my back and hair as he extracted his cock from his fly and pushed it at my mouth. I sucked, all too willing to give pleasure to the man who'd just spanked my bottom for me and plugged my anus. He was already half-stiff, and grew erect in no time, taking me by the ears and spending a moment fucking my head before he finally withdrew.

As Stephen came behind me I glanced back. Sophie and Poppy had pulled their chairs together, hands down the front of each other's school knickers as they watched me punished. Tasanee was staring in fascination as her husband prepared me for use, while Mr Greene had his face hidden in his hands. Mr Petherick was wanking, his thick cock sticking out from beneath his belly with his eyes glued to my bottom. I gave them a sleepy, happy smile and hung my head as Stephen squatted down behind me.

He pushed his cock up into my slippery passage with one firm shove and my fucking had begun, only to stop almost immediately. Still with his cock inside me, he prised my cheeks open and began to pull on the plug, working it in and out to make my anus looser still. I knew what he was going to do. He was going to bugger me, and I was mumbling entreaties I didn't mean as he finally extracted the plug to leave my anus agape and ready for cock.

'No, Stephen, come on, not that . . . oh no . . .'

I broke off with a sigh. He'd put the head of his cock to my open, slimy bottom hole and it was too late, my will to resist completely gone as he gently but firmly forced my hole. Soon the full length of his cock had been introduced to my back passage, leaving me grunting and moaning as I was buggered, all my dignity stripped away, thinking only of how I would look, with my school skirt pinned up and the big white panties pulled down, my hands tied behind my back with my own tie and my bottom all rosy from my triple spanking, and better still, best of all, the man who had spanked me working his cock in and out of my dirty bottom hole.

He was getting faster too, his cock pumping in my rectum to set my feet kicking and my mouth wide as I struggled with the overwhelming sensation of being sodomised. I could feel my ring pulling in and out, and his balls slapping on my empty cunt, driving me higher and higher still, until I was riding at the very edge of orgasm and begging for him to take pity on me, the dirty words spilling from my mouth as my buggering grew harder and faster still.

'Make me come, Stephen, I beg you . . . please, Stephen, touch me off while you're still in me . . . touch my pussy, Stephen . . . touch my cunt . . .'

'She wants a reach round, boys and girls,' he laughed. 'Tell you what, Gabby, I'll do it if I get to finish in your mouth.'

Mr Masham gave a delighted cheer, filling me with new and raging shame even as I was nodding my head in frantic agreement. Stephen slowed down, pushing deep in my rectum as his hand curled around under my belly, manipulating me. My muscles began to jerk immediately, my bumhole tightening on his cock and my gaping vagina closing with a soft, lewd fart. I began to scream, unable to control myself as the climax hit me, so strong and so good, with his cock so deep up me I felt it would come out of my mouth.

Stephen let me ride it, working his cock in my gut and spanking me even as he frigged me off, and holding himself in long after my screams had died to a feeble, exhausted whimpering. As I slumped down over the chair I knew it wasn't over, that I had one last degradation to go, but there was no resistance in me at all. My body lay limp as Stephen carefully extracted his erection from my bottom hole. My mouth came open as he shuffled around to my head. My tongue came out and I was licking his cock, deliberately showing off to them as I lapped at the penis he'd just extracted from my rectum, then sucking as he stuck it in my mouth, glorying in the taste of my own bottom, and of spunk too as he ejaculated down my throat.

I'd been the centre of attention for most of the morning, and was hoping to take a back seat for the afternoon. After lunch we were marshalled on the largest of the lawns, directly in front of the house. Mistress Kimiko was giving instructions to the men, then came over to where Poppy, Sophie, Sabina and I were talking together.

'This afternoon is sports,' she stated.

'We know,' Sabina answered, 'but there's not really much room.'

'There is no problem,' Mistress Kimiko assured her. 'Master has decided each detail.'

'Do we just wear our uniforms?' Poppy asked.

'Panties only,' Mistress Kimiko answered. 'That is normal for English schoolgirls, no?'

'Not really,' Sophie pointed out. 'We used to do gym in our knickers at my school, but we had vests too.'

Mistress Kimiko consulted her clipboard.

'English schoolgirls do sports in just their panties. This is what it says, so come on, chop, chop! Strip off, panties only.'

She turned back towards the men, still reading from her clipboard. I began to undress, eager to avoid further punishment as my bottom was still warm and more than a little tender from the morning's spankings. Sabina automatically assumed a dominant role, watching as we stripped off.

148

'I'm keeping my shoes and socks on,' Sophie stated. 'I don't care what the poison dwarf says.'

'Me too,' Poppy agreed. 'I wonder who wrote all that stuff? What a pervert!'

'Obviously not her,' Sabina put in.

'I think I can guess,' I told them. 'It has to be Jeff. He's the only man I know who thinks like that, well, almost . . . Anyway, he's the Master, you'll find.'

'He's in Japan,' Sophie pointed out.

'That doesn't mean he can't come back, and it explains Kimiko and her clipboard. They must have got together over there.'

'So she gets a sort of Jeff view of the UK,' Poppy mused, 'where everybody's getting spanked all the time and schoolgirls do outdoor sports in just their knickers.'

'Exactly, who else but Jeff?' I confirmed. 'I think I know how it works too, and it's not entirely flattering. He must have hired Wyddon Manor and set up the Institute, but found that Mistress Kimiko and Tasanee were going to be the only girls, so he offered me four places as a birthday present, knowing I could be guaranteed only to bring girls. After all, can you really see him spending nearly two thousand pounds on my birthday present?'

'Well, no,' Poppy admitted, 'especially when he's not around to take advantage of your gratitude and get you to do something really perverted.'

'I think you're right,' Sabina agreed. 'Do you know, one of these days I'm going to take a cane to that fat bastard's arse and see how he likes it.'

'You'd have a fight on your hands,' Sophie pointed out.

'I could do it,' Sabina said confidently. 'He's just a great ball of lard.'

I didn't comment, always keen to allow Sabina to maintain her self-image of strength and dominance, but shrugged off my blouse, leaving myself stark naked except for my white school knickers. Unlike Poppy and Sophie, I was not willing to risk another spanking for leaving my shoes and socks on.

Stephen had disappeared, but emerged from the woods after a few minutes, speaking to Mistress Kimiko before she went to the centre of the lawn and called out in her high-pitched voice.

'Quiet! We are to begin. The first event is outdoor running. All girls and boys must reach the highest point of the woods, where is a bag of ribbons. Each must return with a ribbon. No ribbon and you get the cane. First boy back gets a suck from the last girl back. Understood?'

She read most of it from her clipboard, the game no doubt another of Jeff's perverted inventions. Not that it worried me. I could outrun Poppy and Sophie easily, probably Tasanee too, although remembering the feel of pine needles in my flesh I quickly sat down to pull my shoes and socks back on.

'Are you ready?' Mistress Kimiko called out.

'Not quite,' I pointed out, hastily raising a hand.

'Get set!'

'Excuse me, Mistress Kimiko!'

'Go!'

The others ran, leaving me desperately trying to get the buckle of my shoe fastened. It didn't seem to want to go, and I was panicking, making it all the harder as I pictured myself ending up cock-sucking one more time. By the time I'd finished even Mr Petherick had disappeared into the woods. I dashed after him, watching his enormous backside wobble under his school skirt with horrified fascination.

I overtook him easily, and Mr Spottiswood, but the others were well ahead. I at least knew the path, and managed to overtake Poppy when she took a wrong turning, then Mr Greene. The men didn't matter, only that I wasn't the last girl to come in, but I felt cheated and was determined to win. When I saw Tasanee and Sophie ahead I pushed myself even harder, sprinting with my muscles red with pain and my lungs feeling as if they were about to burst.

Sophie gave me an astonished look as I sped past her, then Tasanee, and Stephen, whose age had begun to tell for all his long legs and masculine strength. Only Mr Masham and Mr Noyles were ahead, both younger and fitter, but as I reached the track at the boundary of the wood I could see them. I was gaining, but I was forced to slow as we turned off to the top of the woods, along a narrow, winding path between huge pines and banks of fern.

Mr Noyles almost ran into me, grinning and holding up a hand clutched full of bright blue ribbons, and I was there, where two walls joined at an open space, with the empty hillside beyond. Mr Masham was there, but already turning away from where a big yellow carrier bag was fixed to the barbed wire topping the wall. He said something I didn't catch and slapped my bottom as he broke into a run.

I burrowed my hand into the bag, but I couldn't feel anything. A horrible suspicion had entered my mind as I peered inside. It was empty, and as I now realised, Mr Noyles hadn't taken just one ribbon, he'd taken them all. It was blatant cheating, and he'd be punished for certain, but if I knew anything about the way Mistress Kimiko worked, and Masters and Mistresses everywhere, then it was highly unlikely that the girls would be spared the cane.

As I sped back the way I'd come I could already feel my fear and shame rising, with an image of Mr Noyles gloating as I bent to touch my toes, had my knickers pulled down behind, screaming as the cane bit down across my naked bottom . . .

It wasn't going to happen. I was going to catch up and make him give me a ribbon, and three more for my friends. I could do it, I knew, if I forced myself, and I was running with every ounce of my strength, driven by anger and fear. A group of the others passed me coming the other way, Sophie pausing to joke about me being in such a hurry when Poppy had obviously lost. I caught up with Mr Masham, who put on a burst of speed and tried to stop me passing him.

He was fast, and my body was telling me to give in, to lie down among the ferns and rest, then just refuse the cane. I couldn't do it, I knew, the spell of the Institute too strong to break, or if not, that breaking it would ruin the rest of my stay. With new determination I snatched at Mr Masham's collar and pulled, wrenching myself past him and sending him sprawling into a stand of ferns, taken completely by surprise. He was calling me a bitch and a cheat as I sped away, but I took no notice. I had glimpsed Mr Noyles ahead, and he was flagging.

I was maybe halfway back, but he'd seen me, and to my horror he didn't turn into the thick of the woods and towards the house, but kept on along the boundary path. To follow might mean I ended up sucking cock, but that didn't matter, not next to the cane, and if I didn't catch him it might very well be both. I was going to though, catching up yard by painful yard, hopeful, then triumphant as I drew close enough to yell at him.

'Give me a ribbon, you cheat!'

He shook his head, too out of breath to answer, but the ribbons were loose in his hand, trailing back. I snatched, missed, and snatched again. This time I caught hold, but he clung on and we'd stopped, both panting for breath as we faced each other, the ribbon stretched taut between us.

'Give them to me!' I demanded. 'You're cheating.'

'No,' he puffed. 'I . . . I want to see you caned.'

'I hate the cane.'

'I know . . . why do you think I want to see you get it?'

'You . . .'

I almost swore, and I could feel the tears of frustration beginning to well up as I tugged at the ribbons. It was futile. He was well over six foot tall, and a man, surely much stronger than me.

'Please?' I begged. 'It's really not fair of you.'

He just laughed.

'Please, Mr Noyles,' I repeated, and my tears had started to come. 'I . . . I'll suck your cock, right now. You can even fuck me, only please let me have the ribbons?'

'Tempting,' he chuckled, 'but I suspect you're going to be sucking me before too long anyway, and more. For now I want to see the tears trickling down that pretty face while Mistress Kimiko canes you.'

I bit my lip, wondering what else I could offer, even the use of my bumhole, although that didn't come far short of taking the cane, especially with him. No, there was only one thing to be done. I hit him.

It wasn't hard, just a sudden jab to his solar plexus, and I felt awful for what I'd done even as I snatched the ribbons from his suddenly limp fingers and ran away. I was terrified for what he might do to me if he caught me, and ran for all I was worth, even though he was clutching himself and gasping with pain. Only the thought that he would have taken pleasure in seeing me cry while Mistress Kimiko beat me saved me from utter self condemnation, but I wasn't going back for anything.

I'd saved myself a caning, and hopefully the others too, but that was all. As I ran back through the woods I passed Mr Petherick, now walking, but only him. My heart sank as I reached the edge of the woods and still hadn't seen Poppy, and sure enough, she was already on the lawn flat on the grass and panting for breath, but there. I collapsed beside her, quickly tucking one of the ribbons into her knickers before Mistress Kimiko could start making demands. Sophie was close too, and I slipped one into her hand, but Tasanee was kneeling at Stephen's feet and before any of us could recover sufficiently to get to her Mistress Kimiko spoke up.

'Gabrielle is the loser then. You are slow, Gabrielle.'

All I could manage was a shrug. I was running sweat, both from my exertions and the heat of the day, and I knew what I was going to have to do.

'Who won?' Sophie asked.

'Mr Masham,' Mistress Kimiko stated.

I hid a sigh. Mr Petherick was approaching, and Mr Noyles behind him, not looking too pleased.

'That bitch Gabrielle hit me!' he protested as soon as he'd reached the lawn.

'He'd taken all the ribbons,' I pointed out. 'It wasn't fair.'

'It's just a game!' he said. 'That really hurt.'

'How much do you think the cane hurts?' I demanded.

'Yes, but that's erotic. You punched me!'

'I'm sorry, OK, but you wouldn't give me the ribbons.'

'That was a bit over the top, Gabrielle,' Stephen put in, 'but I do think you should accept her apology, Clive.'

'I don't think . . .,' Mr Noyles began, then stopped. 'All right, as long as she gives me a suck. I'd have won if she hadn't gone after me. And I want her caned.'

'That's not fair, Mr Noyles,' I insisted, and everybody had begun to talk at once until Kimiko stepped in with her hands raised.

'I will decide. The rules must be followed. Gabrielle has lost and will suck Mr Masham's penis. All runners with no ribbons are to be caned. Gabrielle will suck on Mr Noyles's penis while he is caned.'

Everybody began to talk again, each arguing his or her own point, with the exception of Mr Greene and myself. I was trying to get my thoughts in order, telling myself I'd feel better for sucking off Mr Noyles despite a deep sense of chagrin. After all, I had hit him and the last thing I wanted was any bad feelings when we were all living so close together. Besides, he'd be getting the cane while I did it. I stood up.

'OK, OK, I'll do it, just to show I'm genuinely sorry, but the way Mistress Kimiko set out or not at all.'

There was another flurry of argument, but between Mistress Kimiko and Sabina the men got shouted down, even Stephen agreeing to take a single cane stroke as long as Tasanee was sent inside and he didn't have to go bare. It was also decided that the punishments should be given on the lawn, and Mr Greene was sent indoors to fetch a chair for the canings.

I watched with a lump in my throat as Tasanee and the men were beaten. The two Mistresses created a sort of production line, with Kimiko taking down their trousers or the special girls' school knickers and Sabina applying the cane. She was accurate, but did it mercilessly hard, and I found myself wincing at every stroke, and very, very glad it wasn't my bottom they were being applied to. The only exception was

Tasanee. Stephen insisted on doing her, and as her bottom was already decorated with several sets of welts he was quite gentle with her, or possibly because he'd just learnt how it felt to take a cane stroke from Sabina.

Mr Noyles went last, and he was grinning at me as he mounted the chair, apparently looking forward to the experience. I wasn't, but I knew I had to obey and crawled over to where he was kneeling with his cock and balls sticking through between the rungs of the back of the chair. Sabina was flexing her arm as I took him in, feeling very much that I was being punished as I started to suck.

'The punishment will continue until Mr Noyles has come,' Mistress Kimiko stated flatly and Sabina swung the cane in.

As the cane hit Mr Noyles his cock was jammed into my mouth, but he took it well, barely crying out. It was the same with each succeeding stroke, and he was quickly growing erect in my mouth, obviously enjoying the experience a lot more than he was suffering from it. Not that it made any difference to me. My job was to suck his cock until he came, a fitting punishment for my behaviour.

It wasn't going to be long either, as Mr Noyles began to fuck in my mouth to his own rhythm instead of Sabina's, and to grunt and sigh between the strokes. He even tried to hold off, pulling his cock out to slap it in my face and rub the tip over my cheeks and nose, but with the very next cane stroke he came, as if Sabina had knocked the spunk from his balls. It went in my face, taking me by surprise, some in my mouth, but mostly over my nose and glasses, leaving me barely able to see as I finally rocked back on my heels.

There was a flurry of clapping as Mr Noyles got down, although it wasn't obvious for whom. I stayed put, trying to ignore both my sense of shame and a little involuntary arousal as Mr Masham stepped forward. His trousers were still down, his cock half hard, and the leer on his face was pure cruelty as he approached me.

'That's a fine sight,' he told me. 'I do love to see a pretty girl when she's had her face spunked in. I'm going to do the same, in your mouth and all over your glasses, and then I'm going to make you lick them clean.'

'We didn't say anything about that,' I protested.

'Shut up and suck, bitch,' he rasped.

'Sabina?' I asked, hoping she'd stick up for me.

'Just get sucking, Gabrielle,' she told me.

I threw my hands up in despair, feeling thoroughly done by as I got down on my knees in front of Mr Masham. He was grinning as he flopped his cock out in my face, and showing off as I took him in my mouth, with his belly stuck out and his hands on his hips so that everybody could get a good view of my face wrapped around his penis. They were all watching too, and thoroughly enjoying the show, even Mr Greene taking an occasional peek from between his fingers. I was beginning to feel that I wanted to come, but determined not to give them the satisfaction of seeing me lose control, particularly Mr Masham.

Before long I was sucking on a full erection and bracing myself for a faceful. He began to moan, then to grunt, and suddenly grabbed my head and his cock at the same time, squeezing my cheeks to force me to keep my mouth open as he jerked frantically at his shaft. I saw the spunk erupt from the tip of his cock and closed my eyes as I felt it on my face, hot and wet and slimy, a long streamer laid in my hair and down one cheek, crossing my glasses, a second full in my open mouth and a third exactly in the middle, so that I was left with a blob of it hanging from my nose.

They were laughing and clapping as he squeezed out what was left on to my lenses, leaving me nearly blind. Mr Spottiswood had his cock out and Sophie was wanking him, while Mr Petherick was squeezing his crotch, making me wonder if I was just going to get had again. I took my glasses off quickly, looking at the slippery, greyish white mess the two men had done on them, then turning to Sabina in mute appeal.

'Eat it, Gabrielle,' she ordered. 'Come on, poke out that little tongue and lick it all up. It's good for you.'

'You should eat it then,' I muttered, but too softly for her to hear.

'Do it,' Mr Masham ordered, still breathless from his orgasm. 'Eat my spunk, Gabrielle.'

I made a face, my last, mute protest before I'd poked my tongue out into the sticky filth and began to lap it up. All the men were all staring at me in delight, the girls also, but most of them with disgust as well. They knew what spunk tastes like.

It was impossible not to make faces as I ate it, much to everyone's amusement, and arousal too. Mr Spottiswood was hard in Sophie's hand, and when Mr Petherick transferred Poppy's to his own cock she didn't resist. I continued to lick, dabbing up the blobs of spunk with the tip of my tongue and swallowing them down, grimacing each time but finding it increasingly hard to resist the urge to stick my hand down my knickers and bring myself off.

When Mr Spottiswood was ready Sophie led him forward by his cock and jerked him off into my hair and across one ear, which was the final straw. I put my glasses back on, lifted my head to show off the spunk-smeared mess of my face, stuck my hand down my school knickers, and as I licked up the blob of spunk still hanging from my nose I started to masturbate.

They were all clapping and cheering as I rubbed myself, calling me a slut and a tart. I just pushed my panties down to give them a better show and rubbed harder still, bringing myself quickly up. Mr Masham's cock was still pointing at my face, now limp, but I opened my mouth to let him put it back in. He didn't, but I got Mr Petherick's instead, Poppy masturbating him directly into my mouth as my climax burst in my head and for the fourth time that day a man spunked up in my mouth.

Sabina led me indoors after I'd come, first to help me clean up and then to make me lick her to orgasm on her bed. We stayed cuddled up together for a while afterwards, before returning to the lawn. Either the orders of the day had been forgotten, or the rest of the sports were simply designed for the enjoyment of dirty old men, because Poppy, Sophie and Tasanee were back in their full uniforms and being made to do handstands to show off their knickers.

They'd also been doing exercises in just their panties while Sabina and I had been playing, and we finished off with a game of chase in which the men were allowed to molest any girl they caught. I was good at that, and for once managed to avoid both getting spanked or disgracing myself, but I ended up exhausted. That was it for the day, and we went in to shower and change, both Poppy and Sophie teasing me mercilessly for my inability to control my feelings once I'd got turned on. Mr Greene had brought up clean knickers, but nothing else, leading Poppy to query how we were supposed to dress for the rest of the day.

'Do you suppose the poison dwarf thinks English schoolgirls eat dinner in just their knickers as well?'

'Maybe knickers and a pinny,' Sophie suggested. 'I'm not risking getting hot water down my front.'

'I'm getting back in uniform then,' Poppy stated. 'What about you, Gabby?'

'I'll go in my knickers,' I told her. 'It's cooler. I'm tired and hungry too, so let's make something simple, but lots of it.'

'Bangers and mash then,' Poppy suggested as she fastened her skirt.

'We had that yesterday,' Sophie pointed out, 'and on Saturday.'

'So?' Poppy answered. 'This isn't the Ritz, you know.'

'You should do something different for the three of us, Gabby,' Sophie suggested, adjusting her knickers. 'Some of your fancy French cooking.'

'What if we get caught?' I objected.

'Don't be wet, Gabby,' Poppy answered me. 'Anyway, we won't get caught. They never come in here, and we can eat while we pop in and out to serve.'

I hesitated, but I really did not feel like another evening of bangers and mash, while Poppy was right. Mistress Kimiko was always far too busy eating and showing off her dominance to come into the kitchen while we were cooking and serving. As we finished dressing and trooped downstairs the idea became increasingly tempting. Poppy opened a bottle of wine, which pushed away some of my tiredness but made my hunger keener still, while the sight of all the food in the fridge made my mouth water. I decided.

'OK, I'm going to do T-bone steaks with a Roquefort béchamel, green peas, and I suppose the frozen croquette potatoes will be OK.'

'Yes, please,' Sophie responded.

'Me too,' Poppy put in. 'It's only fair, when they seem to think we ought to live on a diet of spunk!'

160

Sophie laughed and I couldn't help but smile, despite having been the one who'd eaten most of it. They began to peel spuds, leaving me to set everything out so that my timing would be perfect. The steaks weren't good enough to be done blue, but if I got the roux ready in advance the whole thing wasn't going to take more than five minutes; so if we served a simple starter, ate it quickly and hurried back under the pretence of getting the next course ready nobody would even notice.

There were some ready-made vol-au-vents in the freezer and I put them in the microwave. The result looked less than appealing and they tasted of cardboard, but I prepared them anyway, placing four on each plate with a bed of rocket and some baby radishes in the hope that, being British, presentation would be enough for them. By the time I'd finished, the potatoes were on the boil and the sausages sizzling.

I served the vol-au-vents, and was pleased to find them all talking about the day we'd had. Things had got to the stage where none of them bothered to pay more than cursory attention to the maids, and then only for an opportunistic pinch or to make a complaint. Nobody remarked when we returned to the kitchen almost immediately, and I got down to work, finishing my dish just as Poppy and Sophie were scraping the huge saucepan of mashed potato into an equally huge dish.

We turned off the cooker and ate, savouring every mouthful, until all three of us were thoroughly replete. It took a real effort to go back to work, but the mashed potato was beginning to go cold and we at last managed to get ourselves together. I took the sausages, serving first, then Sophie with the beans and Poppy last with the mash. There was a general murmuring of discontent around the table when they realised what they were getting, except from Mr Petherick, who was tucked in as if he hadn't eaten for a month.

I thought we'd got away with it as I took the sausage dish back into the kitchen, my only worry how I was going to excuse myself from eating my own helping. Sophie came in behind me, laughing over what we'd done, but not Poppy, and as I put the dish in the sink I heard voices, angry, then laughing, then a squeal from Poppy, suddenly choked off. I exchanged a worried glance with Sophie.

'Do we run?' she asked, throwing a glance towards the open door and the woods beyond.

'Where to?'

'Just away!'

'In only our knickers?'

She made to speak again, but stopped as the door crashed open and Poppy appeared. She was kneeling on the trolley, stark naked except for pulled-down knickers, her hands tied behind her back with her school tie. They had put a sausage in her mouth, and as I ran to help her I realised she had another in her vagina, stuck so far up that only the rounded, greasy tip showed in the pink of her hole. I'd just taken hold of it when Sabina appeared with the others pushing forward behind her.

'Oh no you don't,' she said. 'She stays like that, and you, Miss Gabrielle . . .'

'Oh shit,' Sophie said softly as we saw where Sabina's gaze was resting, on the three plates we'd eaten from, each with its little piece of bone and smear of sauce.

'What's this?'

'You were eating your own meal?' Mistress Kimiko demanded.

'Why, the greedy little cows!' Mr Petherick exclaimed. 'And steak too, by the look of it!'

'We were hungry,' I tried, spreading my hands.

'Hungry, were you?' Sabina asked. 'So what, you couldn't do us steaks as well?'

'There . . . there wasn't enough Roquefort for the sauce,' I explained.

'Roquefort sauce?' Mr Petherick asked, his voice faint with dismay.

There was a moment of silence, all of them now in the room and staring at the evidence. Then Sophie began to laugh.

'The look on your faces!' she said. 'You ought to see yourselves, really!'

Sabina turned on her, her face full of outrage and disbelief, apparently unable to speak, but Mistress Kimiko succeeded.

'Punishment, all three!' she screeched. 'Stupid bad girls! I thrash you all, dirty pig sluts, worthless . . .'

She'd lost control of her English completely, yelling at us in Japanese, not a word of which I understood except that she intended to beat all three of us severely. I was about to point out that erotic punishment should never be given in anger, but Sabina spoke first.

'Calm down, Kimi. I'll deal with this. So you were the cook, were you, Gabrielle?'

'Yes,' I admitted.

'But I bet it was Poppy's idea to serve us bangers and mash, wasn't it?'

I shrugged, not wanting to get Poppy into any more trouble but knowing better than to lie to her. Mistress Kimiko had gone quiet, and although her eyes blazed with anger she was looking as much at Sabina as us. With what must have been a great effort she brought herself under control, doing her best to save face as she rapped out commands.

'All three of you will be punished. Mistress Sabina will decide the punishments. Meanwhile, Tasanee will cook us some decent food.'

'Yes, Mistress,' Tasanee answered promptly.

'Right then,' Sabina said, and paused, nodding gently as she considered the three of us, for so long that I'd begun to fidget before she went on. 'Sophie, as you seem to think it's funny, let's see you laugh this off. Stephen and Clive, stick her in the outside bin, upside down.'

'Hey, no!' Sophie squeaked, and tried to run.

Mr Noyles shot out a long arm, catching her, and before Stephen had even come around she had been hauled up across his shoulder. She was kicking and squealing, begging and protesting vehemently against her punishment, but Mr Noyles held on while Stephen removed his own tie and Mr Greene's, using them to tie her ankles together and lash her wrists behind her back.

'Panties, Gabrielle,' Stephen ordered.

I slipped them off and watched as he forced them into Sophie's mouth and tied them off with yet another tie, leaving her gagged and helpless. They carried her outside, to where the huge galvanised kitchen bin stood in the service yard. It didn't seem to have been emptied for a while, and the aroma had been growing increasingly rich in the hot weather, which had Sophie thrashing in desperation as they heaved her up and fed her head-first over the edge and into the contents.

She didn't go down very far, but stuck with her head in the rubbish, her bum sticking out with her cheeks wiggling in the big white school panties and her legs waving frantically in the air. Both men were laughing, and paused to enjoy the view before taking an ankle each and tipping her in properly, so that she was half immersed in the rubbish with just her legs sticking out above the edge of the bin.

'Not me, please, Sabina, not in the bin ...' I begged, starting to babble as she turned her cruel smile on me.

'Oh no, not for you,' she said, 'although if you don't take that look off your face I might change my mind. You get to eat the dinner you cooked, that's all.'

'But I didn't, Sabina, I ...'

I shut up. Sophie was still wriggling desperately in the bin and I really did not want to join her. I hung my head instead, accepting my fate.

'Good,' Sabina said. 'Help Poppy down, somebody, and bend her over the table.'

Mr Masham and Mr Spottiswood made quick work of lifting Poppy off the trolley and putting her in place across the kitchen table. With her hands tied she was helpless, looking back with her face full of concern, but made ridiculous by the sausage in her mouth. The one in her vagina showed too, a round, brown dome in the open pink hole, showing just above the edge of her lowered panties. Sabina snapped her fingers at Mr Greene.

'Fetch me a couple of our plates, quickly.'

She strolled across to the fridge, opening it to take out a packet of butter, from which she cut a small knob using the knife from my plate. Poppy watched wide-eyed, her bottom cheeks twitching, and I saw her swallow as Sabina came back behind her. Taking the butter gently between finger and thumb, Sabina used the balls of her hands to spread Poppy's bottom cheeks, exposing the soft, pink star of her anus. She applied the butter to it, rubbing the knob around until it had begun to melt to Poppy's body heat and then easing it slowly up. Poppy's bottom hole was dribbling butter as it closed, but Sabina wasn't satisfied, cutting a second knob and easing it in after the first.

'Your plates, Mistress,' Mr Greene announced.

'Put them on the table,' Sabina answered, not even bothering to look at him.

Both plates held a large mound of mashed potato, a ladle's worth of baked beans and two sausages. Poppy could see, and her eyes were round with horror as Sabina selected the larger of the two sausages. We all knew where it was going, up Poppy's bottom, and I watched it inserted with horrified fascination, her well-buttered ring spreading to accept it with no great difficulty.

As I watched the sausage eased up I was wondering if I was about to get the same treatment, and imagining how I'd look. The sausage wasn't in all the way, but far enough to leave just the fat, rounded tip poking out from Poppy's distended anus, a truly obscene sight, inciting Mr Masham to make a joke so revolting I found myself blushing and looking at the floor. Sabina spoke again as she pulled up Poppy's knickers.

'Stick it out, if you know what's good for you, Poppy.'

Poppy obeyed, sticking her bottom out to make a round, heavy ball in her knickers, with the tips of the two sausages just visible as bulges in the taut white cotton.

'Someone hold her panties open, will you?' Sabina asked.

Mr Petherick obliged, his tongue poking out to moisten his thick, gristly lips as he took hold of Poppy's knickers by the waistband and pulled them wide, far enough so that I could see down, to the top of her crease and the first chubby swell of her cheeks, while a good deal of soft pink girl-flesh was spilling from each leg hole. She gave a muffled sob as she saw Sabina pick up the two plates, and another as the full contents of the first were tipped unceremoniously down the back of her knickers.

'Stick that fat bottom out properly,' Sabina ordered, 'and hold her panties further out, Alan.'

Poppy's face was full of resentment, but she did as she was told, pulling her back in to make her bottom seem bigger and rounder still. Mr Petherick tugged harder on her knicker elastic, holding them open as wide as they would go so that her leg holes pulled out and a mixture of mashed potato and beans began to ooze out at each side. Sabina watched, smiling, then took the second plate and scraped off the contents into Poppy's panty pouch. There was too much, one sausage and a hump of potato sticking out over the top.

'Perfect,' Sabina announced. 'You can let go now.'

Mr Petherick let go, allowing Poppy's knicker elastic to snap shut, or almost, her panties now a little open and sagging under the weight of their contents, with the very top of her bottom crease just showing. The bulge was huge, a fat, soft mound, lumpy in places and wet in others, with juice already beginning to soak through and mashed potato squeezing out from both leg holes. Some had even gone between her thighs, creating a smaller and rather more soggy bulge around her sex lips.

There was obviously far more than her knickers could accommodate, and it was too heavy as well. As we watched, the weight of it was slowly dragging them down, until Sabina was forced to catch hold of the waistband. I had no idea how humiliating Poppy was supposed to affect me, until Sabina looked up.

'On your knees, Gabrielle.'

I nodded weakly, still not sure what she was going to do, but I got down, up close to Poppy until the heavy bulge in her panties was just a few inches in front of my face and the scent of what was in them strong in my nose.

'Now eat it up,' Sabina ordered, 'all of it. I want to see you with the last sausage in your mouth.'

'All of it?' I asked.

'All of it,' she confirmed, 'or I'm going to cane you, then you go in the bin. Take your choice. Shall we have a glass of wine while we watch her, you lot?'

I was left staring at the monstrous bulge in Poppy's knickers as she walked to the fridge. There was more than I could possibly eat, far more, but the thought of being caned and thrown in the rubbish was too much. Bits were falling out of her leg holes anyway, and I couldn't believe Sabina would make me eat what had been on the floor. Maybe if I took it slowly . . .

My tongue poked out and I began to lick at the thin liquid seeping through the cotton of Poppy's panty seat. After a moment I stopped and took my glasses off, then began again, gently nuzzling my face against the cotton, to feel the soft, squashy mess inside and lick up what I could, then nibbling bits of potato from around her leg holes. I never even realised Mistress Kimiko was behind me until I heard her unmistakable voice at the same instant her hand tightened in my hair.

'Eat it!' she snapped. 'Do it properly, Gabrielle.'

As she spoke she pulled my hair, hard, forcing my face against the seat of Poppy's knickers. I felt the potato squash out over my features and I'd been pulled back, no longer able to see, my face caked with mess, and abruptly thrust forward again, only Mistress Kimiko had pulled Poppy's knickers down. My face went between her cheeks, squashed firmly in and rubbing about, all the while with Mistress Kimiko screeching orders.

'Eat it, slut! You like squashed potato and sausages so much, yes? So eat it!'

I tried to, struggling even to get some in my mouth because she was rubbing my face so hard between Poppy's cheeks, but then she'd let go, leaving me to pull back, gasping, my face filthy with mash and beans, my breasts and belly too, from bits that had fallen off. Sabina laughed, and one of the men. I went back to eating, sullenly picking bits of mash and beans off Poppy's bottom and swallowing them down. I felt utterly humiliated and bitterly sorry for myself, my tears starting even as the familiar and treacherous ache began to build up in my sex.

They'd opened the wine, drinking and laughing together as I ate my dinner from my girlfriend's bottom. I could feel my stomach bloating, but they'd got to me, my arousal increasing with every comment at my expense and with every mouthful swallowed down. Tasanee had dinner prepared long before I'd finished, and they ate it around the kitchen table, still watching me.

My control began to go as I started to eat the sausage in Poppy's vagina, sucking it out and biting bits off, my mouth now full of the taste of cunt as well as food. She seemed to have eaten the one in her own mouth, and had begun to moan softly as my lips moved on the flesh of her sex, encouraging me. I began licking, cleaning her bottom cheeks and her crease, even around where her anal ring was still agape on the other sausage. I couldn't see, but I recognised Mr Masham's voice when he spoke.

'I think the dirty bitch is enjoying it.'

'Looks like it,' Mr Spottiswood agreed. 'Butter her up, Sabina, I bet she'd like a sausage up that cute little arse of hers.'

'And her cunt,' Mr Petherick added. 'Don't forget to do her cunt.'

'I'll do as I please,' Sabina answered him, but she'd already ducked down beside me.

I was lost, sticking my bottom out as Sabina pressed a large knob of butter between my cheeks, cold at first, but quickly melting to my body heat and sliding in up my anus. More went up my cunt, a piece big enough to leave me a little stretched until it began to melt, and yet more up my bottom, fingered well in up my rectum. I remembered how it had dribbled out of Poppy's hole and knew it would now be doing the same from mine, oozing yellow and slippery from the tiny central slit of my anus.

My face was deep between Poppy's bottom cheeks, my lips open around the sausage in her bumhole, sucking the tip with unspeakably dirty thoughts racing through my head. She'd begun to giggle and sigh to the touch of my lips and tongue, and to wriggle her cheeks in my face, encouraging me to give her cunt a lick.

Sabina had taken one of the sausages from the mess in Poppy's lowered panties, and put it between my cheeks, rubbing it over my anus and pushing it briefly in up my cunt before returning her attention to the first and dirtier hole. She pushed, and I couldn't help but sigh as my anal ring spread slowly to the pressure, too well buttered to resist as it opened around the tip of the sausage. I felt it start to go in, just like a cock, bloating out my rectum until I was gasping into my faceful of bum and wiggling my bottom for more.

They clapped and laughed to see me so lewd, encouraging Sabina to be dirtier still, buggering me with the sausage while she held my cheeks open so they could all see it moving in and out of my open pink hole. When she stopped she left it deep in, just like Poppy's, which I'd begun to suck on again, letting my fantasies run wild.

'Got the turtle's head, Gabby!' Sabina laughed. 'Go on, eat it.'

I couldn't not obey, pushing in to close my teeth on the sausage in Poppy's anus and pulling it a little way out to nip off the end. They saw that I was chewing and broke into fresh catcalls and cheers, just as Sabina slid a second sausage in up my cunt, filling me in the most delicious way, as if I had two fat cocks up my holes as I ate from Poppy's bottom.

'Eat it all up, then the stuff in her panties,' Sabina ordered. 'I'm going to make you come. Do you want that, slut?'

As Poppy extruded another inch or two of sausage into my mouth I was nodding eagerly, making it break off. I ate it as Sabina's hand found the bulge of my sex, a finger pressing between my lips. Her palm was on the sausage in my cunt, fucking me, her other hand on the one up my bumhole, pushing it vigorously in and out. I began to touch myself, feeling the round, open balls of my buttocks, the swell of my breasts and the hard nipples at the tip of each, my stomach bulging with food as if I was pregnant.

It was all glorious. I was nude, my holes plugged, being fucked and buggered and masturbated all at once and with an audience of men and women to make my exquisite shame all the stronger, and better still, best of all, I was eating mess out of my darling's bottom slit, sucking out the last of the sausage and quickly gulping it down, sticking my tongue deep in up her open, buttery bumhole, licking and sucking and gorging myself as Sabina's hand worked on my slippery, penetrated cunt hole until I came in a screaming, babbling, jerking mess, utterly filthy, utterly humiliated and enjoying every instant of it.

Six

My first thought as I awoke on the Wednesday morning was that it was my day. Whatever was coming, it had been designed for me, by Jeff admittedly, and he had some pretty bizarre ideas, but he also knew my tastes. It would definitely mean going in nappies, of that I could be sure, and after the last two days I could also be sure that the details would be both elaborate and filthy.

Poppy was in bed with me, naked, and I had rather vague memories of sex the night before, with her, Sophie and myself playing together under Sabina's orders. She'd made us kneel in a line for spanking, amused herself with our bodies in a dozen other ways and had each of us lick her in turn, among other things, and that had been after hours of dirty play in the living room.

There had been a lot of wine, also brandy, and my head was a little cloudy as I swung my legs out of bed. I padded nude to the bathroom, indifferent to who saw me. What did it matter, after all? The Institute had got to me, allowing me to relax in a way I can usually only achieve in my special bedroom. Even the men didn't bother me any more, not after seeing them caned, and I had kissed and made up

173

with Mr Noyles, even allowing him to give me a gentle spanking in reparation.

I showered and dried, all the while wondering what was in store for me. Back in the bedroom Poppy and Sophie were both still sound asleep, so I powdered my own bottom, applied a dab of jelly to my anus and slipped into a nappy. Just fastening the tabs at my hips brought my familiar sense of security and arousal up so high I already wanted to play with myself, while my eyes were closed in bliss as I put my hands back to touch the soft, puffy bulge where the nappy material covered my bottom.

My pink woollen booties went on, but that was it, no top. After all, what did it matter if my breasts were bare? Nobody minds a baby with no top on. With my dummy in my mouth I was done, feeling silly, excited and most of all free. I quite wanted to serve the morning coffee the way I was, so everybody could see, even if it was a bit out of role. Mr Greene had got there first, carrying the tray upstairs as I went down. On it was a baby bottle, full of milk, which I accepted, sucking contentedly on the teat as I went outside into the cool morning sunshine.

If being bare except for my nappy felt good indoors, it was twice as good outdoors, with a delicious element of naughtiness added to all my other feelings. I made a point of walking down to the bottom of the garden, where there was a risk of me being seen from the road, gaining me a sharp thrill every time a car approached and I had to duck back behind a hedge. Soon I was laughing for my own behaviour, and I'd completely forgotten that I was supposed to be helping with breakfast, or anything else.

When I finally returned to the house after walking right around the boundary path for the sheer joy of it I found Sabina already on the lawn, in her deckchair with Mr Greene on all fours to one side of her, acting as a table for her glass of orange juice. Mistress Kimiko was also there, reading from her clipboard, and dressed in a smart blue nurse's uniform. She addressed me immediately.

'There you are, Gabrielle. It is your day today.'

'I know.'

'Then you should be ready. You are dressed at least. So now . . .'

She broke off as Poppy and Sophie came out from the house. Like me, both wearing nothing but nappies and booties, but as I caught a movement in the open doorway behind them I conjured up an unappetising image of Mr Petherick clad the same way. Fortunately he wasn't, nor were any of the other men. Mr Greene was in his maid's outfit, but the rest were in white coats, as if the staff of a home for the mentally disabled had assembled on the lawn. Stephen emerged last, also in a white lab coat, but rather spoiling the image of a group of mature and sensible professionals because he was leading Tasanee by the hand and she was stark naked expect for a pink pull-up decorated with tiny yellow ducks encasing her hips and sex.

'What are we doing, exactly?' I asked Poppy as she joined me.

'We're going to get a medical,' she said.

'How do you mean a medical?' I asked.

'Search me,' she answered. 'That's what the poison dwarf said at breakfast, that's all. I suppose they'll want to stick thermometers up our bums, that sort of thing.'

I cast Mistress Kimiko a glance, wondering if Poppy was right. It didn't sound too bad, and at least it would be painless. Kimiko wasn't looking at me, but tapped her pen on her clipboard as she spoke.

'As I said at breakfast, today is for Gabrielle. We have seven doctors, more than was expected, so Mistress Sabina and I are to be nurses, and present at all times. There are five doctors that way, and we can make five tasks. Who will want to take the girls' temperatures?'

'Told you so,' Poppy whispered. 'I hope you're lubed up?'

'Yes, but they're not going to miss a chance to do that anyway, are they?'

All five men had raised their hands, but Mistress Kimiko pointed to Mr Noyles.

'You have big fingers. You are good. Who would like to make the cunt investigation?'

'I'm not quite sure that's the correct medical term,' Stephen stated, 'but I'd be glad to do it.'

'Cunt investigation, Mr Stanbrook,' Mistress Kimiko said, making a mark on her clipboard. 'Inoculation must be Mr Masham.'

My sense of well-being had been fading rapidly as she spoke, to be replaced by alarm.

'Gynaecology? Inoculations?' I queried. 'And why Mr Masham?'

'Mr Masham's a dentist.'

'Why doesn't that surprise me? And even if he is, I'm not sure about having him stick needles in my bottom, because that's what's going to happen, isn't it?'

'Bound to be,' she assured me. 'It wouldn't be any fun to stick them in our arms, would it?'

'Thanks, Poppy.'

'Come on, Gabby,' Poppy urged. 'It's just for fun.'

'Well . . . OK, it wasn't quite what I was expecting, that's all. Can't I have a sugar lump instead?'

'No you can't!' she retorted and smacked my thigh.

'Shut up, you two!' Mistress Kimiko snapped. 'Who will give them their enemas?'

'I'm good at that,' Mr Petherick offered.

I didn't like to think why.

'Enemas from Mr Petherick,' Mistress Kimiko said, 'so Mr Spottiswood must take their samples, yes?'

'Oh yes,' Mr Spottiswood said eagerly. 'I can do that.'

I was suffering from a slight sinking feeling as the men began to laugh and joke among themselves over what they were about to do to us, and I was also aware that if the same thing had been suggested when I'd first arrived I would have backed out immediately.

'Who's coming to me first then?' Mr Noyles asked, rubbing his hands.

'The order is set,' Mistress Kimiko told him. 'First they give their samples. Second is their enemas. Third, their temperatures are taken. Next the cunt investigation. Inoculation is last. Come with me for your equipment. You girls, wait until I call you. Sabina, you should be in your uniform.'

'Don't get pushy with me, Kimi,' Sabina answered, 'or you may end getting the same as the sluts.'

Mistress Kimiko gave her a furious look but started for the house with the men trailing after her. Sabina swung her legs off the deckchair, gave a lazy yawn and followed, clicking her fingers for Mr Greene. He obeyed instantly, attempting to crawl and carry her orange juice at the same time, a comic sight she missed completely because she didn't even bother to look back.

I was left standing on the lawn, wondering what I'd let myself in for and trying to tell myself it would be OK once I was properly turned on. My delight in nappies is really very simple. It allows me to regress, shedding all responsibility, and while it is very definitely sexual, my ideal is to be brought off under

177

my nurse's fingers while being changed. Unfortunately nobody I've ever met provides my ideal complement but invariably wants to spank me, humiliate me in a whole assortment of ways, or in this case do horrible medical things to me.

'Why couldn't they just put the four of us in a cot or something?' I sighed.

'I suppose the men have to get something out of it,' Sophie pointed out. 'After all, they're the ones who're paying.'

'Like Gabby said, we're really here for their entertainment,' Poppy put in. 'I mean, the poison dwarf says we have our special days, but really it's more like the days when advantage is taken of our special fantasies. Jeff, huh?'

'He means well,' I pointed out, 'it's just that he tends to apply his own sexuality to other people's fantasies.'

'So we end up as spunk receptacles for a load of dirty old men?'

'Like you don't love it!' Sophie laughed.

'OK, it's good,' Poppy admitted, 'but I'm going to watch when Sabina canes him.'

'She's not really going to try to, is she?' I asked.

'She says so,' Poppy assured me, 'and I think she means it.'

'Having all the men grovel to her has gone to her head,' Sophie put in. 'I think she's beaten all of them, even Stephen if you count that weedy cane stroke, and we end up as her whipping girls!'

I nodded. Part of the entertainment the night before had been Sophie and Poppy being spanked and given six of the cane apiece from Mr Masham and Mr Noyles. As Sophie said, Sabina had been giving increasingly free rein to her dominance since we'd been at the Institute, but that was really only an extension of the way she'd been moving ever since we'd known her.

'Excuse me,' Tasanee broke in gently as Poppy and Sophie began to argue about whether or not Sabina was capable of making Jeff submit to the cane. 'I have not been in a diaper before. What do we do, please?'

'It's only a diaper if you're in the States,' Poppy pointed out. 'Over here it's a nappy. Basically, if nature calls you don't have to bother to go to the loo.'

'Excuse me?'

'You can pee in it, if you'd like to,' I explained.

'Or poo,' Sophie added, 'although I'd like to see the men's faces if you did!'

They both laughed, but Tasanee merely looked puzzled.

'It is a punishment, to be made to do our toilet in them?' she asked.

'That depends how you look at it,' I told her. 'I find that makes me free, you might feel it was a punishment.'

She nodded gravely and would have continued, but Sabina had come back out from the house. In place of her casual clothes she was now in an abbreviated nurse's uniform, but still managed to project an air of dominance despite the skirt being so short her knickers showed. She hadn't been able to get the front done up either, or she hadn't tried, with the zip open to her navel to show off the inner curves of both full, golden-brown breasts.

'Bloody Jeff!' she protested as she reached us. 'Look at this thing! He knows my size.'

'I think he must have got everything in job lots,' I suggested.

'Yeah?' she responded. 'Well I'm going to make him wear it when he arrives, while I cane him.'

'He'd never get it on,' Poppy pointed out. 'Maybe Mr Petherick's schoolgirl outfit?'

'Whatever,' Sabina answered. 'OK, who's first? You have to be last, Gabs. Come on, Tasanee, time to let the perverts have their fun with you.'

Tasanee went with her, as meekly as ever. The three of us began to talk again, but I was beginning to get that distinctive nervous apprehension that comes with waiting at a dentist's, or at a doctor's when you know the treatment is going to be painful or unpleasant. I'd started to need the loo too, and was wondering if I'd get a spanking from one of the nurses if I went in my nappy, and if so, whether it would be for the best to help me cope with the medical inspection.

Time began to drag, and yet Sabina seemed to be back almost immediately, now with Mistress Kimiko's tawse, which she used to smack Sophie indoors. The upper windows were all open, and at a cry in Tasanee's distinctive tone Poppy gave me a nervous grin, which I returned. If Sophie had been taken in to give her sample that meant Tasanee was in the enema room, making me wonder what part of the process had caused a girl who could take the cane in near silence to cry out.

Sabina came back almost immediately, using the tawse across Poppy's thighs as she too was herded indoors. I was left alone, looking up to the windows, from one of which I could hear Mr Petherick's voice, then Poppy's, unclear but expressing maybe disgust and protest, then a sudden sharp smack and a cry. My stomach had begun to flutter, with the thought of things being inserted into me running through my head; fingers, nozzles, probably a speculum, undoubtedly one or more cocks.

At last Sabina came out for the third time and it was my turn.

'There's a bit of a queue building up for the enema room,' she told me, 'but you may as well give your sample.'

She sent me on my way with a smack of the tawse across my nappy seat and laughed when I ran to avoid getting another on the back of my legs. I climbed the stairs, to find Sophie and Poppy standing in the corridor, both looking rather sorry for themselves. All the rooms opposite the ones the men normally occupied had each been given a sign. The first said urology.

'In you go,' Sabina said as she came up behind me.

I entered the room, to find Mr Spottiswood seated in a chair with a small table next to him. On the table was a single, large glass, empty but somewhat wet inside.

'Ah, baby Gabrielle,' he said, 'now I do hope you won't make a fuss over this like the others?'

'Not if she doesn't want the tawse across her thighs,' Sabina warned as she came in behind me.

'I'm sure she'll be a good girl,' Mr Spottiswood said. 'She is usually the most obedient of them, except for Tasanee perhaps. Very well, Gabrielle, off with your nappy and you're to provide me a specimen in that glass.'

'Yes, Doctor Spottiswood,' I answered, wondering why Sabina had had to smack Poppy, who wasn't usually shy.

I took off my nappy and put it down on the bed, which gave no more than a pleasant touch of exposure and a little shame. Both feelings grew as I squatted down with the glass in my hand, spreading my sex to Mr Spottiswood's goggle eyes. It took a little concentration to let go, but I managed and was enjoying the exhibition I was making of myself as my pee gushed out into the glass beneath me. I was quite full, and by the time I'd finished the glass was close to overflowing, drawing a slight blush to my cheeks as I offered it to Mr Spottiswood.

'My, you have been a thirsty girl,' he said, taking the glass and lifting it to the light. 'Hmm, nothing wrong there, it seems. Good rich yellow, and very clear. Excellent.'

He held out the glass to me and I took it, not quite sure what I was supposed to do, but after a moment he spoke.

'Drink it up then.'

'Drink it?' I queried.

'No fuss, I think we said,' he answered, grinning. 'Pee pee is good for you.'

'No . . . yes . . . but . . .'

'Drink it, Gabrielle,' Sabina said from behind me, her voice full of warning as she stroked the tawse gently up my back.

'OK, I'll drink it,' I said quickly.

There was a choking feeling rising in my throat as I put the glass to my lips, smelling the warm, hormonal scent of my pee even before I tasted it. Both of them were looking at me, and it was hard to be sure whose face showed more cruelty and satisfaction for what they were making me do. Now I knew why Poppy had had to be smacked, but it was pointless to protest. She'd been smacked and she'd still had to drink her pee.

I tipped the glass, tasting my rich, acrid piddle, a little, then more as it began to flow into my mouth, and I was gulping at the glass, eager to get it over with as soon as possible and wishing I'd had a pee in the garden after my morning bottle. Halfway down I began to choke, but forced myself to go on, telling myself it wasn't so very different from having Poppy pee in my mouth but unable to shake off my feelings of humiliation. Both Sabina and Mr Spottiswood watched in unconcealed delight, their eyes fixed on me until I'd swallowed every last drop.

'I said she'd be the easy one,' Sabina remarked as I finished. 'Right, Gabby, into the enema queue.'

'Hang on,' Mr Spottiswood said. 'There's no rush is there? I could just do with a blow job after that.'

'There's no rush at all,' Sabina agreed. 'Go on, Gabby, get sucking.'

'Why's it always me?' I protested as Mr Spottiswood flopped out his cock and balls through the opening of his lab coat.

'Shut up and suck, Gabrielle,' Sabina ordered, 'and don't be a selfish bitch. Have you been caned, or strapped?'

'No,' I admitted, and hung my head.

'Then suck . . . his . . . cock,' she said firmly.

She'd taken me by the hair, twisting me around and rubbing my face against Mr Spottiswood's bulging genitals until I opened up and took his already half-stiff penis into my mouth. He immediately began to masturbate, tugging at the inch or so of shaft sticking out from my lips, while Sabina held me firmly in place, pulling my head up and down so that rather than sucking I was getting a face fuck.

'That was good,' he sighed. 'Four little sluts drinking their own piss . . . four little sluts drinking their own piss. What a sight!'

I couldn't argue, and not just because my mouth was full of rapidly expanding penis. He was right, and I was wishing I'd been made to watch the others do it before having to drink my own; Tasanee, then Sophie, then my own Poppy, each with her face screwed up as she swallowed down her own urine, and then me, made to do exactly the same, only in my case I had to suck off the man who'd made us do it as well.

'In her mouth or in her face?' Sabina asked as Mr Spottiswood began to grunt and tug faster, his hand knocking on my nose and lips as he moved towards orgasm.

'Her mouth,' he grunted, 'right down the little piss mop's throat . . .'

He broke off with a grunt and he'd done it, forcing me to swallow as best I could with Sabina still bobbing my head up and down on his erection. It didn't work, my cheeks bulging with spunk as my mouth filled and the whole filthy mess exploding from around my lips as he jammed himself deep, all over his lab coat and all over his balls.

I came up coughing, spitting spunk and mucus, only for Sabina to thrust my head down again, rubbing my face in the mess to smear it all over my glasses until I'd opened my mouth and was struggling to lick it from Mr Spottiswood's rubbery ball sack.

'How does it taste, Gabby?' Sabina laughed. 'A mouthful of your own piss, and now spunk on top. Go on, lick it all up and swallow it down, piss mop. That's a great description of her, Ken, it really suits her. That's what you are, Gabrielle, a piss mop. God I love tormenting you.'

She was still holding me in place, and kept me there until I'd licked up as much of Mr Spottiswood's spunk as possible, then holding my nose until she was sure I'd swallowed my filthy mouthful. He'd watched it all, grinning inanely at my humiliation and discomfort until Sabina was finally satisfied. I was shaking badly as I put my nappy back on, close to tears, but with my inner thighs wet and slippery with my own juice. Poppy was alone in the corridor, and turned me a smile as I came out.

'They made you drink it?'

'Yes, and suck Mr Spottiswood off.'

'That's why you're last. After all, it's your day.'

'I seemed to get most of it on your day, and Sophie's.'

'Only the dirty stuff, and you must admit a lot of that's been your own fault.'

I nodded, knowing that she was at least partly right. Certainly I'd been extremely foolish to let my sympathy for Mr Petherick get the better of me during the pig-sticking, and I didn't suppose for a moment it would make the enema he was about to give me any easier to take either.

'I can still taste it,' Poppy said.

'At least you didn't get a mouthful of spunk as well.'

She grimaced, just as the next door opened. Sophie emerged, shook her head and blew her breath out. Her nappy was unfastened at one side, with her hand down the back to let her itch her bottom hole.

'The bastard's using toothpaste as lube,' she said. 'Just to make our bumholes sting.'

Poppy winced, but Mistress Kimiko had come out of the enema room.

'Silence in the queue!' she snapped. 'Poppy, you are next. Sophie, go into proctology.'

I was left in the corridor, feeling sorry for myself but unable to deny the responses of my body. They knew how to handle me, particularly Sabina, and there was no denying my feelings, or how good my orgasm would be when I was finally permitted to get there, yet that did not stop me feeling immense chagrin for the journey. Besides, it was supposed to be my day and yet it looked as if I'd have to make as many as five men and maybe two women come before I was allowed to do so myself.

Mr Petherick's voice was audible, gloating and lecherous, as Poppy was given her enema, also

Mistress Kimiko, with her sharp commands, all punctuated by the occasional soft gasp and a good deal of whimpering, then a gushing, splashing noise and I realised they'd made her expel in front of them. It was about what I'd been expecting.

Sabina came out of the urology room after a while, applying a swat to my bottom as she passed and disappearing into the second last room, where Tasanee was presumably being given her 'cunt investigation'. Mr Spottiswood also emerged, but only to go downstairs. No sooner had he gone than Poppy emerged from the enema room, wide-eyed and shaking her head as if in disbelief, with her discarded nappy hanging from one hand.

'What a bastard,' she sighed. 'Your turn, Gabby.'

'Gabrielle!' Mistress Kimiko screeched, and I walked into the enema room.

I closed the door behind me and took in my surroundings. Mr Petherick and Mistress Kimiko were standing together with their backs to the window, creating a bizarre contrast between his blubbery bulk and her tiny delicacy. As with the other room, there was a table and a chair, also a bed. In this case the chair was in the middle of the room, its back towards me, while on the table a squat stand supported a thing like a hot-water bottle but with a long, transparent tube extending from the bottom. The tube ended in a bulbous nozzle, still smeared vivid blue with the toothpaste from a half-empty tube beside the stand. There was also a one-litre measuring jug and two buckets, one full of water, one discreetly covered with a cloth. I forced a smile, awaiting my orders.

'We have decided it will be amusing to watch you do it yourself,' Mistress Kimiko announced, 'but also, Mr Petherick is going to fuck you.'

My mouth came open in automatic protest, not so much for what she'd said, but the way she'd said it, as if submitting myself to Mr Petherick for sex was something I had no say in whatsoever, nor would even think of refusing. What stifled my words was him, producing a dirty little chuckle as he opened his lab coat to expose his cock, already hard in excitement. It was going up me, as simple as that. He also had his fat, hairy ball sack out, and bounced it in his hand as he spoke.

'Get in position then, darling. I want to see you put the tube up your bottom.'

'She must fill the reservoir first,' Mistress Kimiko pointed out.

I knew, and hadn't even intended trying to escape my fate. Taking up the bucket, I filled the litre jug and the enema bag in turn, leaving it bulging and fat. Only then did I remove my nappy and get into position on the chair, the way I was obviously supposed to, kneeling with my bottom stuck out so that my open cheeks were on show to both Mr Petherick and Mistress Kimiko.

'You will lubricate your arsehole with toothpaste,' she instructed, 'and put the bulb right in before you turn on the water.'

Both their faces were full of glee as they watched me prepare myself for my own enema, hers sharp and bright and evil, his red and puffy and full of lechery. I knew the toothpaste was going to sting, but as I squeezed a thick worm out on to my bumhole it only felt cold and squishy. That was deceptive, because as I pushed a little into my hole my ring had already begun to feel hot, and grew hotter as I rubbed the paste in, until my anus was burning and so loose I thought I was going to lose control and soil myself in front of them without needing the enema.

'Now the nozzle,' Mr Petherick demanded, stroking his cock as he spoke, 'right in up that darling little bottom.'

I obeyed, taking the enema nozzle, touching it to my now inflamed anus, poking it in and pushing it deep, until I felt my ring first open and then close around the bulb designed to hold it in place in my rectum. Mr Petherick gave an excited grunt at the sight of me with the tube protruding from my anus, and another as I turned the tap on.

As always, there was no sensation at first, but I knew my rectum was slowly filling with water, and that was enough to set me sobbing as I turned away from my audience and shut my eyes in shame for the thought of being watched as I gave myself an enema. Had it not been erotic I wouldn't have minded so much, but it was. I had my bottom stuck out with a hose in my anus and my wet, ready sex on open view to a girl and a man, a man with an erect cock, a man who was about to fuck me, and I'd now realised he intended to do it while I took my enema. My eyes came wide once more. I had to look.

He was standing up, cock in hand, the fat purple head pointed directly at my open bottom. I heard my own sobs escaping my lips as he came forward, to poke it between my cheeks, rubbing his helmet on the junction between the nose and my bumhole even as I began to feel the pressure of the water in my rectum. His cock went lower, rubbing between my lips and for an instant I was gasping in helpless ecstasy. Then it was up my hole, pushed deep to fill me and turn my gasps to sobs once more as he began to fuck me.

With his cock in up my cunt the bloated feeling in my rectum immediately doubled, and grew faster as he moved inside me. I could feel the weight of the water, and that awful helpless feeling as the urge to evacuate grew stronger. He'd taken hold of my hips, his huge belly now resting on my upturned buttocks as he fucked me, make me gasp and whimper.

Soon I began to wiggle my toes against the pressure in my gut, to shake my head and clutch at the back of the chair. My rectum felt bloated, and every push into my cunt made it worse. My belly had begun to bulge and grow round, wobbling to the rhythm of my fucking, as were my breasts. My anus was burning, the bulb now threatening to pop out as the pressure grew, squeezing out a little, but stuffed back up every time Mr Petherick pushed into me.

Now I knew why Tasanee had cried out, the twin sensations of my straining rectum and the big cock moving in my cunt far more than any girl could be expected to handle. I wanted to scream, and began to babble useless pleas and utter obscenities, alternately begging him to stop and to fuck me hard, to pull the hose free and fill me up until the water began to bubble out of my mouth and nose . . .

'I'm there . . . oh you dirty little darling, you dirty, filthy little darling!' Mr Petherick grunted and I realised he'd come inside me.

He pulled out, and I knew immediately that there was no way I could possibly hold the tube in up my bum without his gut to wedge it in place.

'It's going to happen!' I squealed. 'Get the bucket!'

I didn't wait for them to respond, but grabbed for it myself, sticking it over my bum without even bothering to remove the towel, and only just in time. The nozzle exploded from my anus, followed by everything else, in one great noisy burst. My bottom was on full display, with the dirty water and lumps of solid gushing from my open anus, to their delight. Mistress Kimiko was laughing, Mr Petherick looking on with a gloating amusement, sending the blood rushing to my cheeks, and yet even my shame for evacuating in front of them was mild compared with my overwhelming sense of relief.

'That's the best one yet,' Mr Petherick chuckled as I sat down on the bucket to let the rest of my enema out.

'Tasanee made a bigger fuss,' Mistress Kimiko pointed out.

'Yes, but I like the way Gabrielle hates it but can't stop herself getting turned on.'

That wasn't strictly accurate, but it was obviously what he wanted to believe. I didn't dare get up, with my bottom hole still wide open and sore from the toothpaste, while as I knew from experience enemas have a nasty habit of taking you by surprise just when you think you've finished expelling. Mr Petherick was watching me.

'I wish my cock stayed hard after I'd come,' he said wistfully. 'I could spend forever fucking in that darling little pussy of yours.'

'You weren't supposed to be fucking in it at all,' I pointed out. 'You were supposed to be giving me an enema.'

'You get so juicy,' he told me. 'I can't resist you. Waste not, want not, as they used to say.'

He was beaming, immensely happy with himself and clearly oblivious to the thought of what he'd just done being wrong in any way at all, or even excessive. That made what little resentment I had left hard to sustain, and I found myself smiling back.

'Wipe your bottom, Gabrielle,' Mistress Kimiko ordered. 'Mr Noyles will be ready for you.'

She passed me a roll of loo paper and I added one more touch to the complete destruction of my dignity by wiping my bottom in front of them. I knew Mr Petherick would want to see, and did it facing away

190

from him, but I hadn't anticipated Mr Greene also getting an eyeful when he came in.

'May I have your bucket please, Mistress?' he asked.

I nodded, astonished to be called Mistress when I was stark naked except for a pair of little pink booties and in the act of deliberately wiping my bottom in front of a dirty old man, but he seemed to believe in female superiority regardless of the circumstances. He even averted his eyes somewhat as he took the bucket.

'Thank you,' I said automatically as I reached for my nappy.

I'd been addressing Mr Greene, but it was Mr Petherick who answered.

'Don't mention it, always happy to oblige.'

He was still chuckling to himself as I put my nappy back on and left the room. There was nobody else about, although I could hear noises from the last two rooms. Next was Mr Noyles, and a thermometer up my bum, surely easy enough to take after being made to drink my own piddle and having my bottom flushed out?

Sabina was with him, seated on the bed with her legs crossed so that her tiny nurse's skirt had ridden so high her stocking tops showed, while her zip was even further down than before, with one dark brown nipple just showing at the side. Mr Noyles himself was seated on the chair, stirring a large thermometer in a cup of what seemed to be vodka.

'Ah, Gabrielle,' he said, 'no, no, you needn't take your nappy off, just bend down and touch your toes, with your bottom towards Nurse Sabina. Yes, that's right, good girl, stick it well out.'

I did as I was told, offering them my bottom. Sabina took hold of my nappy seat, moving it aside to expose my slit and my anus. Mr Noyles gave a lewd chuckle at the sight, then spoke.

'A little more lubricant, I think, nurse.'

'Certainly, Doctor Noyles,' Sabina answered.

She had my anal jelly, and I held my position as a blob of it was applied to my bottom hole. It was cool and slimy, also deliciously soothing after the heat of the toothpaste and the soreness of expelling my enema. I couldn't hide a sigh as Sabina rubbed the jelly in, poking one finger a little way into my anus, only for Mr Noyles to take over. I squeaked in surprise as he immediately pushed his larger, thicker finger deep up my bottom.

'Yes,' he remarked thoughtfully after a moment. 'Surprisingly tight, considering she is such a slut. Do you have her sodomised often?'

'Only occasionally,' Sabina replied, 'but she keeps herself lubricated and I sometimes have her wear beads or a little plug.'

I'd begun to blush, not surprisingly, but Sabina still had Mistress Kimiko's tawse and I didn't dare move.

'She seems in good condition,' Mr Noyles went on, 'a very neatly formed anus too. Is she naturally pink, or does she bleach?'

'She's naturally pink,' Sabina replied.

'Pretty,' Noyles replied, 'although I do like it when white girls have dark bumholes and feel they have to explain that it's just the way they are, not that they don't wipe properly. Do you wipe properly, Gabrielle?'

'Yes!' I protested, now blushing crimson. 'And . . . and it didn't say anything about an anal examination.'

His finger was deep up my bottom, feeling around in the flushed-out cavity of my rectum. Neither of them bothered to answer me, but as Mr Noyles shifted his position on the bed his lab coat fell open and I saw that, like Mr Petherick, he already had his cock out. Sabina took hold of it, wanking him gently, and at last he pulled his finger out of my bottom.

Sabina continued to nurse his erection as Mr Noyles retrieved the thermometer from the glass of vodka. It was an old-fashioned glass one, with a bulb the size of a large marble full of red alcohol and a long shaft nearly as thick as his finger. He glanced at it briefly, shook it, then put the bulb to my anus. I felt the glass, hard and extremely cold from the sudden evaporation of the alcohol. My ring opened to the pressure and my lips parted in a soft gasp, but it went in easily, slid deep up into my rectum.

I could only imagine how I looked, bent down with my bum stuck out and my nappy pulled to one side with a thermometer protruding from my lubricated anus. They seemed to find it funny anyway, chuckling together as they watched the temperature rise, peering close, until finally Mr Noyles spoke up.

'Exactly normal. Excellent. That's four very healthy young girls we have here. Now, I confess that having all those bottoms in my face has rather affected me, so if you wouldn't mind giving me release, Nurse Sabina?'

'Certainly, Dr Noyles,' Sabina said sweetly. 'Would you like to do it over her bum, up her bum, or just in my hand?'

'Wank me up her bum, would you?' he drawled. 'I think I'll give her a cream pie.'

'Not up my bum, Sabina,' I protested. 'I really don't feel like being sodomised just now. I'm sore, and . . .'

'Stop whining, Gabrielle,' she laughed. 'He only wants to put his helmet in your hole while I toss him off, nothing to make such a fuss about. Now stay still.'

I gave in, thinking of the tawse, and took a grip on the table, trying not to pout as I steadied myself to have my bottom hole masturbated in. He came close, Sabina leading him by his cock, and I was grimacing as I felt the roundness of his head against my bottom hole, convinced he was going to bugger me anyway. As she began to tug on him, with her fist smacking between my cheeks, I was waiting for him to ram it up at any moment, which forced me to keep my anus loose, because I know full well how carried away men can get once their cocks are in up a tight, warm hole. They don't think about whether it hurts the girl or not.

'That's good,' he sighed. 'I'm going to spunk, Sabina . . . I'm going to spunk right up her arsehole . . . oh, yes, right up it. You're an angel, Sabina . . . a true angel . . .'

As I received a dose of come in my anus my main emotion was resentment. I was the one bent over to have my bottom spunked up, but Sabina was the angel. Yet it was all I could do not to reach back and rub myself as Sabina squeezed out the rest of the come from Mr Noyles's cock into my open, sloppy hole, and that didn't stop me blushing crimson as he spoke again.

'Squeeze your arse, Gabrielle, make yourself squirt the spunk out. I love to watch that!'

'Go on, do it!' Sabina ordered, laughing.

Before I could stop myself I'd tightened my anus. There was a squishy noise as a little fountain of come erupted from my anus and on to my cunt, leaving me stickier than ever and blushing hotter than ever as they laughed over the show I was making of myself. At last Sabina adjusted my nappy, covering me once more, and I was left to go.

My legs felt weak as I walked the few steps next door. Stephen was waiting, looking thoroughly pleased with himself, and making no effort whatsoever to hide the rigid erection sticking up from between the sides of his lab coat. Mr Noyles's spunk was dribbling out of my anus and into my nappy, and I wasn't sure if I wanted to wipe or have a cock stuck up my bottom, something of which must have shown in my face.

'Feeling a little uneasy, Gabrielle?' Stephen joked. 'Well, I'm sure I can do something about that, if only to make it worse. Lie on the bed, please, head downwards.'

I obeyed, even putting my own feet into the heavy leather restraints he had fastened to the bedstead. He gave an approving nod for my obedience and began to fasten them, trapping one ankle and the second, to leave me with my legs spread wide. There were cuffs at the top as well, and I placed my hands in them, so that once he'd fastened those too I was completely helpless.

'We'll need your nappy open, of course,' he said, and pulled the tabs wide to tug it free from between my legs.

Now my sex was exposed, open and moist to his gaze and to his hard cock, also my slimy bottom hole.

'My, you have been a busy girl,' he remarked, glancing down to where Mr Noyles's spunk was still oozing slowly from my anus, which would no longer close properly.

He spent a moment just staring at me, drinking in the details of my naked body as if filing them away for future reference. I had no choice but to lie as I was, my body open for him to do with as he pleased. At last he spoke.

'So then, your cunt investigation, as Mistress Kimiko so charmingly puts it. First, let's have a look inside you, shall we?'

I managed a feeble nod, not that he needed my permission. He wasn't paying attention anyway, but had taken a disposable plastic speculum from a box, which he gave a liberal coating of lubricant before once more turning to me.

'Not that you aren't nicely juicy anyway,' he remarked, 'but these things should be done properly.'

As he spoke he had touched the speculum to my sex, cold and hard and slippery with jelly. I barely felt it go in, but only as my hole began gradually to stretch with the wider part of the shaft, and more so as he began to turn the screw, speaking again as he worked me open.

'Let's see if we can get a really good gape, shall we? You're a little tighter than your friends, I think, but with your height I'd like to imagine you could accommodate rather more.'

I didn't bother to contradict him, but was panting softly as my cunt spread wide to the speculum. Already I was stretched beyond the capacity of the thickest cock, and growing wider, until my pants had turned to gasps and I felt as if an express train could happily have used me as a tunnel. Still Stephen twisted the screw, until I was wriggling on the bed and shaking my head in reaction.

'That's it, as wide as you'll go,' he said, peering in up my open hole, 'or at least, as wide as the speculum will go. Hmm, I can see the neck of your cervix, just like a little pink arsehole. Do you know that when a woman comes her cervix goes into a sort of spasm, as if trying to suck up the pool of spunk that's hopefully just been made in her?'

'Yes,' I managed.

'I've always wanted to see that,' he continued, and he'd begun to rub a knuckle on my clitoris.

There was nothing whatever I could do, my vagina stretched open to his view as he casually brought me off, using his hand to manipulate my cunt until I came. As the spasms began to run through my body he was still staring up me, his eyes bright with interest and amusement, his grin growing to a childish glee as I hit my peak and he watched my cervix suck and pull at the bottom of my gaping hole.

I cried out in mingled frustration and ecstasy as I came, with my hands and feet jerking in my bonds and my pulsing bumhole squeezing out the last of Mr Noyles's spunk into my nappy. Stephen had been nursing his cock as he brought me off, and the moment I'd finished he spoke.

'I have to fuck you, right now, Gabrielle.'

He snapped the lock on the speculum, making me gasp as the pressure keeping my straining cunt wide suddenly vanished. Even when he'd taken it out I didn't close properly, still wide as he climbed on top of me, his body between my thighs, his cock probing for my hole, and up me. He held me as he fucked me, kissing me too, and I'd quickly given in, allowing my mouth to open under his as he pumped into me, struggling for friction in my slippery, abused cunt hole. When he stopped I thought he'd come, but as his mouth pulled from mine the expression on his face was not of pleasure, but frustration.

'Damn,' he swore, panting, 'I knew I shouldn't have come with Tasanee. I'm going to have to do it up your bum, Gabs . . . I just can't get the friction.'

I tried to protest, but all that came out was a weak moan. Not that I could stop him, bound hand and foot with his weight on me as he guided his helmet to my bum hole. As with Mr Noyles, he put his helmet in a little way first, just enough to open me a little, and rubbing in my ring as he masturbated himself back to full erection. Only then did he put it up, grunting and pulling on my shoulders as he forced my anus, until at last I felt his scrotum press to the turn of my cheeks and knew he was up me properly.

'That's better,' he sighed. 'Nice and tight, oh that does feel good, Gabrielle.'

He'd began to move his cock in and out, just slowly, making my ring pull and squashing his balls into the crease of my bottom. I let my mouth open as his pressed to mine, kissing with increasing passion as I began to enjoy my buggering despite myself. It felt too nice to resist, with my bottom in the soft material of my nappy and my slippery anus penetrated. I was pulling on my bonds, enjoying my helplessness but wishing I could hold him too, tight in my arms, before he ejaculated in my rectum, which he was about to do.

The pushes had become harder, his kisses also, and deeper, until he was forcing the breath from my body with every thrust and it felt as if the head of his cock was about to come out of the top of my head. I felt his body go tight, he jammed himself in up to the balls and I knew he'd done it, the second man in a matter of minutes to ejaculate up my bottom. He was at least gentle as he withdrew, and dabbed me clean with a tissue before releasing me. I was left to fasten my nappy as he sat back in the chair with a happy sigh, then spoke.

'That was excellent. I must say, whoever's in charge of this operation comes up with some great games.'

'It's Jeff Bellbird,' I told him, 'and I'm only surprised he's not here to enjoy them himself.'

'Thank him for me when you see him then,' he replied. 'Do you mind if I come and watch you get your injection?'

'You might as well,' I answered, although my stomach had begun to flutter again on being reminded about Mr Masham and his needle. 'It's not as if I've got any modesty left, is it?'

He simply laughed and kissed me as I got up. Again there was nobody in the corridor, but I could hear voices from the next room, Sabina's, then a slap and a squeak from Poppy. They weren't the only ones in there either. Mistress Kimiko and all the other guests were packed into the small room, even Mr Greene. I managed a smile, trying not to feel embarrassed and telling myself that a little jab with a needle was nothing after what had just been done to me.

That didn't stop my flesh crawling as I saw Mr Masham. He was standing by the window, in his lab coat like the others, and with a syringe already in his hand, pointed vertically upwards as he expressed a spurt of fluid from the long, vicious-looking needle at the tip.

'Ah, my final patient,' he said, nodding at me.

'Um . . . hang on a second,' I protested. 'What is it in the syringe?'

'Isotonic saline,' he assured, 'nothing to worry about. Now come along, let's not have any fuss. If you could put her in the straps, please, nurse.'

'Straps?' I queried, but Sabina was already coming towards me, and Mistress Kimiko too.

I'd begun to shake as they took hold of me, my fear impossible to hold down despite telling myself it would only be a moment of pain. Not that I normally made a fuss about injections anyway, or not too much, but this was different. I was already having to force myself not to start babbling as Sabina and Mistress Kimiko led me to the chair and forced me into a kneeling position across the seat. They had leather straps, which were folded around my back and thighs, securing me to the chair with my nappy-clad bottom stuck out towards the door. My arms were pulled up into the small of my back and strapped together and I was well and truly helpless, shaking and on the edge of panic as Mr Masham came towards me.

'Take her nappy off, and give her a swab,' he instructed.

Sabina responded, quickly pulling my nappy tabs loose to expose my bottom one more time, then applying a ball of cotton wool to the top of a half-bottle of over-proof vodka, which she used to swab down a spot at the very crest of my right bottom cheek. Mr Masham was now behind me, with both my cunt and anus on show to him and fully vulnerable, only it wasn't his cock I was scared of, but the syringe in his hand.

'Just a little prick,' he chuckled. 'Then a big one.'

I barely heard, my eyes shut tight and my whole body shaking hard as he took a big pinch of my bottom flesh, gave my cheek a little wobble, then plunged the needle home. He laughed as he did it, a sound of such vindictive cruelty I just burst into tears, all the pent-up emotions of the morning coming out in one great gush. I felt the fluid begin to go into my bottom flesh as Mr Masham depressed the plunger, sobbing as I took it and finishing with a little choking gasp as he pulled the needle from my flesh. Poppy ruffled my hair and I managed to look up through hazy eyes as Sabina swabbed the puncture mark in my bottom. It was over, except perhaps for attending to Mr Masham's cock, something I was too far gone to refuse. Sure enough.

'Good girl, Gabrielle,' Sabina chuckled, 'that wasn't so bad, was it? Nearly done, but it's only fair you satisfy Mr Masham, isn't it?'

'OK,' I managed, 'he can have me. Why not, when everybody else has?'

'Not quite everybody,' she pointed out. 'OK, she's all yours, Derreck, but up her bum, OK?'

'Gladly,' he chuckled, and he began to fondle me behind.

'Hold on,' I managed, 'not up my bottom again . . . please, Sabina?'

'Oh yes, Gabrielle,' she answered, 'up your bum, right up your bum. I love watching you while you're buggered, you know that.'

'Yes, but I've just been buggered, and given an enema. I'm sore!'

'Not as sore as you're going to be,' she laughed. 'Come on, Derreck, pop it in.'

'Sabina!' I protested as she began to rub his half-stiff cock against my bottom cheeks.

'Do shut up, Gabrielle,' she chided. 'Nappies suit you, you know. I've never met such a baby! Anyone would think you'd never had a cock up your bum before, the fuss you make.'

'You try it some time!'

'I'm not into it,' she answered casually, 'and don't be insolent.'

She slapped my cheeks, and again, still rubbing Mr Masham's cock against my bottom and between my cheeks as she spanked me. Nobody else said a word, but just watched as I was prepared for my buggering, although Sophie had Mr Spottiswood's cock in her hand and was stroking it gently.

'Are you going to be good, or do I have to give you a few strokes of the tawse?' Sabina demanded.

'I . . . I'll be good,' I sighed, and I'd given in, hanging my head as Mr Masham's cock grew between my bum cheeks.

She was rubbing his helmet on my anus, and he'd began to push, opening me together. I made myself relax and he began to force himself up, squeezing his cock into my rectum an inch at a time until at last the full bulk was inside me, stretching my aching ring wide and filling my whole body with that dirty, bloated feeling which comes no other way. I was gasping as he began to bugger me, and as his hand reached under my belly I knew I was lost. He was going to bring me off in front of all of them, to add that final, filthy touch to my disgrace by making me come with his cock up my bottom, both to shame me and to enjoy the feel of my anus in spasm on his shaft.

As he buggered me he was laughing, and still groping me too, slapping my bottom and fondling my breasts, spreading my cheeks to watch my anus pulling in and out on his cock and calling me a bitch and slut and a whore. I didn't even see him pick up the syringe again, but I felt it as he jabbed the needle deep into my bottom flesh. As I screamed his laughter grew truly deranged, but I was too far gone to mind, my head full of dirty thoughts as I was buggered, of how I'd been made to drink my own piss, how I'd been given an enema and made to squirt it out of my bumhole with people watching, of how I'd had my cunt stretched and fucked, my anus probed, invaded, exposed, spunked in, and finally my bottom punctured as I was buggered.

He still had the needle in me, and nobody tried to stop him, each and every one of them enjoying the show. I was going to come anyway, screaming out my passion as his fingers worked on my sex, and as he began to push more firmly into me his balls had began to touch me too. That was too much, the final filthy detail that pushed me over the edge, to have his heavy, bulging scrotum pressing to my cunt as he masturbated me, to my empty cunt, empty because the cock that should have been up it was in my bottom hole instead.

202

My screams got louder, I was kicking in my straps and writing on his cock, my anus now in full, powerful contraction on his shaft as my orgasm tore through me. He pulled the needle free, only to plunge it deep in my flesh once more. As I screamed to the sudden pain my climax hit a new high, just as I heard him grunt, felt him jam deep, and I knew I'd given myself the final, delicious indignity and milked his cock up my own rectum with my contractions.

The medical left me completely exhausted and extremely sore. I left the others to it and retired to take a long, hot bath, followed by applying about half the tube of soothing cream to my poor aching bottom, especially the hole. Despite the state I was in my head was still full of dirty thoughts, which simply wouldn't go away, and it took a conscious effort not to masturbate again once I was alone in my bed. I needed something though, just to cope with my raging feelings, and slipped into a new nappy, which I was fastening just as Mr Greene came into the room with my lunch.

He was angling to be tossed off, but I'd had enough of men and shooed him out. I felt an inevitable touch of guilt, but told myself that as Sabina seemed to be enjoying exerting her sexual control over the men so much she could do it instead. Her behaviour was actually a bit of a sore point, because however much I'd enjoyed it at the end, she had been completely merciless with me, amusing herself with my body just as much as any of the men.

She had always liked to exert her dominance and actively enjoyed being cruel to me, which I'd always found well worthwhile in return for her services as my nurse, often involving things that it was a lot to ask of anybody. Unfortunately she had grown rapidly worse since arriving at the Institute, while she'd only really attended to me when she felt I needed to be punished or for her own sexual satisfaction.

I put the thought aside as I ate my lunch, reasoning that there was very little to be done about it and that no doubt our relationship would return to normal once we were back in London. Thinking of that made me remember that we only had one more day in Wales, and it was that which made me get out of bed when I'd finished instead of going to sleep with my thumb in my mouth, which was what I felt like.

Everybody else was still in the dining room, and to judge by Mistress Kimiko's shrill screeching and the smack of leather on flesh one of the girls was being given the tawse. I wasn't really in the mood for company, let alone finding myself on the receiving end of a punishment, while I was very sure indeed that I wouldn't be allowed to escape the Institute without at least one proper beating. The atmosphere had got to me so heavily that I felt it would be right, perhaps that I even needed it as the climax of my stay, but now was not the time.

I wandered out into the woods instead, allowing the turmoil of my feelings slowly to settle down. What remained was a strong but gentle need to indulge my own fantasy for being in nappies rather than the one Jeff had worked out for me. After all, I'd been taking my nappy on and off continuously, but nothing I'd done had really focused on the fact that I was in it, or the implications of that. Unfortunately the morning had left me drained, both mentally and physically, so what I really wanted was impossible. I contented myself with thinking about how I could do it the next morning, perhaps before anyone else was up, because there are some things simply too intimate to be done in front of men, or at least the men at the Institute.

The day was less hot than before, with cloud blowing in from the west to leave the space under the pines just a little too cool. I walked out to the edge of the wood and found myself a place where I could sit in the broken sunlight and just think without any risk of being disturbed. With no watch on and half asleep anyway, I'd soon lost track of time, and turned back for the house only when the sun had gone in behind the shoulder of the hill.

I was back in the mood I'd been in that morning as I walked, enjoying being in nothing but my nappy and generally at peace with the world. Still not really in the mood for company, I went in through the service yard and upstairs, hoping that Poppy might be in our dormitory so that we could have a private cuddle without any men to interfere. She wasn't, but I could hear voices from outside and went to peer from the window. Stephen, Tasanee and Mistress Kimiko were talking together, while Sabina was amusing herself with the others. She had Poppy and Sophie kneeling on the grass, both now stark naked, and was explaining the rules of a game to the men.

'. . . so if you can keep it in the air for ten seconds you get a blow-job, thirty seconds and you get to fuck one of them, a minute and you can do whatever you like. OK?'

Mr Greene made some objection I didn't catch. The other four nodded eagerly. Sabina was holding a big, multicoloured beach ball, which she threw to Mr Masham, then snapped her fingers, pointing at the ground as she addressed Mr Greene.

'OK, you grovelling little worm, if you don't want to play you can be my seat. Get down on all fours.'

He obeyed instantly, dropping to the grass so that she could sit on his back. As she lowered her bottom on to him his expression was ecstatic, but she took not the slightest notice, instead consulting her watch as Mr Masham lifted the beach ball and poised it on his nose as if he were a performing seal.

'Ready,' Sabina said, 'steady . . . wait for it. Go!'

Mr Masham let go of the ball, struggling to balance it on his nose, and on his face as it promptly rolled off. I couldn't help but laugh at the sight, and feel amusement for the way Sabina could make them perform ridiculous tricks with the promise of sexual favours from the three of us. Not that I was going to join them and end up in another round of cock-sucking and other rude behaviour, especially when with my luck I'd probably end up being buggered by Mr Petherick.

That wasn't going to stop me enjoying the show, and after servicing five men that morning I didn't even feel bad about leaving Sophie and Poppy on their own. It was exciting, too, to see what they'd have to do, and when Mr Masham dropped the ball after just under half-a-minute there was a little lump in my throat.

'Congratulations, you get a bj,' Sabina laughed. 'No, not yet, because the winner gets first choice of the girls. Where the fuck is Gabby, by the way?'

I moved back a little from the window, watching around the side of a curtain as Mr Masham tossed the ball to Mr Petherick. He proved remarkably good at it, his broad, fat face providing an ideal platform for the ball, so that once he'd got it resting over one eye it was obvious he'd be able to keep it up for as long as he pleased. When Sabina called the minute I saw Sophie and Poppy exchange a wry glance and I found myself more grateful still that for once I was going to get away with it.

Mr Noyles took the ball and made a complete mess of it, performing a bizarre, capering jig as he attempted to use his long beaky nose to prevent it rolling off his face. He failed almost immediately, but Sabina called out eleven seconds anyway, which I was sure was a cheat. Mr Spottiswood then took the ball, and he too proved clumsy, but did at least manage a real ten seconds. Sabina was slapping her thighs with laughter as she watched his antics, and had to pause to get her breath back before she could deliver the final verdict.

'Very good, boys! Alan is the winner then, and gets first choice of the sluts. Who's it to be?'

Mr Petherick was beaming as he waddled to where Sophie and Poppy were kneeling, and took one of his chins between forefinger and thumb as he considered them. Both had hung their heads, and I could well imagine they'd each be hoping the other would get chosen so that she could play with somebody at least marginally more attractive. At last Mr Petherick spoke up.

'I'll have Poppy,' he said, 'and she can bring me off between those lovely fat tits.'

'You heard the man,' Sabina stated, and clicked her fingers at Poppy.

Poppy rose, pouting a little, and allowed Mr Petherick to lead her to where a low wall marked the far edge of the lawn. He had to lean back to get his cock and balls out properly because of his overhanging belly, and even then Poppy couldn't get them between her breasts. Sabina wasn't helping either, laughing at their attempts, until at last Mr Petherick spoke up.

'You're going to have to suck me hard first, Poppy.'

'Do it,' Sabina ordered before Poppy even had a chance to answer.

After an instant of hesitation Poppy went down, licking and sucking at Mr Petherick's balls as well as his cock as Sabina guided her by the hair. The others had gathered around to watch too, but there was none of the reticence the men had shown at the beginning of our stay. Mr Petherick was soon hard, his erection easily long enough for Poppy to fold her breasts around despite the swell of his belly.

Poppy began to jiggle her breasts against his cock, bouncing them in her hands and slapping them together, so that her nipples were rubbing on his belly as well as his cock in her cleavage. When he began to get urgent she changed her technique, making a cock-slide for him as he pumped up and down with his helmet emerging from between the fat pink pillows of her breasts with every pump. After that it didn't take long, his cock quickly erupting to splatter her breasts and face with droplets of come, which Sabina made her lick up before speaking to Mr Spottiswood.

'You're next, Ken. Do you want Sophie, or perhaps Stephen will lend you Tasanee?'

'Sophie will do nicely,' Mr Spottiswood answered, reaching out to take her hand.

As Mr Spottiswood sat down Sabina had already turned to Stephen.

'Tasanee can do Derreck then, if that's OK?'

'Be my guest,' Stephen responded, and sent Tasanee on her way with a pat to her rump.

Sophie already had Mr Spottiswood's cock in her mouth, and Tasanee soon joined her, leaving Mr Noyles, who Sabina promptly turned to.

'How about you then, Clive? Gabby's gone into hiding by the look of it, but how about Kimi here? I bet you'd love to see that pretty painted mouth with your prick stuck in it?'

'Yes, of course . . .,' Mr Noyles began, only to be interrupted by a screech from Mistress Kimiko.

'I am a dominant! I do not do this disgusting act, so if you want Mr Noyles sucked off, Sabina, you do it yourself.'

Sabina just laughed.

'Oh come on, Kimi, you've got to get down and dirty some time.'

'You suck his filthy penis. I am dominant,' Mistress Kimiko insisted. 'You love to wank on men's cocks, like this morning, and I am sure you like to suck them too.'

Sabina shrugged and was about to turn back to Mr Noyles, but seemed to think better of it.

'So what?' she demanded, speaking to Mistress Kimiko. 'Do you think you're better than me?'

'Answer this question yourself,' Mistress Kimiko stated.

'I'm asking you,' Sabina repeated. 'Do you think you're better than me?'

The East End was beginning to come out in Sabina's voice. If I'd been Mistress Kimiko I'd have backed down very quickly indeed. Either she didn't realise, or she was too confident in her own dominance, but she answered back, and there was contempt in her words as she spoke.

'Who took down her panties for a tawse stroke, yes? Not me, Sabina, but you. Underneath, you are a slut, that is all. I am a dominant, a true dominant.'

'And that makes you better than me, does it?' Sabina demanded for the third time.

The others had stopped, Sophie frozen with her open mouth an inch away from Mr Spottiswood's cock, a string of saliva still connecting her lip with his helmet. Stephen made to say something, but before he could speak Mistress Kimiko had turned on her

209

heel, her chin raised in contempt as she started for the house. For a moment Sabina just stared, then followed, grabbing Mistress Kimiko by the shoulder and spinning her around.

'I asked you a question!' she snarled.

'Get your hand off me!' Mistress Kimiko snapped. 'You know the answer, I think . . . slut.'

'Fuck you, you little bitch!' Sabina spat, and her hand had closed on Mistress Kimiko's wrist.

Mistress Kimiko tried to jerk away, but Sabina held on easily. My hand had gone to my mouth as Sabina ducked down, butting her shoulder into Kimiko's midriff and lifting. As Mistress Kimiko was hauled into the air and across Sabina's shoulder she went wild, screaming in fury and kicking her legs in every direction. Sabina barely seemed to notice, her face set in a determined scowl as she stamped across the lawn to where Mr Spottiswood still sat with his cock out, but with the astonishment on his face giving away to amusement.

'Put me down!' Mistress Kimiko screeched, and gave a yelp of surprise as Sabina did exactly that, dumping her burden on the lawn from the full height of her shoulder.

Sabina sat down on the wall, and before Mistress Kimiko could get her breath back she'd been rolled over, face down on the lawn. Sabina's face was a sneer as she reached down to twist one hand into her victim's hair.

'What are you doing?' Kimiko screeched. 'What are you doing? Get off me, you fat bitch!'

'What am I doing?' Sabina sneered, as her hand locked into the waistband of Kimiko's leather shorts. 'Can't you guess? I'm going to spank you, you little bitch, and just for calling me that, it's going to be bare.'

Sabina simply picked Kimiko up bodily.

'No!' Kimiko screamed, using every breath in her lungs as she was laid into spanking position across Sabina's lap. 'No! You can not! You can not! You can not!'

'Oh yeah? Watch me,' Sabina answered, and began to tug down Mistress Kimiko's shorts.

Kimiko went berserk, screaming what I suppose were threats and insults in Japanese, thrashing wildly with all four limbs, attempting to kick and scratch. Sabina ignored it, cool and determined. She realised the shorts weren't going to come down with the button done up, but that didn't stop her. Changing her grip, she tucked her arm around the struggling girl's stomach and quickly flipped the button open. Kimiko began to babble in Japanese as she felt her shorts come loose and her desperate thrashing grew wilder still, but it made no difference.

She was bared, her shorts hauled off the tiny, squirming buttocks, easily until a little crease had come on show, and then with a series of hard jerks as she snatched back for her waistband. A high, word-less scream broke from her lips as her bottom came fully bare, round and pale in the sunlight, and it had been done. She didn't give in though, still fighting and still trying to pull her shorts back up as Sabina adjusted her position, bringing a knee up to force Kimiko's bottom cheeks into greater prominence and show off the little bare cunt between.

'Gather rounds, boys!' Sabina laughed, and placed her hand on Kimiko's naked bottom, making the little cheeks wobble. 'Here goes, high and mighty Mistress bitch-slut Kimiko, you're going to get a spanking, a bare bottom, public spanking, which is just what you need!'

Every one of Sabina's words was full of relish and of mocking laughter as she gave the little round cheeks another playful wobble. Kimiko emitted another furious scream, spat out a sentence in Japanese and then found her English again.

'Stop! This will stop now! Put me down, fat bitch! Stop, or I'll . . .'

'Or you'll what?' Sabina sneered.

'I will tell the Master!' Mistress Kimiko screamed. 'He will beat you! He will beat you good!'

'Yeah, right,' Sabina answered. 'Bring him on, and I'll whip his arse for him too.'

With that she applied the first smack, and Mistress Kimiko was being spanked. It wasn't hard, just a pat really, but it didn't have to hurt, it just had to be done. Mistress Kimiko screamed again, expressing so much raw fury it made me wince. Sabina just laughed, tightened her grip and began to beat out a steady rhythm on Kimiko's writhing buttocks. The more Kimiko screamed and swore the more Sabina laughed, and the harder Sabina spanked. The little round cheeks began to go red, and to part, showing off pouted, hairless cunt lips and a pale brown anus.

'There we are boys!' Sabina crowed, spanking harder still. 'The great Mistress Kimiko's bare arsehole, on show today only, so get a good long look while you can!'

The men didn't need telling. They had already clustered round. Stephen looked a little doubtful, and Mr Greene was staring in shock, but the others were drinking it up, their faces alight with cruelty and amusement as they watched the spanking, and not one of them with so much as a shred of sympathy. Poppy and Sophie were no better, watching in smug satisfaction as the woman who'd punished them so frequently was given a dose of her own medicine, and even Tasanee had a quiet smile on her delicate face.

I'd have been no better, and I didn't call out despite being shocked by Sabina's behaviour, which was completely unacceptable. Like the others I watched, feeling increasingly guilty but with my eyes firmly fixed to the spanked girl's jiggling bottom cheeks and the ruder details between. I told myself that if Sabina tried to make Kimiko do anything with a man I would go down and stop it, but that was all.

It wasn't necessary. The instant the spanking was over Kimiko jumped up and ran for the house, not even pausing to pull her shorts up properly, but clutching them in one hand so that her audience were treated to a last show of wobbling red bottom cheeks as she fled. She'd never stopped fighting, but her face was streaked with tears, and I decided I should go and talk to her.

I knew how it would be, because I'd been in the same state myself. At first she'd be bawling her eyes out, when she really needed to be left alone, but as she began to calm down she would probably want somebody to talk to. I would wait.

Outside, Sabina was talking earnestly to Stephen while the others laughed and joked about the spanking. Sophie was already stroking Mr Spottiswood's cock and clearly turned on. So was I, despite my bad feelings, the urge to touch myself warring with my guilt for wanting to come over the memory of Mistress Kimiko being spanked so firmly across Sabina's knee.

After a while Sabina went inside. I sat down on my bed, telling myself I wasn't going to masturbate and would wait ten minutes to allow Kimiko to get over her tantrum before I went to speak to her. I took off my nappy, which didn't seem quite the thing to be wearing if I was going to have a serious conversation with Kimiko, and put on a dress instead.

I spent the ten minutes alternately checking the time and watching Sophie suck Mr Spottiswood's cock, then made for Kimiko's room. The door was slightly open, but I hesitated outside, listening. I could near faint, liquid noises and the occasional low moan, but it wasn't right for crying. Puzzled, I pushed the door open, to find Kimiko on her bed as I had expected, and rubbing her smacked bottom, also as I had expected. What I hadn't expected was that she would be twisted around with her face buried between Sabina's thighs, licking cunt.

Seven

The following day everything had changed. I had to shelve my plans for sneaking off into the woods for a little nappy play when Mr Greene came in about an hour before I would have expected him to tell us that we were to get dressed and assemble in the living room. He'd brought the coffee up, but I was still half asleep as I went to shower, with the memories of the evening before only slowly filtering into my head.

After catching Kimiko licking Sabina I'd backed away quietly, leaving them to what was obviously a very private moment. Kimiko had still been crying, but there had been no doubting the enthusiasm with which she'd been applying her tongue to Sabina's sex. I was surprised, but not completely astonished, because I'd seen similar phenomena before among clients. Other the years I could recall five of them who'd been outwardly homophobic in an attempt to suppress their desire for their own sex, four males and one female, but had eventually come to accept it. On only two occasions had their conversion been sudden, but it was always emotionally powerful, especially their first homosexual experience.

Evidently Kimiko's repeated assertion of the purity of her dominance had concealed a powerful desire to submit, and as is so often the case, once the change was made she embraced it wholeheartedly. She'd come downstairs naked and on a collar and lead borrowed from Stephen and spent the rest of the evening at Sabina's feet. The men had been delighted, all except Mr Greene, who seemed to be close to tears. Mr Masham and Mr Noyles had spent the evening trying to cajole Sabina into giving them Kimiko for their amusement. They'd failed.

We girls had been luckier. Sabina had taken Kimiko to bed and invited us to watch, with her door locked but making very sure the men knew what was going on. Kimiko had been made to show us every detail of her body, spanked and finally put on her knees to kiss Sabina's bottom. Now with Kimiko thoroughly enslaved, Sabina had wanted body worship from all four of us, and she'd got it, for two solid hours. It had been fun, but focused solely on her, so once the three of us had finally been dismissed to leave her with her new plaything we'd had a much better time in our dormitory, playing cards for gentle spankings and licks before tumbling into bed together.

I'd also remembered that it was supposed to be the Master's day, but I had no idea what that was supposed to involve, beyond Jeff turning up and being absolutely filthy with us. To judge by the clothes Mr Greene had brought up when I came back into the dormitory Jeff had developed some sort of military fetish. Each of us had a green army jacket, tight at the waist and flared over the hips, and a smart little hat in the same material with a cockade of white feathers at one side. That was it, no knickers or even socks, so we were presumably supposed to go bare from the waist down. I didn't mind that, but I was still hoping to get some time to myself later, so I put on a fresh nappy, sure that it would be seen as naughty rather than an attempt to cover up. Poppy put on her school knickers, but Sophie just went bare.

Most of the others were already downstairs, drinking coffee and talking among themselves, mostly speculation as to what was going on. I took the only remaining armchair and Poppy cuddled up on my lap, her bare bottom and the rear view of her cunt clearly visible to the men. Sophie sat down on the arm with her arm around my shoulders. Sabina came in last, also in a tailored army jacket, but with a skirt to match and captain's pips on her shoulders. Kimiko was on her lead, and nude.

'Settle down chaps,' Sabina joked, 'orders for the day and all that. Kimi, run along and make another pot of coffee. Chop chop.'

Kimiko was sent towards the kitchen with a smack to her bottom. Everybody else went quiet, and I saw that Sabina had the yellow clipboard.

'Today was to have been the Master's day,' she announced, 'but there has been a change of plan. Today is my day. I'm an unattached girl, aren't I?'

She glanced around as if seeking a challenge but nobody spoke up and she continued.

'Just to be sure you all back me on this, here is what was going to happen if I hadn't dealt with Kimi's bottom yesterday afternoon. It doesn't affect you men very much, as you'd simply have been left to your own devices, but each of the girls was to be taken to the stable block and given what was called the Room 101 treatment, which basically means a heavy session of whatever you like the least. Poppy was going to have her head shaved and spunked on. I'm not going to tell you what he was going to do to Sophie in case it gives any of you ideas, and I'm looking at you, Derreck Masham. And Gabrielle, you were to be tied by your wrists and hung from a hook

217

in the ceiling with your feet on two blocks of wood for forty-eight strokes of the birch. Oh, and they were going to gag you to keep you shut up while you were whipped.'

I felt myself go cold inside at the thought, mainly for the pain, far, far more pain than I could take, let alone find erotic, but also because I obviously wasn't supposed to get any say in the matter. Something wasn't quite right though, because while Jeff was an out-and-out pervert he was also my friend and I couldn't see him doing anything so nasty to me, or Poppy and Sophie. I found myself wondering if he really was the Master, or if I'd been completely wrong.

'What a bastard!' Poppy whispered.

'What happens when this Master bloke turns up?' Mr Masham asked Sabina.

'The Master,' Sabina answered, 'is a man called Jeff Bellbird, and I suggest we give him a dose of his own medicine. When he arrives, you men jump him, we tie him up, and I personally will give him the spanking of a lifetime. He can watch too, while we all have fun in the evening.'

'What's he like, this Jeff?' Mr Masham queried.

'A big fat bastard,' she told him, 'a right lard tub.'

'So what's in it for us if we help you?' Mr Noyles demanded.

'What's in it for you is that you get to play with these sluts,' she answered, waving a hand in the general direction of my chair, where Poppy still had her bare bottom stuck well out, 'and believe me, they're going to be grateful.'

'That's true,' Poppy admitted.

I had to agree. Any man who saved me from a severe birching deserved anything he asked in return.

'OK?' Sabina asked, and there were no objections. 'Good. Once we've dealt with the Master, we have

Sabina day, and this is how it works. The five girls are my personal property. You can look all you like, but nobody is allowed to touch under penalty of the cane, two dozen strokes, delivered hard, and I do mean hard. The only exception is for Stephen with Tasanee, and Stephen is allowed to pet the others but not fuck them or anything, except Kimi, who's mine. Then, if you've been very, very good to me all day, and generally behaved yourselves including doing all the meals and housework, then, in the evening I will allow you privileges with the girls. I might even lend a hand myself, if I'm feeling generous. Got that?'

There was a bit of muttering among the men, but they accepted it. Sabina seemed to assume that the rest of us would go along with it, and it was certainly better than being strung up for the birch. Kimiko came back with the coffee and Sabina went into a huddle with Stephen, Mr Masham and Mr Noyles, discussing how to trap Jeff. I wasn't entirely happy with the situation, and waited until they'd made their plans before catching up with her as she went out to the loo.

'Are you sure about this, Sabina?' I asked. 'Wouldn't it be better just to tell him we won't co-operate?'

'He was going to birch you, Gabby,' she pointed out.

'Well, yes, but I can't see Jeff doing that. Maybe to scare us, but he wouldn't go through with it. Are you sure this isn't just about wanting to get your revenge for the time he spanked you?'

'What if it is?' she demanded. 'And not just that, no. He's got it coming to him!'

'I reckon he deserves everything he gets,' Sophie put in as she joined us. 'What was he going to do to me?'

'It's pretty nasty,' Sabina responded.

'But what?' Sophie demanded. 'Come on, I've taken pretty well everything, so what's the big deal? I mean, he can't actually hurt me, can he, and I've always got my stop word.'

'OK, if you insist,' Sabina told her. 'He was going to tie you up in one of those old zinc tubs and pour out a box full of spiders on you. I'm not sure he believes in stop words.'

Sophie had gone white, and looked as if she was about to be sick. I put my arm around her shoulder to support her as Sabina gave a shrug.

'I said it was pretty nasty.'

'I can't see Jeff doing that,' Poppy protested. 'I didn't think he even knew Sophie's scared of spiders and bugs and stuff.'

'Somebody must have told him, I suppose,' Sabina answered, and disappeared into the loo.

'I'm really not sure about this,' I told Sophie.

'Oh come on, Gabs,' she urged. 'How many times has Jeff spanked you, and worse?'

'Quite often, but . . .'

'And it's not your thing, is it?'

'I don't mind spankings, not all that much, as long as it's not too hard . . .'

'Yeah, and he was going to string you up from a hook and birch you?'

'Do you really think he'd do that?'

She shrugged.

'Maybe, maybe not, but I don't see what the big deal is about tying him up and giving him a spanking, not after all the stuff he's done to us.'

'I still don't know . . .'

I broke off because Mr Masham and Mr Noyles had come out of the living room. Sophie tried to follow Sabina into the loo, only to discover that the door was locked. I made for the kitchen, as without Kimiko to organise things it didn't look as if there was going to be a proper breakfast. While I ate a riesling sorbet I mulled the situation over in my mind and quickly decided that the less I had to do with it the better. Sabina was showing off her dominance, as she quite often did, and especially in the presence of men. Her plan for the day didn't sound all that much fun either, while the entire holiday had been focused on punishment and sex, dirty sex admittedly but not really dirty enough for me. I wanted to play in my nappy.

The only problem was what they were planning for Jeff, and I really couldn't believe he would have broken our limits the way he'd said. He'd probably just done it to scare us and make it easier to take when he spanked us and buggered us, which was much more the sort of thing he was into. Also, he could look after himself. He was fat, but he was also heavily built, younger than them, and spent his time doing paintball and other outdoor sports.

If I hung around too long somebody was sure to catch me and I'd end up spending the day at Sabina's beck and call, so with only a slight twinge of conscience for Jeff I slipped out of the back and into the woods. Just knowing what I planned provided a deliciously naughty thrill, but I knew it was best not to rush it. Instead I would let things build slowly to a natural peak. Dinner the night before had been steaks with boiled potatoes and peas, after Poppy had been told very firmly what would happen if she made bangers and mash again, with a jam roly-poly to follow. I'd eaten plenty, and it was beginning to tell.

There was one part of the wood I'd yet to explore, the edge of which overlooked the road by which Jeff would arrive and where I remembered the map showing a small stream coming down from the hillside. It also had a stand of younger pines, which would be perfect to hide in if anybody came looking for me, so I set off in that direction. My ill feeling from the morning faded gradually as I walked, with the solitude having its natural effect.

I'd remembered the stream correctly, and while it formed the border of the wood and presumably the boundary for Wyddon Manor, it had cut deep into the ground, forming a series of pools and little waterfalls among rocks and little patches of soft grass, completely hidden from even a few yards away. It was perfect, and better still because I could sit at the top of the bank and see the road below me and for a long way up the valley, so that nobody could possibly come across me unexpectedly except through the forest, which was an acceptable risk.

In fact it was rather an exciting risk, because only the other guests could catch me; whoever it was would be sure to want to take advantage of me, and I would be in a very vulnerable situation indeed. As I chose a place to sit from which I could watch the road as I waited, but with only the upper, and decent, part of my body showing, I began to speculate on who would be best.

Poppy would be fun, because I could be completely uninhibited with her, but there was no denying that somebody less familiar would bring out stronger feelings. Sophie would also be good, at least if I was in a mood to share my experience, but after everything that had happened during the week I felt more inclined to be put upon. Sabina would enjoy herself with me, and undoubtedly add some element of punishment, perhaps being made to hold my nappy down while I was smacked, but she wouldn't use her hand so it was sure to be a painful experience.

Neither Tasanee or Kimiko was much use in the circumstances, except to add to my sense of shame, and for sheer embarrassment any one of the men would provide more than all the women together. Stephen would be bad enough, but he was too into control and dominance, while what I wanted was somebody dirty. Mr Greene was no use, and Mr Masham was too like Stephen in his tastes. Of the other three, Mr Spottiswood was quite dirty but really more into putting girls to his cock. Mr Noyles had really enjoyed himself with my bumhole and might want to go further, while Mr Petherick had given me my enema. One or other would be best, but it was hard to choose between them.

My bladder had begun to feel tight, and I wondered if it would be nicer to just let go and enjoy the freedom of peeing in my nappy, or to wait until I couldn't hold on any longer and get off on the feelings of helplessness and shame instead. I'd just decided to do it right away and spend some time walking with my wet nappy on when I saw a car slowing for the curve in the road. My arousal was getting so strong I was tempted to stand up and walk into the wood, so that the driver would see I was in a nappy under my uniform jacket, but he was past before I could pluck up the courage.

I told myself I'd do it for the next car, as long as it was driven by a single man, which set my tummy fluttering deliciously as I waited. The first was a people carrier and I let it go, the second a customised 4x4 full of rowdy young men, which I felt was tempting fate, but the third was ideal, a small, red hatchback with a single figure visible in the driver's seat, a single, bearded figure, and as it drew closer I recognised Jeff Bellbird. I stood up, waving frantically, and when he didn't slow down I flipped up the front of my jacket so that as much bright-white nappy material as possible was showing against the green and brown of the wood.

He slowed and stopped, pulling off at the side of the road. As he climbed out and over the wall with some difficulty he seemed bigger and more like a bear than ever, a very happy bear, because his face was split by a huge grin. I waved again, and only then realised that I was giving a nappy show to another car which had come the other way. As I ducked back down I was blushing and smiling, also wondering if Jeff would like to play with me.

'Hi Gabs,' he greeted me as he lumbered up, 'all on your own?'

'I just came out to play a little,' I told him. 'Not entirely though. I'd better warn you that they've got it in for you at the house.'

'Eh?'

'It's all rather complicated, but basically Sabina wants to punish you, and she's bribed some of the men to tie you up so she can give you a spanking. I don't think she ever really got over that time you did it to her.'

He laughed.

'Bring 'em on, we'll see who gets spanked!'

As he spoke he'd dropped into a peculiar pose, with his massive legs spread so that his belly hung between them, his arms also open wide and his fingers splayed as if about to grapple somebody. You could have fitted Mr Petherick inside him with no bits sticking out for a start, and there seemed to be an awful lot of muscle beneath his bulging fat. Suddenly I couldn't see the men at the house even daring to try, let alone restraining him successfully, while on a more personal level it was impossible not to feel a thrill for his sheer animal power. He was full of energy too, restless and speaking in short, clipped sentences.

'I'm in the company sumo team,' he explained, straightening up and giving me a brief, formal bow.

'So I see,' I answered. 'I don't think anyone's going to be spanking you in a hurry, not if you don't want them to.'

'She can do me if I can do her afterwards,' he said. 'I'd love to get that one squealing, she's far too up herself. Shall we go to the house then?'

'Maybe in a bit,' I answered, picking a celandine in what I hoped was a suitably coquettish manner. 'I thought, maybe, you'd like to play with me for a bit, just the two of us . . . I'd like to say thank you for your birthday present.'

'Oh yeah, you can do that all right,' he answered.

'OK,' I promised, 'but one question first. Were you really going to hang me up for a birching whether I wanted it or not?'

'Eh? I never said that.'

'It was on Mistress Kimiko's clipboard, Jeff.'

'Who's Mistress Kimiko?'

'The woman . . . you really don't know, do you? Was it you who set the Institute up?'

'No, not me,' he said, and if he was lying he was a very good actor. 'I met this bloke in Japan, virtually anyway, in a chat room. I was explaining how the pig-sticking game works. He was telling me how he'd set this Institute place up, but he didn't have enough girls. I said I'd get him some if he gave me a few free places.'

'Which you gave me as my birthday present?'

'Yeah,' he answered, completely casually. 'I should have been here too, but the mainframe went down at work, and . . .'

'So you don't know anything about what's been happening over the last few days?'

'A load of pervy stuff, I suppose. I put down all the stuff you're into, like going in nappies and how

225

Sophie likes to be a schoolgirl and all, and gave him all the advice he could need.'

'But you're not running it?'

'No.'

'Who is then?'

'Search me. He called himself Vertigo on the net, but he knew what he was talking about so I reckoned it would be safe.'

He was telling the truth, leaving me wondering who the real Master was and why he wanted to punish me so viciously, also relieved that it wasn't Jeff. I kissed him and sat down on a rock but was quickly interrupted.

'I've got something to show you. You'll love it!'

I'd been about to tell him what I wanted to do, and was left feeling slightly frustrated as he went down to his car and back, only to return with something that made my eyes pop. It was cane, quite thick and with one end bound in leather for a handle, also dark, with age and presumably the sweat of both users and victims.

'It's Japanese cane,' Jeff said enthusiastically, 'the genuine article. Bare your bum and I'll give you a few strokes.'

'I'm not sure I could take it, Jeff,' I said hastily. 'It looks really painful.'

'Come on, Gabs, just a couple of strokes,' he urged. 'I'll warm your bum for you first.'

'No thanks.'

'Aw come on. I'm dying to get to grips with that perfect little bum.'

'It's not that I don't want to play . . . in fact, I . . . I was about to wet my nappy,' I admitted, blushing despite myself.

'Cool. Suck me hard and I'll watch, then give you a couple for pissing yourself.'

'You can watch, of course, and I don't mind sucking,' I answered, 'but not the cane, please? It hurts so much.'

'I won't do it hard,' he promised, then stopped briefly. 'Look, think about it, yeah? For now get your mouth around my fuck stick.'

I nodded, sure that once his cock was in my mouth he'd soon forget about caning me.

'I like the little army jacket,' he said as I got down on my knees in front of him. 'Open it up, yeah? Get your tits out.'

I nodded, unfastening my jacket and opening the front to let him see my breasts as he pulled his cock and balls from his fly. He began to play with himself as I teased my breasts a little, each watching the other. Just him being there was making me feel released in a way I couldn't have done with any of the other men, so that I felt I could give free rein to the dirty thoughts building up in my head rather than simply act as a receptacle for somebody else's lust. Even the thought of the cane was adding a little thrill of fear, and I thought of how I'd have to be a good little cock-sucker to avoid it.

'Take your trousers and pants down,' I told him.

He responded eagerly, pushing everything down to his ankles and lying back, his massive thighs spread with his genitals hanging between them, his balls stirring within the bloated, gingery sack of his scrotum, his already swollen cock moving sluggishly. I crawled forward, drinking in his male scent for a moment before I began to nuzzle my face against the soft, fleshy mass in front of me, then to kiss, and to lick, before taking the bulk of his penis into my mouth and sucking.

'You're eager,' he sighed.

I nodded on my mouthful and began to move my head up and down, enjoying the feeling of having a man's penis growing in my mouth as I let my hands wander over my own body, touching my dangling breasts and the gentle swell of my belly, the edge of my jacket to feel the way it flared out around my hips, my nappy-clad bottom, my bare legs. When Jeff was close to full erection I took him in hand, transferring my mouth to his balls, ever dirtier as I kissed them, sucked them, and moved lower still, to the deep, musky crease between his vast buttocks.

'Ah, you gorgeous little slut,' he sighed, 'go on, do it, Gabby, lick my arse.'

He didn't need to tell me. Already my tongue was burrowing between the cheeks of his bottom, pushing in to find the little fleshy dimple of his anus and to lick it. A shudder ran through me as I began to tongue his bottom hole, something not so far from orgasm, and for the sheer filthiness of what I was doing. He groaned in pleasure and spread his thighs wider still, inviting me to get my tongue in even deeper. I pushed it up, tasting him, kissing his anal star, then lapping at it, my hand now on the front of my nappy, massaging my cunt through the thick, puffy material.

'Stop,' he grunted, 'if you don't get your tongue out of my arsehole I'm just going to spunk on your head.'

It would have been good, to feel his come splash into my hair and over my face while I licked his anus, but my nappy was still clean and I was sure it would be my last chance to soil it, at least in Wales. My hand was still between my thighs as I pulled back, gasping a little as our eyes met.

'God, but you're dirty, Gabrielle,' he sighed. 'Go on then, piss yourself and I'll fuck you while you've still got your nappy on.'

As I'd suspected, he'd forgotten all about my beating. I nodded in response and moved back a little, rolling over on to all fours to lift my bottom for him, and looking back. He began to nurse his erection as he watched me, and I thought of where his cock would be going once I was wet, up me, with my nappy pulled aside to show off my ready cunt. With that I let go, sighing as my pee squirted out, gushing into my nappy with a hissing, bubbling sound. I put my hand between my thighs, to feel the material swell and bulge, growing quickly heavier as my piddle filled it, until the whole area beneath my cunt and my cheeks felt fat and squashy.

'I've done it,' I told him. 'I've wet my nappy. Look at me.'

'Undo the tabs,' he replied, 'show me properly.'

I obeyed without hesitation, trembling hard as I unfastened one nappy tab and then the other, to peel open the back and show off the squashy, yellow material where the inside had soaked up my pee, my bare bottom with the skin wet and glistening, and as I stuck my bum out a little more, the rear lips of my wet, ready cunt and my dimpled anus.

'Gorgeous,' he breathed, coming forward with his cock still in his hand, 'that is so dirty. Let me touch.'

His hand had found my bottom even as I nodded my permission, to stroke my pee-soaked cheeks, tickle between them, cup my cunt and slip a thumb up into my hole, tickle my anus for a second time, and then begin to spank.

'Naughty, naughty, Gabrielle,' he chided. 'Imagine it, a big girl like you wetting your nappy, you definitely deserve to be spanked.'

His slaps were hard enough to sting on my piss-wet skin, but I wouldn't have stopped him for the world. It felt too good, to have my bottom smacked for wetting my nappy, and with the back down so I was his completely, to look at, to touch, and if he felt I needed punishment, to spank. His cock was bumping my thigh as he masturbated, bringing me a yet nicer image, of being spanked and then having the man who'd done it come all over my hot red bottom.

'So naughty,' he sighed, spanking harder, 'so very naughty. Now let's get this bum nice and warm . . .'

'Oh, yes, please, very warm. You can spank harder, if you like . . . Spunk over my bottom, if you like . . .'

'Uh, uh, not yet. I want to cane you.'

'No, Jeff . . .'

'Sh, Gabrielle. You've been bad, and you're going to be caned.'

'No, Jeff, please!' I begged, but he had put one massive hand around my waist, holding me firmly in place as he reached for the wicked Japanese cane.

'No, Jeff, please,' I repeated, starting to panic for all my arousal. 'Not the cane . . . not the cane!'

I was sobbing, but he held me tight, putting the cane down in the crook of my knees as he began to spank me again, harder now.

'Please, Jeff!' I whined, starting to wriggle and kick. 'I've managed to avoid this all week, and . . .'

'I know,' he said happily. 'I put that in your instructions. Maybe I should have had "Reserved for Jeff" stamped on your bum, yeah?'

'That was really sweet of you,' I said, my voice quick and urgent with my rising panic, 'but really, you don't need to . . .'

'Uh, uh,' he interrupted. 'I think I do, and I think you know it, deep down.'

'No, Jeff . . .,' I babbled, but it was a lie.

I just needed to be properly taken in hand, exactly the way he was doing, my fear pushed aside by a strong, no-nonsense man and my bottom properly taken care of. Still I wriggled in his grip, unable to accept my own needs without at least a token fight, and as he tightened his hold on me and spoke again it was as if he could read my mind.

'Wriggle all you like. Cry if you want to, OK?'

My answer was a squeak as he planted another hard smack on my bottom, this time full across the seat. It stung crazily, bringing my fear higher still, but I was too far gone to try to stop him, just whimpering pathetically as he picked the cane up.

'Just six,' he said, and he brought it down across my bottom.

I cried out, in pain and despair and frustration, but mainly for my utter helplessness, both physical and mental. He had me completely, beating my pissy wet bottom with my cunt and bumhole on show to him, and for all he'd done to me I knew I'd be accepting his cock in one or the other just as soon as I'd been well thrashed. With that thought I burst into tears, but Jeff knew me too well to be put off by my crying, and simply brought the second cane stroke in.

'I love it when you cry,' he sighed. 'Come on, let go, show your emotion.'

As he spoke he gave me the third stroke, and the instant my cry of pain had died in my throat I went to pieces completely, howling my head off and beating my fists on the rock, kicking my legs and blubbering so hard I was blind with tears. The snot was bubbling from my nose and the spittle running down my chin, and as the fourth cane stroke bit down across my bottom fresh piddle squirted from my open cunt and into my nappy. The fifth followed, and the sixth, immediately, another and another, and I'd gone wilder still, now in a truly pathetic, uncontrolled spanking tantrum, all four of my limbs waving in every direction as he beat me.

'You said six!' finally managing to get my voice

231

back through the snot and tears and the huge lump in my throat.

The beating stopped.

'Oh yes, so I did,' he chuckled, and let go of me.

I stayed as I was, gasping for breath with my head hung down, my mouth slack, unable to see for my tears. My bottom was burning, and so was my head, full of awful consternation of what he'd done to me, self-pity too, but I wasn't moving from my kneeling position until the rock-hard cock now prodding against my thigh as Jeff began to masturbate once more had been pushed deep in up my body.

That was what I expected, but to my surprise he fastened my nappy again, then spoke.

'Now the rest, if you can. I want to see your nappy bulge.'

My response was a fresh sob, even though it was exactly what I'd been planning for myself. I was trembling badly as I tried to relax, not an easy thing to do when I'd just been thrashed and was being watched even when it was Jeff. His eyes were fixed to my nappy seat, already fat and heavy with my piddle, and shortly about to be worse, while his cock already looked fit to burst.

'Go on, Gabby,' he urged, 'do it, fill your nappy for me. I really want to see you do it.'

I nodded weakly, and gave a low whimper as I began to push. My rectum was full, and I knew I could do it, with just a little effort, and as I squeezed I felt my load shift inside me. Still it wouldn't come, and I had to remind myself that it didn't matter how dirty I was in front of Jeff, that he could cope, that he loved to watch me pee, to bugger me and stick his cock in and out of my open, sloppy hole. Again I squeezed, and now it was easier, the mass in my rectum pressing against my anal ring.

232

'It's coming,' I sighed as my bottom hole started to open, and I was doing it, about to soil my nappy deliberately as a man masturbated over the sight.

'Good girl,' Jeff gasped as I felt the first, fat piece squeezed out between my bottom cheeks.

The mess touched my nappy and I was dirty, the first piece sticking between my cheeks as my anus closed. Now it was too late, I'd messed myself and there was no going back. Again I pushed, squeezing more out, a second heavy lump, a third, and it had begun to come easily. I was sobbing as I did it, and shaking my head for the raw power of my emotions, but I could no longer have stopped myself if I'd wanted to. My nappy had begun to fill and to push out behind, bulging to my growing load, ever heavier. It was now completely obvious what I'd done, and Jeff was wanking furiously with his eyes fixed to the tell-tale lump in my nappy seat.

I closed my eyes in bliss and let my mouth come wide as I pushed out yet more. My full load was now in my nappy, a warm, squashy mass between my bottom cheeks and over my cunt, heavy and moist, a sensation impossibly rude and impossibly desirable, but as I was about to reach back to masturbate as I showed off to him, Jeff spoke.

'I'm going to fuck you, Gabby, just the way you are.'

I didn't need telling, but quickly scrambled over to a bit of soft grass between the rock. He was coming after me even as I got into a kneeling position with the fat, heavy swell of my nappy seat stuck up for him beneath the hem of my jacket. I looked back, catching a last sight of the straining erection I was about to have plunged up me before he was behind me. He began to prod his cock at my bulge, squashing it against my bottom, before suddenly jerking my nappy seat aside. I was whimpering as he held me like that, his cock in his hand, his eyes feasting on my bare, slippery cunt and the wet brown star of my anus.

'Do it,' I begged. 'Put it in me, Jeff, up my bottom if you want, but do it . . .'

My words broke to a grunt as his helmet found my cunt, filling me as he pushed up, his fat belly squashing out the contents of my overfilled nappy. I could feel it as he started to pump into me, squelching in my hole and squeezing out around the mouth. That was too much, immediately. My hand went back, thrust down my sodden, bulging nappy front and I masturbated, alternately rubbing my clit and touching where his cock was in up my hole. I was wishing he had two cocks, or that there was a second man there to bugger me. As the first twinges of orgasm hit me I realised that was what I needed more than anything, and I was clutching at his cock to try and stuff it up my own bottom and babbling obscenities.

'Up my bottom, Jeff . . . bugger me, go on, do it, bugger me . . . fuck my bottom hole . . . fuck my dirt box, Jeff.'

I was screaming the final, filthy words, and I'd got his cock out of my cunt. He gave a pleased grunt as I moved him to my anus, rubbing his helmet on my slimy, open ring. I pushed, loosening myself in my effort to accommodate him. He pushed back and I felt my anus spread to his cock, opening easily until my ring was taut around his shaft. I could feel the weight of his cock inside me, stiff and heavy, my rectum bloating out as he filled it, all the way in, until his balls were pressed half to my empty cunt and half to my soiled nappy seat.

'You . . . you'd better come if you want it while I'm up your arse, Gabs,' he panted, 'because I'm going to spunk . . . I'm going to spunk right up your dirty arsehole.'

My hand was already on my sex, two fingers stuck briefly up my cunt to feel that I was empty where a girl is supposed to be fucked and full where she isn't, before I was masturbating again, my fingers working furiously between my lips as Jeff's cock pumped in and out of my bumhole. I was screaming, and begging for every filthy degradation I could imagine as my contractions started again.

This time there was no going back. I was coming, my buggered bottom hole in hard spasm on Jeff's erection. From his gasping and grunting I knew he had come too, spunking up in my rectum to add the final, filthy touch to my buggering, or almost final, because I wanted to suck his cock. He gave a yelp of surprise as I pulled off him and swivelled round, still rubbing at myself, my orgasm rising to a new peak as I saw erect cock, steaming gently in the pale Welsh sunlight, slimy with my juices, spunk still dribbling from the tip, all of which went in my mouth.

I sucked and swallowed, again, and again, as I rode what must have been the longest orgasm of my life, with peak after peak tearing through me, with every filthy detail of what we'd done fixed firmly in my head; sucking his cock and licking his anus, soiling my nappy and being fucked in it, making him bugger me and having him come in my rectum, and lastly sucking his dirty penis clean for him.

Finally I was forced to stop or black out, and there were lights in my head as I sat down with a squelch. Jeff fell back too, to lie gasping on the grass. He was staring at me in amazement, and I eventually managed a weak grin.

'I . . . I got a little carried away there, I think,' I told him.

'That's just fine,' he answered. 'You get carried away any time you like.'

'Thanks,' I told him.' Not many men could cope with that.'

He just shrugged, as if to say that most men were simply beneath notice. I badly needed to clean up, and the moment I had the energy I crawled into the stream. Jeff joined me and we helped wash each other, including having thick fingers pushed in up my vagina and anus as I knelt with my bottom below the surface of the water. He had some whisky in the car, and I made him fetch it, taking a couple of swallows as I sat on the sunlit rocks to dry off. I also explained the situation at the Institute in greater detail, but he merely laughed.

'So I get a spanking from your Sabina. Big deal, but they'll have to take me down first.'

'Don't worry,' I assured him. 'I'll explain, but anyway, Kimiko's probably told them the truth by now.'

'Whatever,' he answered.

Not wanting to litter, I made Jeff fetch a plastic bag from his car for my soiled nappy and we set off for the house with me now naked from the waist down. Despite having just come, Jeff kept pawing my bottom or making me walk ahead so that he could admire the way my cheeks showed under the hem of my jacket, apparently far more interested in me than in what might happen at the house. Only when we reached the lawn did he react at all, squaring his shoulders as he considered the men assembled on the lawn.

'Stay here,' I told him.

They were standing in a ring, watching as Sabina gave Sophie a spanking, bare across the knee with her uniform jacket turned up to show off the full expanse

236

of a very pink bottom. None of them was even looking in our direction, and I was just yards away before anyone saw me.

'Jeff's here,' I announced, 'but he's not the Master.'

Even as I spoke I realised he'd ignored my advice and come up behind me.

'Nice bum, Sophie,' he commented. 'I hear you want to deal with me too, Sabina?'

Sabina gave him a surprised look, but it was me she answered.

'Gabrielle, you treacherous little bitch!'

'I'm sorry,' I said, 'but what you were doing wasn't fair.'

She was going to reply, and she looked genuinely angry, but before she could choose her words Jeff spoke up again.

'I'll do you a deal, Sabina,' he offered. 'If all six of you guys can take me down you can do what you like, but if they can't, I get to spank you, on the bare, and tits out too. Oh ... and a blow job afterwards.'

The expression on Sabina's face changed to outrage, and again she seemed unable to find words to express herself.

'Come on,' Jeff urged. 'Six on one, huh? That's got to be good odds.'

'I ...,' Sabina managed, as Sophie took her chance to get up and scamper away, rubbing at her red bottom. 'Fuck that, you deserve everything you get, so no deals.'

'I tell you, he's not the Master,' I insisted. 'Ask Kimiko.'

Kimiko was there, but she merely hung her head to the ground, saying nothing. Mr Masham and Mr Noyles had already begun to advance on Jeff, but slowly, while the other men were holding back.

'I really wouldn't,' Stephen advised. 'I know Jeff, and . . .'

Mr Masham chose that moment to dart in, snatching for Jeff's wrist. Jeff merely stepped aside and gave the smallest motion of one massive arm, which sent Mr Masham sprawling on the lawn. Mr Noyles tried to grapple from the other side while Jeff was distracted, and very briefly managed to get a grip before being swung off his feet and also deposited on the ground.

Jeff moved into his sumo stance, squatting down with his massive legs splayed and his arms ready to catch anyone who dared come close. Mr Masham was rubbing a bruised shoulder and didn't seem inclined to continue, while Mr Noyles seemed to have changed his mind. None of the others looked at all interested in trying their luck.

'Come on,' Jeff urged. 'All six of you.'

'Just do it, you cowards!' Sabina snapped. 'Call yourselves men?'

'Yes, but if he really isn't the Master . . .,' Poppy pointed out.

'Shut up, Poppy,' Sabina ordered. 'Go on, you lot, get on with it. Any man who gets in there and they can have Gabby all night, anything they want, even up her arse.'

'Been there, done that,' Mr Masham said. 'How about we get to fuck you, Sabina?'

'Piss off!' she answered him.

'And I get to spank you if I win?' Jeff chuckled. 'Come on, boys, she gets it either way, win or lose. That's what we want to see, isn't it?'

'Go fuck yourself, Jeff,' Sabina raged. 'Come on, you pathetic little wimps, take him!'

None of the men moved, but Jeff had begun to advance on Sabina, who quickly got up from the chair she'd used to spank Sophie.

'You can't, you wouldn't dare!' she squeaked.

'Try me,' Jeff answered, 'and don't bother to run either. You wouldn't get five yards in those boots.'

He was right, because Sabina's knee-length leather boots were only military in style, and rendered completely impractical by four-inch spike heels.

'I can kick you though,' she warned.

'You can try,' Jeff answered and made a sudden snatching motion with one hand.

Sabina made a face and continued to back away, her expression growing more panic stricken as she watched Jeff's slow advance. At last she spoke.

'OK, OK, I'll take your deal. If you can handle all six men you can spank me, but not hard!'

'Suits me,' Jeff answered. 'I just want that big black bum bare and wriggling, that's all.'

'Bastard,' Sabina answered.

'And don't forget my blow job,' Jeff reminded her.

Sabina made a face again, then an urgent motion to the men. None of them looked very keen, but it was Mr Masham who spoke up.

'What's in it for us?'

'I told you,' Sabina answered him. 'Anyone who helps gets one of the girls for the night.'

'I sleep with Tasanee anyway,' Stephen pointed out.

'It's not a big deal is it?' Poppy added. 'I mean, I'll go to bed with Derreck if he likes, but frankly, if he's going to fuck me anyway, I'd rather it was done in front of people.'

'What then?' asked Sabina.

'We get you, that's what we want,' Mr Spottiswood pointed out.

'What?' she demanded. 'So it's Jeff or all six of you?'

'Five, Mistress,' Mr Greene put in. 'I could never take unfair advantage of your divine body.'

239

'Just fuck off, will you, you pathetic specimen!' Sabina raged. 'If you think I'm so bloody perfect, help take Fat Jeff down. I . . . I'll ride you around the lawn . . . or spank you in your maid's uniform . . . you can kiss my arse . . .'

'Sounds good to me,' Jeff put in. 'I'm up for a lick of your bum, Sabina, if it's going, or you can sit on my face while you toss me off, if you like.'

'You're a pervert, Jeff Bellbird,' Sabina stormed.

'Thanks,' he said, grinning. 'So come on then, what's it to be?'

Sabina made to answer, but suddenly threw her hands up in the air, and her tone had changed completely when she spoke.

'OK, OK, I give in. You can spank me, just not hard.'

'And my bj?'

'OK! You really are an utter bastard though.'

'Maybe,' he admitted, and sat down in the same chair Sabina had spanked Sophie on just minutes before. 'Come on then, over you go. Undo your trousers, but don't take them down, that's my job.'

Sabina's face was set in fury as she unfastened her smart green uniform trousers, and her hands were shaking so badly she fumbled the button twice before it came loose. Jeff waited patiently, with the rest of us quickly gathering around. I decided not to mention that Jeff had come with me just a half-hour earlier, and despite quite a lot of guilt I knew I wouldn't be doing anything else to change her fate either.

'Green suits you, you know,' Jeff remarked casually as Sabina came close to him, 'makes your bum look even bigger, and I do like a nice big arse on a girl.'

As he spoke he'd taken a handful of Sabina's bottom, gently kneading one heavy cheek. She stood rigid, but unresisting, as he guided her down across his knee. Her bottom looked huge in the tight green army trousers, a sphere of heavy flesh barely contained by the thin material, which seemed as if it would split at any moment. Jeff turned her jacket up to show the full expanse of her cheeks.

'Now that is what I call a bum,' Mr Masham remarked. 'Go on, Jeff, spank it.'

'Patience, patience,' Jeff chuckled. 'You're forgetting the unveiling ceremony. Right, trousers down, Sabina, let's see what you've got on underneath.'

A tiny whimpering noise escaped Sabina's throat as Jeff took hold of the waistband of her trousers. They were tight, and hard to get down, so he had to tug at them repeatedly, only slowly exposing the smooth, dark meat beneath. Her whimpering grew stronger as she was laid bare, but Jeff took no notice, gradually revealing the full chubby globe, until Sabina was nude behind, with both cheeks fully out of a pair of minuscule yellow panties that provided only the absolute minimum of modesty.

'Sweet,' Jeff remarked, wobbling one big cheek, 'sweet and juicy. Now, let's have these little panties down, shall we?'

Sabina didn't even protest at her stripping. She knew knickers come down for spanking, and that any attempt to keep them up would only get her laughed at. Jeff did it slowly once again, sticking his thumbs into her waistband and peeling them down, with what would have been the seat on any proper pair pulling slowly from between her big cheeks. She was too meaty to be showing more than a hint of cunt, even with her knickers pulled right down, but I was sure we'd be seeing more once the spanking got under way and she started to kick.

'Nice arse, Sabina,' Mr Noyles spoke up.

'Glorious arse,' Jeff agreed, placing one huge hand on each of Sabina's bottom cheeks and starting to knead.

'You said a spanking,' Sabina protested. 'Do you really have to touch me up too?'

'Yes,' Jeff said emphatically. 'Having a grope is all part of the fun. Oh, and you just reminded me, I said tits out, didn't I?'

Sabina gave a single, forlorn sob as he began to fiddle with her jacket. It took him a while, and she had to lift her chest to let him do it, but soon her jacket had been turned right up to expose her back and midriff. He unclipped her bra and flopped her breasts out for a brief feel before returning his attention to her bottom, only now with one of her bare breasts squashed out on his leg and the other dangling beyond.

'That's how to spank a girl,' Mr Noyles said enthusiastically, 'bare bum and tits out too. Lovely.'

'When she spanked Kimiko, she showed us her bumhole,' Mr Spottiswood pointed out.

'Good point,' Jeff admitted. 'One bumhole coming up.'

Even as he spoke he had hauled Sabina's cheeks apart. She gasped as she was put on show, with the jet-black dimple of her anus pulsing slightly in her agitation as the men peered close to get a good look. Her sex showed too, the full, brown lips pouting out between her thighs. She was distinctly puffy, and a dab of wet over her hole betrayed her arousal.

'Look how wet she is,' Mr Spottiswood commented. 'She's no better than the rest of them.'

Jeff moved his fingers lower, spreading out the wet, pink centre of Sabina's hole and peering close. She began to wriggle, but he simply pushed one arm down on to the small of her back, holding her firmly in place as we inspected her sex.

'You're right,' Mr Masham remarked. 'She's as big a slut as any of them.'

'Do you suppose all girls get wet just by being stripped off?' Mr Petherick queried.

'No, they have to be into it,' Stephen pointed out, drawing a murmur of agreement. 'It's just that girls like Sabina, or Kimi, need an excuse to give in to what they really need.'

'That may be true sometimes, but . . .,' Poppy began.

'Nearly always,' Sophie cut in.

'I think it's natural for women to want to be spanked,' Mr Masham added, 'but not that many have the inner strength to acknowledge their desires.'

'There's a lot in that,' Jeff agreed, adjusting Sabina's position a little to let her second breast flop out over his thigh. 'I mean, there's no denying that being spanked turns women on, physically, so it's really just a case of having the courage to make the mental connection, while . . .'

'Will you get on with it!?' Sabina stormed. 'Please?'

'Yes of course, sorry,' Jeff chuckled, let go of her bottom and laid in.

Sabina must have been regretting her demand from the first smack. It didn't look particularly hard, but with Jeff's huge hand and the sheer weight of his arm it obviously hurt. She began to kick immediately, with her smooth brown thighs starting to work in her well-lowered knickers and the army trousers, although she was doing her best not to make a display of herself.

Her resolution didn't last long, her gasps and sobs breaking to yelps and curses, then to a full-blooded squealing mixed with furious swearing as Jeff set up a fast, vigorous rhythm on her bouncy cheeks. She began to beat her hands on the grass beneath her, and

243

to shake her head, with her breasts jumping in every direction and her kicking growing more frantic by the moment. We stood back a little, not wanting to catch a stray boot, but we could still see everything, with her jet-black bumhole winking between her cheeks to every smack, and her increasingly juicy cunt on open display between her thighs.

'A real spanking tantrum, beautiful,' Mr Spottiswood sighed. 'Harder, Jeff, really make her kick.'

'No, you said . . .,' Sabina gasped, only to break off in a pained squeal as the next slap caught her full across her cheeks. 'You pig! Stop, please stop . . . I'll suck you . . . red, Jeff . . . please . . . red!'

He'd brought her spanking to a crescendo as she spoke, but with the last word she burst into tears and he stopped. She immediately went limp, making no protest as he gently caressed her bottom, stroking both full dark cheeks, and she only gave a low moan when he eased a finger between them and up what was obviously a very wet hole.

'I think you're ready,' he said. 'Right, on your knees. I may be a bit slow, but it's nothing against you. I just gave Gabby a bum shag.'

I felt the blood rise in my cheeks, but nobody was looking at me. Sabina had crawled slowly off Jeff's lap and into a kneeling position, turning her tear-streaked face up to his. She made no effort to cover her breasts or bottom, knowing full well she'd only be made to take them out again. Jeff looked immensely pleased with himself as he pulled out his cock, then his balls, almost as an afterthought. Sabina hesitated, gave a last, shame-filled glance to her audience and went forward, taking Jeff's cock in her mouth.

She'd promised to do it, but there had been no protest, no reluctance, not even an attempt to be allowed to do it in private. Even with the tears still trickling softly down her face it was clear that she wanted to be sucking cock, and in front of an audience. Not one of us spoke as Jeff slowly began to grow to erection in her mouth, although I saw that Mr Spottiswood had guided Poppy's hand to his cock. It was still a little shock when my wrist was taken in Mr Petherick's soft, clammy hand and put to his crotch, but I squeezed obligingly, finding him already half stiff in his pants. I took him out, and his hand had gone to my bare bottom as I began to masturbate him.

Sabina was completely lost, now on all-fours with her breasts swinging to the motion of her cock-sucking and her bottom raised for all to see, the flush quite evident on her spanked cheeks and both her anus and her distinctly slippery cunt on open show. I was wondering if any man would dare to mount her and fuck her, also if it was fair to let it happen when she'd only agreed to do Jeff. Mr Masham had his cock out, Sophie was stroking Mr Noyles's crotch and Stephen had Tasanee on her knees, licking his balls as he masturbated. Only Kimiko wasn't busy with a man, but the meek expression on her face had gone, to be replaced by something of her old viciousness as she spoke up.

'Give her bukkake . . . your spunk in her face. This is what she should get. I tell you why. She lied about all the tortures, to make you help her with Jeff.'

I saw Sabina stiffen, but she didn't stop sucking, even as Kimiko went on.

'Really, you were just to be threatened, and given the choice to dominate instead, to dominate Mr Greene.'

Mr Greene was nowhere to be seen.

'We'll worry about him later,' Sophie suggested. 'Let's give Sabina her bukkake. She really scared me.'

'Me too,' Poppy agreed, and began to lead Mr Spottiswood forward by his cock.

Sophie paused only to extract Mr Noyles's erection from his trousers, and when Mr Masham beckoned to Kimiko she came. Mr Petherick stepped forward too, and Sabina was surrounded by a forest of erect cocks.

'Do it,' Jeff said suddenly, 'suck us all off, Sabina.'

Her response was a little mewling sound around her mouthful of penis, and as Jeff pulled her off her face was full of consternation. She glanced around, began to speak, only to be cut off as Sophie guided Mr Noyles's cock into her open mouth.

'That's right, suck it,' Sophie said, 'you really deserve this, Sabina.'

Sabina shook her head, but she was sucking, and as her hands were guided to other cocks she took hold, tugging Jeff and Stephen over her breasts and into her own face. Mr Petherick had started to groan and was groping my bottom hard, so I tugged faster and was almost immediately rewarded by a jet of spunk erupting from his cock, full in Sabina's face. She pulled off Mr Noyles, her face screwing up in disgust, but Sophie had pushed her head close, allowing me to milk the rest of Mr Petherick's come out into her hair and across her forehead, then pop it in her mouth to be sucked clean.

She did it willingly enough, for all the expression on her face, and even took it down. Watching her swallow spunk triggered Mr Masham, whose cock erupted in Kimiko's hand to spray thick white come into Sabina's hair, down her back and over the heavy, naked globes of her bottom. Mr Spottiswood's cock had been thrust into her mouth even as Mr Petherick's left it, and he too came, down her throat, across her nose and one eye, then full into the other eye.

I saw the spunk squash out from under one eyelid as she quickly closed them, only to have Stephen come in her hand, splashing her breasts and face, then Mr Noyles, full in her open mouth and across her cheek and neck. Only Jeff hadn't come, and she went back down on his cock, her face now a mask of spunk as she began to suck once more.

'Come on, you girls,' Jeff urged. 'Lick it off.'

Poppy went first, lapping at Sabina's face and Jeff's cock simultaneously. I knew what I wanted, and had got down behind her before anyone else could steal my place, to take hold of the full, brown ball of her bottom, first to kiss and lick at the blobs of spunk spattering her still-hot flesh, then burrowing between to drive my tongue up into the dark, wrinkled bumhole I'd been made to lick so often but could never tire of. Sophie joined me, her tongue applied to Sabina's sex and we were licking together.

I heard Jeff grunt and knew he'd come in her mouth, but it wasn't over, Sabina still sucking and swallowing down his sperm as best she could while wriggling her bottom in our faces. Sophie licked harder, right on Sabina's clitoris, and I was burrowing my tongue as deep up her bottom as it would go. She started to come, her cheeks contracting in my face and her anus in spasm on my tongue tip, which I kept in, and moving, until I was sure she was completely finished.

She collapsed on the lawn, and so did I, my thighs spread wide for all to see as my hand went between them, masturbating openly until I in turn had brought myself to a badly needed orgasm. It was short and sharp, very different to the one with Jeff, but left me feeling equally content, and all the more so when I heard Sabina's voice.

'OK,' she said softly, 'you've had your fun with me, and I admit it was nice. I hope you're satisfied.'

There was an immediate chorus of agreement, ending with Poppy volunteering to fetch some water and a flannel. I sat up, feeling a little dizzy, but smiling as I watched the men put their cocks away. Everything seemed to have worked out well, although I wasn't entirely happy about Jeff's behaviour.

'You wouldn't really have done it against her will, would you, Jeff?' I asked.

'Nah, of course not,' he laughed. 'I was calling her bluff.'

'You are a real bastard!' Sabina gasped, flicking away a tendril of spunk that was hanging from one still engorged nipple.

'You two should kiss and make up,' I suggested.

Despite Poppy's best effort, Sabina's face was still a mess, but after just a moment's hesitation Jeff leant down to give her a kiss on the forehead, selecting about the only square centimetre of skin not soiled with spunk and saliva.

'Friends?' Jeff asked.

'Friends,' Sabina agreed.

Poppy had come back out, with tissues as well as a bowl of water and a flannel. I was feeling in need of a shower, but decided to wait a little, so took some tissues. No sooner had I begun to clean up than Mr Masham spoke up from where he'd gone to stand on the low wall we had been using for spankings.

'I think you girls better get indoors. Somebody's coming.'

Sabina, Kimiko and Tasanee were all nude or near nude, and quickly ran in. I went to where Mr Masham was standing, sure only that my upper body would be visible. A car had parked at the bottom of the drive and a man was getting out; middle-aged, thin and no great height, but with a distinctly stern expression on his face.

'Who's this, do you suppose?' Mr Spottiswood asked.

'I suppose he must be this Master bloke,' Jeff suggested.

'He doesn't look much,' Poppy put in.

'A lot of dominant men are really weedy,' Sophie responded. 'It's the small man complex, I suppose.'

'Do you want us to tie him, Sabina?' Mr Masham asked.

There was a touch of hurt pride in his voice, and in Mr Noyles's as he answered.

'Yes, go for it.'

I was going to say something, but then I thought of how it would have felt to be hung from my wrists and whipped with a birch by a man who didn't have the decency to ask my permission or allow me a stop word. Being fair and nice was all very well, but the Master definitely needed a lesson in how he could treat people, if only for the sake of women he might be in a position to dominate in the future. Besides, Mr Masham and Mr Noyles had already set off among the hedges.

'I'm in,' Jeff stated. 'Give me your panties, Poppy.'

Poppy didn't question him, but quickly peeled off her knickers. Jeff took them and lumbered after the others, ducking low between a pair of hedges before he vanished from sight.

'Make sure it really is him!' I hissed, but too late.

I considered going indoors, suddenly very much aware of my bare bottom and pussy, because while it did seem likely that the man was the Master he could perfectly well be some local official, or simply a driver who'd got lost or had car trouble. When I heard a shout and the sound of a scuffle from towards the road I changed my mind, grabbing instead a towel somebody had put out to sunbathe.

There was silence again, then Mr Masham and Mr Noyles appeared. Last came Jeff, who was carrying their victim over his shoulder. The man had been bound with the ropes intended for Jeff, and had Poppy's knickers stuffed in his mouth for a gag. Whoever he was, he was very unhappy indeed about his capture, struggling desperately with the face a rich red and his eyes popping with anger. They popped still more when he saw Poppy and Sophie, neither of whom had bothered to cover up.

'So this is the Master?' Sophie sneered. 'So what, you were going to put spiders all over me, were you?'

'And shave my head?' Poppy demanded. 'Let's get his trousers down, Sophie, and see how he likes a bit of his own treatment. Dump him on the lawn, Jeff.'

Jeff complied happily, dropping the man from his full height. Poppy and Sophie closed in and quickly had the man's trousers and underpants down, exposing a set of rather scrawny genitals and setting him thrashing even more desperately than before. Sabina had come out again, now reasonably decent, and stood looking down on our captive.

'Let's take turns to spank him,' Sophie suggested. 'You can go first, Sabina.'

'I want to shave his pubes,' Poppy added, 'and maybe piss on him.'

The man's struggles were now demented, but there was nothing whatsoever he could do as Sabina rolled him on to his front, lifted his middle by the ropes binding his arms and began to slap at his bottom. I was having trouble not laughing, just for the faces he was pulling as he was spanked, but it died in my throat as Kimiko came running from the house, screeching at the top of her voice.

'Stop! Stop! Stop! What are you doing!? That is Mr Llewellyn, the owner of the house!'

Sabina had applied two more forceful slaps before what Kimiko had said sank in. Her manic grin faded, to be replaced by a look of serious concern.

'You're fucking joking?' she demanded.

'No, this is Mr Llewellyn!' Kimiko assured her. 'There is no Master. I . . . I had to make him up, so you would do as you were told, and dominate Mr Greene. It is Mr Greene who was in control. This is Mr Llewellyn!'

'Oh shit,' Sabina stated, and released her grip.

Mr Llewellyn collapsed back on to the grass, where he continued to wriggle frantically, with his cock and balls flapping from side to side. For a long moment everybody was silent, until Sabina's voice finally broke through.

'Shit! What do we do now?'

'Leave?' Jeff suggested.

nexus

The leading publisher of fetish and adult fiction

TELL US WHAT YOU THINK!

Readers' ideas and opinions matter to us so please take a few minutes to fill in the questionnaire below.

1. Sex: Are you male ☐ female ☐ a couple ☐?

2. Age: Under 21 ☐ 21–30 ☐ 31–40 ☐ 41–50 ☐ 51–60 ☐ over 60 ☐

3. Where do you buy your Nexus books from?
☐ A chain book shop. If so, which one(s)?

_____

☐ An independent book shop. If so, which one(s)?

_____

☐ A used book shop/charity shop
☐ Online book store. If so, which one(s)?

_____

4. How did you find out about Nexus books?
☐ Browsing in a book shop
☐ A review in a magazine
☐ Online
☐ Recommendation
☐ Other _____

5. In terms of settings, which do you prefer? (Tick as many as you like.)
☐ Down to earth and as realistic as possible
☐ Historical settings. If so, which period do you prefer?

_____

☐ Fantasy settings – barbarian worlds
☐ Completely escapist/surreal fantasy

- ☐ Institutional or secret academy
- ☐ Futuristic/sci fi
- ☐ Escapist but still believable
- ☐ Any settings you dislike?

_____

- ☐ Where would you like to see an adult novel set?

_____

6. In terms of storylines, would you prefer:

- ☐ Simple stories that concentrate on adult interests?
- ☐ More plot and character-driven stories with less explicit adult activity?
- ☐ We value your ideas, so give us your opinion of this book:

_____

_____

_____

7. In terms of your adult interests, what do you like to read about? (Tick as many as you like.)

- ☐ Traditional corporal punishment (CP)
- ☐ Modern corporal punishment
- ☐ Spanking
- ☐ Restraint/bondage
- ☐ Rope bondage
- ☐ Latex/rubber
- ☐ Leather
- ☐ Female domination and male submission
- ☐ Female domination and female submission
- ☐ Male domination and female submission
- ☐ Willing captivity
- ☐ Uniforms
- ☐ Lingerie/underwear/hosiery/footwear (boots and high heels)
- ☐ Sex rituals
- ☐ Vanilla sex
- ☐ Swinging
- ☐ Cross-dressing/TV

☐ Enforced feminisation
☐ Others – tell us what you don't see enough of in adult fiction:

_____
_____
_____

8. Would you prefer books with a more specialised approach to your
   interests, i.e. a novel specifically about uniforms? If so, which
   subject(s) would you like to read a Nexus novel about?

_____
_____
_____

9. Would you like to read true stories in Nexus books? For instance, the
   true story of a submissive woman, or a male slave? Tell us which
   true revelations you would most like to read about:

_____
_____
_____

10. What do you like best about Nexus books?

_____
_____

11. What do you like least about Nexus books?

_____
_____

12. Which are your favourite titles?

_____
_____

13. Who are your favourite authors?

_____
_____

14. **Which covers do you prefer? Those featuring:**
    (Tick as many as you like.)

☐ Fetish outfits
☐ More nudity
☐ Two models
☐ Unusual models or settings
☐ Classic erotic photography
☐ More contemporary images and poses
☐ A blank/non-erotic cover
☐ What would your ideal cover look like?

_____

15. **Describe your ideal Nexus novel in the space provided:**

_____

_____

_____

_____

16. **Which celebrity would feature in one of your Nexus-style fantasies?**
    We'll post the best suggestions on our website – anonymously!

_____

THANKS FOR YOUR TIME

Now simply write the title of this book in the space below and cut out the
questionnaire pages. Post to: Nexus, Marketing Dept., Thames Wharf Studios,
Rainville Rd, London W6 9HA

Book title: _____

NEXUS NEW BOOKS

To be published in March 2007

BEASTLY BEHAVIOUR
Aishling Morgan

Genevieve Stukely is working as an erotic dancer in the American west when she learns that her uncle is dead and that she is to inherit the family estate on the borders of Dartmoor. Only when she returns to the mother country does she discover that Sir Robert Stukely did not die simply of old age, but was found with an expression of utmost terror frozen on his features. Nearby were the footprints of a gigantic hound.

Now Mistress of Stukely Manor and known to have a colourful past, Genevieve quickly finds herself the centre of attention for half the rakes and ne'erdowells in Devon.

Beastly Behaviour follows the Truscott saga into its fifth generation with a tale of bizarre lust and Gothic horror drawn from several historical and literary sources to make it one of the most elaborate erotic novels ever published, to say nothing of being also irredeemably erotic.

£6.99   ISBN 978 0 352 34095 5

CITY MAID
Amelia Evangeline

City Maid recounts the erotic adventures of an innocent young woman in Victorian London. When Eleanor enters service in the Hampton household she has no idea that beneath the façade of respectability the house is a secret world of lust and depravity. Her mistress, Lady Hamilton, soon teaches Eleanor her position in the sternest and most shocking manner. Immediately, Eleanor realises to her horror that once you've felt the thrill of submission, life will never be the same again.

£6.99   ISBN 978 0 352 34096 2

RUBBER GIRL
William Doughty

The *Nexus Enthusiast* series brings us a definitive work of fiction about the hugely popular world of rubber fetishism. In *Rubber Girl*, Jill has an overwhelming fetish for rubber – the sight of it, the scent of it, the feeling of its texture around her skin, its aerodynamic and aesthetic qualities as a sensual fabric and second skin for her voluptuous body, as well as its flexible properties for restraint and bondage. And her neighbour Matt is drawn into her shiny latex orbit when she combines her love of rubber with his weakness for female domination. Kinky Sue, who has a crush on Jill, is the next to join in the perverse and rubbery games in an isolated country house in Dorset, equipped with stables. Together, they reach the very heights of rubber fetishism.

£6.99   ISBN 978 0 352 34087 0

If you would like more information about Nexus titles, please visit our website at www.nexus-books.co.uk, or send a large stamped addressed envelope to:
  Nexus, Thames Wharf Studios,
  Rainville Road, London W6 9HA

NEXUS BOOKLIST

Information is correct at time of printing. To avoid disappointment, check availability before ordering. Go to www.nexus-books.co.uk.

All books are priced at £6.99 unless another price is given.

NEXUS

☐ ABANDONED ALICE	Adriana Arden	ISBN 978 0 352 33969 0
☐ ALICE IN CHAINS	Adriana Arden	ISBN 978 0 352 33908 9
☐ AQUA DOMINATION	William Doughty	ISBN 978 0 352 34020 7
☐ THE ART OF CORRECTION	Tara Black	ISBN 978 0 352 33895 2
☐ THE ART OF SURRENDER	Madeline Bastinado	ISBN 978 0 352 34013 9
☐ BELINDA BARES UP	Yolanda Celbridge	ISBN 978 0 352 33926 3
☐ BENCH-MARKS	Tara Black	ISBN 978 0 352 33797 9
☐ BIDDING TO SIN	Rosita Varón	ISBN 978 0 352 34063 4
☐ BINDING PROMISES	G.C. Scott	ISBN 978 0 352 34014 6
☐ THE BOOK OF PUNISHMENT	Cat Scarlett	ISBN 978 0 352 33975 1
☐ BRUSH STROKES	Penny Birch	ISBN 978 0 352 34072 6
☐ CALLED TO THE WILD	Angel Blake	ISBN 978 0 352 34067 2
☐ CAPTIVES OF CHEYNER CLOSE	Adriana Arden	ISBN 978 0 352 34028 3
☐ CARNAL POSSESSION	Yvonne Strickland	ISBN 978 0 352 34062 7
☐ COLLEGE GIRLS	Cat Scarlett	ISBN 978 0 352 33942 3
☐ COMPANY OF SLAVES	Christina Shelly	ISBN 978 0 352 33887 7
☐ CONCEIT AND CONSEQUENCE	Aishling Morgan	ISBN 978 0 352 33965 2
☐ CORRECTIVE THERAPY	Jacqueline Masterson	ISBN 978 0 352 33917 1
☐ CORRUPTION	Virginia Crowley	ISBN 978 0 352 34073 3
☐ CRUEL SHADOW	Aishling Morgan	ISBN 978 0 352 33886 0

NEXUS CLASSIC

----------- ✂ ------------------------------

Please send me the books I have ticked above.

Name   ....

Address   ....

           ....

           ....

           .... Post code ....

Send to: **Virgin Books Cash Sales, Thames Wharf Studios, Rainville Road, London W6 9HA**

US customers: for prices and details of how to order books for delivery by mail, call 888-330-8477.

Please enclose a cheque or postal order, made payable to **Nexus Books Ltd**, to the value of the books you have ordered plus postage and packing costs as follows:
  UK and BFPO – £1.00 for the first book, 50p for each subsequent book.
  Overseas (including Republic of Ireland) – £2.00 for the first book, £1.00 for each subsequent book.

If you would prefer to pay by VISA, ACCESS/MASTERCARD, AMEX, DINERS CLUB or SWITCH, please write your card number and expiry date here:

....

Please allow up to 28 days for delivery.

Signature ....

Our privacy policy

We will not disclose information you supply us to any other parties. We will not disclose any information which identifies you personally to any person without your express consent.

From time to time we may send out information about Nexus books and special offers. Please tick here if you do *not* wish to receive Nexus information.   ☐

----------- ✂ ------------------------------